Born in the West Midlands, Marg
on the move between England an
landscape, environment and peop
early influences now come into her
lived in London, primarily workii
as a child protection worker, then as a psychotherapist. She
now lives in Bristol, and feeling more settled she has turned
from writing non-fiction to fiction. *Echo* was inspired by her
work as a psychotherapist. It is her second novel and focuses
on the difficulties in growing up. Like her first novel, *Between
the Shadow and the Soul*, it is a psychological thriller, but with
a dash of magical reality.

To find out more about Marguerite and her work, visit
her website: www.margueritev.org.

Ja Tony & Jenny,

With love from Marguerite

15.12.15

ECHO

MARGUERITE VALENTINE

SilverWood

Published in 2016 by SilverWood Books

SilverWood Books Ltd
14 Small Street, Bristol, BS1 1DE
www.silverwoodbooks.co.uk

ISBN 978-1-78132-415-8 (paperback)
ISBN 978-1-78132-416-5 (ebook)

British Library Cataloguing in Publication Data
A CIP catalogue record for this book is available from
the British Library

Set in Sabon by SilverWood Books
Printed on responsibly sourced paper

For all those women whose courage, humour and endurance against adversity remains unacknowledged.

'Her Kind' – *Anne Sexton (1928–1974)*

I have gone out, a possessed witch,
Haunting the black air, braver at night;
Dreaming evil, I have done my hitch
Over the plain houses, light by light:
Lonely thing, twelve fingered, out of mind,
A woman like that is not a woman, quite.
I have been her kind.

Part One

I started off as an Echo. That was the name my mother gave me but it was a long time before I knew why. After all her name was Phoebe, not Narcissus and besides, that would have been too obvious. Maybe she didn't know herself, but whatever her reason, once I knew, I had to change it. What we're called is important and I didn't want to be an Echo or an echo – if you get my drift.

Growing up is hard. That's why people write and make films about it, but for some, like me, it was worse than hard. It was excruciating. My mother used to say girls, and by that she meant me, are moody. More moody than boys? Who knows? Who cares? I'm still moody despite reaching my mid-twenties, so no changes there then.

Thinking about my life, things began changing in a big way from when I was nine. From then on, every summer we'd leave London to spend our holidays in Wales in a farmhouse with a group of surrealist artists. The farmhouse was in a tiny hamlet called Ffridd on the Welsh side of the River Severn, not far from Chepstow. My mum's interest was in surrealism, especially female surrealist art, and this became a major influence while I was growing up. During those Welsh summers I developed a different take on reality, as in, there's no real in reality; it doesn't really exist. I put this down to having been surrounded by her arty friends and listening to their conversations.

My mum said she found her artistic inspiration there, but she wasn't a real artist. Her actual job was teaching Classics at a posh girls' school in Hampstead. Apart from that, she liked the weird and wonderful which is maybe why others found her fascinating. I didn't. Not while I was growing up. She constantly gave me grief; for nothing usually, and, the older I got, the worse she got. She'd take one look at me and then she'd start. We both should have been awarded a George Cross; her for sniping and me for survival under enemy fire.

The first summer we stayed in Wales, Philomena, one of the artists, told me how to get to the river estuary. I remember that place vividly. It was so different from London. I used to cycle there. I loved the loneliness and silence, the absence of colour, the mud, and how its flatness merged into the sombre sky so you couldn't tell one from another. It was another world and until I left London I didn't know such places existed. It was eerie. I rarely saw anyone and only the occasional cry of curlews broke its quiet solitude. It was in the tidal range of the River Severn and someone told me that the river had the second largest rise and fall of water in the world.

This captured my imagination. I would dream of the river swallowing the fields and land, rushing into villages and towns and pushing inland into the woods until eventually the waters would recede, leaving the creek, lonely and isolated, with only the mud, the reed beds and the birds for company.

The creek felt like the beginning and the end of the world and I took to visiting at dawn or late evening. The changing light made it more mysterious and I loved being there by myself. I'd listen to the bird song and the wind sighing and stand in the reeds and watch the movement of the tides and the thin, brackish water slide and swirl through the reeds. Sometimes I'd wait and watch the water creep over my shoes until it was almost too late. Then I'd run, I'd run fast before the waters swept me out to the sea far away.

My mother didn't like me going there. She said the tides were dangerous and that the water could move fast, faster than I could run, but I didn't listen. I didn't believe her and even if I had, she couldn't have stopped me. But that was a long time ago and it's all different now. They've built another bridge since then. A long elegant bridge, one that's upriver and stretches between the two countries of Wales and England and carries an eternally restless line of cars and lorries throughout the day and night. I don't mind because it means my creek and the woods around will stay secret forever and I need solitude now, as I did then.

My mum had found Ffridd through reading the back pages of the *London Review of Books*. It's where people advertised for relationships, places to rent, and courses to attend. I was with her when she first spotted it. She read it out to me. It was a short ad and it said the artist owners of a renovated Welsh farmhouse were looking for two temporary tenants over the summer. It said personality and an interest in the arts were the most important qualities but also paying the rent reliably and regularly would be regarded positively. My mum thought that meant they wanted somebody unconventional – but not so they forgot to pay the rent.

There was an interview for prospective tenants. That was strange. After all you don't normally get interviewed for a holiday, but then everything about them was strange. I remember my mum saying the wording of the whole advertisement was a contradiction in terms, but it didn't stop her. She went right ahead and wrote back. She was intrigued. The idea of living in Wales over the summer appealed to her and she was determined to get out of London during the holidays.

And because I was still young, I had to go with her. She wasn't in the habit of consulting me. Usually I did what I was told to do, although you'd never think that, the way she carried on. The woman who'd placed the ad was called Philomena and her partner was Gareth and they were both artists, although in a different way. Philomena was a photographer and painter and Gareth a poet. He was introduced to us when we went for our interview, but other than that most of the time he kept out of our way.

When Philomena got to know my mum, she told her, who later told me, they had an open marriage which was apparently alright with her. They both had a rule not to bring their lovers home so maybe that's where he was when he wasn't writing – making love to someone else. He was always busy. He seemed pleasant enough, although at first I found him uninteresting.

Amazing really, when you think about it, how feelings change. When I got older, say from about the age of fourteen, I found him anything but uninteresting. I'd found one of his love poems which he'd left out on the kitchen table. Philomena was out and it was obvious the poem wasn't about her because of the way he described this woman. He'd called the poem 'The Girl in the Flowered Dress' and once I'd started it, I had to read it to the end. It was so beautiful, so romantic, so full of yearning that it made me wonder if he'd made her up, because she sounded so wonderful. Almost too good to be true. But, made up or not, from then on this poem made me look at Gareth in a new light and I began observing him.

Eventually I came to the conclusion that although he looked normal, underneath he was seething with passion and that, together with being unfulfilled, was what drove him to write love poetry.

I noticed he didn't smile much. His face was craggy and lined as if he'd suffered – like most poets – and he had intense blue eyes and long wavy brown hair which he brushed away off his wide forehead. He wasn't very tall but well proportioned and how he moved reminded me of a flamenco dancer that I'd seen once at Sadler's Wells. He had that kind of powerful body and a primal energy and I'm saying that because one of our teachers had a thing going for a flamenco dancer and that's how she talked.

After spending many hours night and day secretly watching him, and trying to find out how old he was, I concluded he was very attractive in a poetic, shambolic kind of way. However, and unfortunately, due to circumstances beyond my control, hormonal, some might say, this interest in him eventually transformed into a full-on obsession and chaos ensued.

His partner, Philomena, was, in contrast to this imagined woman in a flowered dress, larger than life both literally and metaphorically. There was absolutely nothing mysterious about her. She was who she was, nothing more, nothing less. She was a big woman and seemed mostly to wear one of two outfits, although once I did see her in a type of cruise ship outfit as if she were an extra from a forties black-and-white film. Usually she wore baggy blue linen trousers which she never ironed and only occasionally washed and these were always worn with a sun-and-sea faded pink drill top, the kind members of the boating fraternity wear. If it got cold this was exchanged for a navy, oiled-wool, sailor's sweater. She always wore those utilitarian Birkenstocks on her feet, which I thought were particularly hippy and unattractive and when the temperature dropped she put them on with striped socks. That was how she dressed for her art work.

Her best outfit was a large flowing dress made out of ruby red velvet. She wore this barefoot when she (and sometimes Gareth) had supper with their friends in the house or the garden. It must have taken yards of material to make that dress, and she'd wear it with stunning jewellery handmade by one of her friends. My favourite piece was an emerald-and-amethyst butterfly but she didn't stop at that for decoration, she'd wind a paisley scarf round her light brown hair, art nouveau style, and finish off the outfit with jangling, Celtic-designed, silver bracelets on her arms. Despite her size, she was scarily and exotically eye catching. Her voice was also gravelly or vulgarly rough, depending on your point of view, and that was because she'd smoked a lot and over the years this had coarsened her voice. She could be as noisy and raucous as her geese, and had a laugh that could strip off wallpaper. My mum hit it off with her straight away.

When we went for our interview, she'd asked my mum if she had a memorable painting, one she particularly liked. My mum told her she had, but this could change any time. Her current favourite, she said was 'Eine Kleine Nachtmusik' by an American woman called Dorothea Tanning. I noticed Philomena look startled and asked why she liked it. I was alarmed about how she'd answer because my mum had shown it to me and talked about it before, so I already knew what she thought. The painting was seriously weird. I didn't want her thinking we were mad because then we'd never get to be Philomena's tenants and after seeing round the farmhouse, I'd already decided I wanted to give it a go.

But there was no stopping her. My mum said she liked it because she liked paintings by artists of their dreams, that she loved the irrational and art that turned reality and the expected on its head. She went on to say how beautiful the giant sunflower was lying on top of the stairs but there was something spooky about the two young girls, one of them with her hair standing on end as if terrified out of her mind, and the other apparently in a state of ecstatic reverie leaning half-naked against a closed door.

Philomena must have known this painting because she asked her what she thought lay behind the door. My mum said it could represent the entrance to the unconscious and that the unconscious was the root of creativity, but it was hard sometimes to access. She sounded so serious and intellectual, which I knew she could be sometimes, because of the people she mixed with and the way she talked to me, but every time she got off on one like that, she embarrassed me.

Luckily Philomena didn't seem bothered. She just laughed. She said she always found a whisky chaser or a spliff were good routes to the unconscious when she was painting. Then she turned to me because I think she'd forgotten I was there, and she didn't want me to feel left out.

She asked me what I thought but I didn't like being the

focus of attention so I said, as if I was dumb, I didn't think, which wasn't quite true and then I asked, as a distraction, how far away were we from the sea. Philomena said there was no sea nearby, unless you included the Bristol Channel, but there was an estuary which ran into the river and then into the sea and I could go there instead. She told me about a bike I could use and that she'd tell me how to get there when we came to stay. I gathered from this we'd passed her test for acceptability.

She continued staring at me. Then she took out a cigarette from a silver case, tapped the cigarette on it, lit up and still looking at me through the smoke as she blew it out towards the ceiling, she said, 'You're a strange child, Echo. You know more than your years. There's a wild streak in you. But I like you.' Then she said, 'You don't look like your mother. Are you more like your father? Where is he?'

I looked across at my mother but she was eyeballing me in that way only my mother could. It was the look of the gorgon and any minute longer I could turn into petrified stone. I said, 'I don't know,' but before I could say any more my mother said, 'Actually, she does look like me. We don't talk about him. He's an irrelevance. Echo and I just get on with our lives. I've told her as much as she wants to know and it's far better that way, isn't it, Echo?'

I knew she didn't expect an answer so I just looked stupid and kept my mouth shut. That was all that was required. Then, turning again to Philomena, my mother said, 'Men can be so needy and clingy, don't you think?'

Philomena said nothing but she caught my eye and I could have sworn she gave me a wink. It lasted a nanosecond.

My mum asked if she'd chosen anybody else and Philomena said she'd had lots of people replying, but most were unsuitable because she could see they'd complain a lot, or they were humourless, or boring, but there was a photographer she liked, who she thought would fit in. Her name was Gaby, short for Gabriella, and she came from

Cardiff. She'd gone to pick up some stuff but she'd be back later and we could meet her.

Philomena had the idea that the three of them could form a female artists' 'cross fertilisation' collective. When she said this, I said, 'Do you mean like the bees?'

I was trying to be funny but it failed because she took no notice. Maybe she didn't hear. But for a few years that's what they became, an artists' collective.

While they were doing their art, they usually forgot about me but I was still part of what was going on. What they didn't know was that as a reaction to being ignored or bored, I'd sometimes pass the time by observing them. Watching people when they don't know they're being watched is fascinating. For a while it was my favourite hobby, because if you think about it, it's a version of bird watching. The difference being, instead of birds you watch people. You can learn a lot about them. For example, I discovered most people put on an act, they perform as if they have a secret audience that they've made up.

My mum lived for those summers. The farmhouse was along the Welsh Borders, two or three miles from the River Severn and a bit like a French gîte, only the rent was cheap. It was a long, low dilapidated building with peeling pale limewash the colour of goats' milk and surrounded by an anarchy of planted beds and natural woodland. To reach it, first you had to drive through fields, opening and shutting each farm gate as you entered and left, until finally you'd get to the farmhouse, swing open the farm gate, drive in, and park on a corralled square of rough grass. A raucous cackle of white geese would rush towards you with their heads held high in that imperious way geese have. Over the years I learnt not to be intimidated.

The original building was many centuries old but the various owners had added to it so that inside it was like a maze of disconnected groups of rooms. I liked the central sitting room best because it was big and interestingly atmospheric.

It was dark, with a low ceiling and tiny windows set into the thick walls. Philomena used to place a white ironstone jug with the flowers of the season on one of the window sills, and the light from outside streamed in illuminating the flowers as if they were other-worldly or like an illustration from Blake's poetry. Books were everywhere, on the floor, on the sofas, on top of cupboards, and on spare window sills. Randomly placed Liberty-style oriental rugs covered the stone flagged floor and the two large, feathered, sagging, faded red sofas overflowed with variously coloured cushions.

At the heart of this room was an enormous wood-burning fireplace. Built into the wall and on each side of it was a space for a person to sleep during the depths of a bitter winter. You had to be small to fit in there. Most people were too big, but I wasn't, not when we first started going there. Whatever the season, whatever the time of the day or night, there was a perpetual smell of wood smoke and it must have been this that discoloured the lime washed white walls. These were hung with photographic prints and paintings, some of which were very strange.

The three women, Philomena, Gaby and my mum got on really well. I'd hoped Gaby would have a daughter so I'd have a friend my own age, but she didn't. She was a teacher like my mum and once, when I asked her why she didn't have a child, she said seeing children all day and every day at work was enough, and she didn't want any at home. I thought she was rude, so I said that's just how I felt about grownups, but I'd never had the choice. I told her grownups were everywhere constantly interfering in my business and telling me what to do and what to think. Gaby looked at me and I could see she was wondering whether I was serious which I was, but it didn't bother her. She just smiled at me. She was alright really. She was pretty with round dark eyes, a heart-shaped face and long dark hair and she usually wore jeans and a man's shirt. The shirt was too big for her. It had stripes and swamped her. I asked her whether she had Birkenstocks like Philomena

17

and she said she had, but she preferred flip flops because she could easily slip them off her feet and walk on the grass. I told her to be careful of the wasps because I'd been stung on my foot once doing that. The wasps drink the dew on the grass, I said, and I asked her if she knew about that. She said she'd be careful.

Gradually the three women became like some kind of art collective in the way Philomena had wanted, and they developed an informal routine. They did their art in the day and they cooked together in the evening and if the weather was good, we all ate outside 'al fresco'. I hadn't known what that expression meant but my mum told me. They seemed to get on well and sometimes as it got late they drank lots of wine and they'd get noisier and noisier and more and more argumentative, but they were never nasty with each other. Amazing really. They were so enthusiastic. They showed their art to each other, talked about it and compared it with other women artists' work.

As for me, I was just left to get on with it and nobody bothered me or asked what I was doing. Neither did they ask Gareth for that matter. As the sole man he was an outsider but he didn't seem to mind. He kept out of their way most of the time and so did I. As the only child I was also an outsider, but because my mum was a single parent and we lived together in London I'd been used to her talking to me as if I was grown up. She'd also expected me to look after myself so I thought of myself as older than I really was. Consequently, sometimes I thought I knew it all. But I didn't. I found I had a lot to learn.

I was thirteen and it was the fourth summer we'd holidayed in Wales. I'd taken to visiting the creek almost every day, but I never saw anyone there. I didn't mind, because I thought of it as my personal property and if I didn't go at least three times a week, I suffered withdrawal symptoms. I went whether it was sunny, raining or windy, but as we were always there in August the weather was never bad enough to stop me completely.

I'd cycle the two or three miles down the back lanes and leave my bike under a particular tree. It was old, with a huge branch which had partially collapsed and lay close to the ground. It was perfect as a hiding place. Then I'd walk down the one and only path to the creek to check out if there was anything new. I was looking for interesting-looking stuff washed up by the tide, or dropped by the birds or the wind. The women at the farm photographed or painted what they called 'found objects'. They saw all kinds of abstract shapes and creatures in pieces of driftwood and what to a normal person looked ordinary and boring would become a piece of sculpture or a picture in their hands.

Entering that wood for me was like entering a mysterious other world. It was a place for dreaming and I loved its solitude. I spent long hours just messing about, not doing anything in particular. But one day I met a boy called Ifan and from then on things changed in a big way.

The day had been beautiful and it was late in the evening. It was still warm and the trees were filled with birdsong, the fire of the falling sun lit up their leaves and tiny insects swirled and moved like clouds of golden dust between them. The tide had been up and the water was pulling back from the reed beds to begin the long journey to the sea. As I got nearer to the river I heard someone singing in Welsh. I didn't know the song or understand the words, but I was astonished because this was what they called border country and it was rare to hear Welsh.

I stopped and listened. The song was hauntingly sung, almost as if it might be a poem. I was used to the frantic noise and pop music of London and this was so different, I was entranced. Then I saw him. A boy a little older than me, kneeling over a pool formed by a submerged tree root with a stick in one hand. He'd made a little raft and put a frog on the raft and courtesy of this boy, the little creature was being pushed along on the water and having a free ride. I stared at him.

Although I'd thought I was totally silent as I approached him, he must have heard me or sensed my presence. He stood up, looked straight at me, but before I could speak, he ran off. There was just enough time for me to see him. He looked old-fashioned, almost as if he didn't belong round there. His hair was blond and straight. It fell into his eyes, and looked as if someone had put a bowl on his head and cut his hair all round it. His eyes were grey-green. He reminded me of a Viking, or a Russian, the type I've seen since in a Tarkovsky film. He was well dressed in jeans and a check shirt with short sleeves and was taller than me. The speed of his disappearance left me feeling bewildered. I must look scary, I thought. I even wondered whether I'd imagined him, but because it was so rare to meet anyone, I wanted to see him again and find out more.

There was something different about him and that attracted me. Only the raft with the frog drifting away on the tide showed he was real.

Following that chance meeting, I made sure to be at the same place at the same time the next day, but there was no sign of him. I searched the estuary in case he was hiding somewhere and one day I found his den. It was in the middle of a group of bushes, hidden in the undergrowth and I felt sure it was his. I had to crawl past prickly blackberry bushes to reach the hollowed-out centre and inside, resting on the grass, was an old square tin with a picture of a boy with round red cheeks eating a biscuit. I opened the tin and found a bar of chocolate wrapped in a plastic bag and sellotaped down.

I sat for a moment wondering if he'd put it there. I wanted it to be a present for me and that was why he'd wrapped it so carefully, to stop foraging animals eating it. I waited for him until dusk hoping he'd come but he didn't appear, so I decided to eat some of the chocolate, so he'd know I'd been there. Then I cycled back to the farm. I was so happy I'd found his den.

When I got back to the farm the women were sitting outside in the garden with some visitors. Gareth was there too. They'd put a long table out on the grass. There was loads of food and wine and they seemed slightly drunk because they were laughing uproariously at everything. Philomena briefly said 'Hello,' and my mother told me there was food in the kitchen, but other than that, they took no notice of me.

The kitchen was like the rest of the farm, cluttered, only even more so. The walls were painted golden yellow so it always looked bright and the cupboards and shelves were burnt orange except where they were pale turquoise. As well as the usual cooking utensils you find in kitchens, everywhere you looked there was interesting stuff. Ornamental cockerels and pottery pigs and one of the walls had been painted with a dazzling mural of strutting peacocks. But pride of place, which you couldn't miss, was a life-sized ostrich with a human face, made out of straw. Philomena had put bead necklaces round its neck and a notice which said 'this is not an ostrich' which apparently was some sort of surrealist in-joke, and then Gareth put a trilby hat on its head.

The kitchen table still had the debris remains of their supper and I noticed a plate of food left out for me by my mum, but I didn't fancy it. I opened the fridge door to see what else was there and saw she'd cooked one of her specialities: Florentine biscuits.

However critical I became of my mother, I'll give her this, she was an inspired cook. I ate three of them, then helped myself to a bowl of Greek yoghurt sprinkled with sesame seeds, stirred in honey that smelt and tasted of thyme, and drank some pomegranate juice. It was all delicious. I picked out four of the best-looking remaining Florentines and wrapped them in foil for my secret friend in the estuary. I planned to leave them in the den first thing with a note saying I hoped my new friend liked them, and they were from me, Echo.

The thought of returning to the den was so exciting that, to make sure I arrived early, I set my alarm for five o'clock. Everyone was still asleep when I left the farm and there was no one to stop me so I didn't even have breakfast before I left. I just upped and went.

By the time I got to the creek the sun had risen. I hid my bike under a bush and looked around for the path. The estuary that morning was magical. It radiated with a mysterious otherworldly light, and I felt very happy, even though I had trouble finding the den again. It was hidden away from the path and in a particular clump of undergrowth but once I'd found it this second time, I saw there was a way of always locating it. Standing like a sentinel on the path was a twisted old hawthorn tree with grey-green lichen growing on its higher branches and this marked the place where you had to crawl through the bushes. I bent down and ducked underneath. It didn't occur to me that anyone might be around already because I was so early, but suddenly I heard someone crashing through the bushes in the opposite direction to me.

It could only be him. I shouted out, 'Hey, it's me. The girl you saw yesterday.' There was no response. 'I took some of your chocolate from your tin but I've got some biscuits in exchange. My mum made them. They're delicious.'

I stopped to listen for a reply but there was total silence so I guessed that's what he was doing too. Listening. Then I shouted, 'My name's Echo. What's yours?'

Nothing. I began to think perhaps it was an animal I'd heard but there was no way of knowing for sure so I decided to leave the Florentine biscuits in his tin anyway and I got out the note I'd written for him. It just said they were for him from me and I put that in the tin too.

I was so fed up and disappointed I hadn't seen him. I wanted to talk to him. It was then I realised how lonely I was. I didn't like being on my own all the time and I'd been looking forward to today. I felt restless and I didn't know what to do with myself. It wasn't worth going back to the farm because the women would be busy with their art so I wandered through the woods for hours in the hope of seeing him.

Eventually I found myself back at the den. It was mid-afternoon by then and I was hungry so I thought to open the tin again and eat one of the biscuits I'd left for him. After all, he wouldn't know I'd left four and three was enough anyway. I prised open the tin thinking I hadn't remembered it as being so tight.

My note was still there but all the biscuits had gone. I turned the note over and written in a neat hand was, 'Thank you very much for the biscuits. They were lovely. Ifan.'

Reading that note made me feel really, really happy, especially now I knew his name. I was full of hope. Soon I'd see him and we could talk. I stood holding the note and walked back to the path, but as I made my way something hit me on the back of the head.

I rubbed my head and looked on the ground to see what it was. A conker. I'd been hit with a conker. I looked around wondering if it had dropped off a tree but there were no conker trees, and besides it wasn't the conker season. It could only be Ifan, or perhaps, I thought, a squirrel had dropped it on my head by mistake. I bent down to pick it up and as I did another two hit me on the head. The sky was raining conkers. I began giggling.

I picked one up and I called out to no one in particular, 'Don't you know people can get knocked out with conkers?'

I heard a suppressed laugh and looked up into the trees. I could see him. Ifan. He was high up, standing in one of the branches close to the trunk and laughing. When he saw he'd been spotted he began climbing down, but this time he didn't run away, but stood in front of me grinning. He spoke first.

'You've got a funny name,' he said.

'Yes,' I said. 'It's my mother. I don't know why she called me Echo.'

'What's your surname?'

'Morgan.' I put my hand out and said, 'Nice to meet you. I thought I was the only one here.'

Ifan said, 'Well, you're not. There's me. Where do you live?'

'In a farmhouse at a place called Ffridd, it's about three miles from here, but I'm only here in August. The rest of the time I live in London.'

'I saw you last year but you disappeared. I thought you must have been here just for the day, then a few days ago I saw you again. You were hiding your bike, but I didn't want to speak to you, not until I knew you were okay.'

'Oh,' I said and because I didn't know what else to say, I added, 'I heard you singing.'

'What about it?' He smiled. He looked pleased.

'I liked it and so did the frog. What's it called?'

He gave me a look. 'Calon Lân.' Then he grinned, 'Shall I sing it again?'

'No, no thank you. Where did you learn it?'

'At school and with my dad, when we go to the rugby.'

'It's nice. Have you got a bike?'

'Yes, I live in the opposite direction so I cycle here too. I liked your biscuits.'

'My mum made them. I'm glad you liked them and you think I'm okay.'

We looked at each other. He was standing quite close to me and that made me feel shy.

'Do you want to see the best trees in this wood? There's some good climbing ones near here and you've got jeans on, and there's places to mess about along the river.'

'A tree. I've never climbed one. I don't know what to do.'

'Never climbed a tree?'

'No, there's not many where I live, not in Stroud Green.'

'I'll show you, it's easy, follow me, do what I do. Ready?'

I was ready. We became friends. Looking back to that time, we were both lonely and neither of us felt we fitted in although it was a while before Ifan told me about himself. Left alone by the women at the farm, I came and went as I wanted. I was happy with Ifan. We'd go for bike rides, paddle in the shallows of the river, climb trees and I'd bring food from the farmhouse for our picnics. We were good together and the estuary became our playground. Ifan was a year older than me but sometimes he seemed a lot older, although in those early days I didn't know why, nor anything about his past.

At the end of that summer, and after I'd returned to London, I missed him. He'd become my best friend. I'd find myself thinking about him and I wished he lived in London like me. I knew very little about him and I wanted to know more, like where he lived, who his parents were, and if he was an only child. I'd not told him anything about myself either. He'd never asked so I'd never said. It was as if we lived in some kind of bubble and the world outside was of no consequence.

The following summer I couldn't wait to meet up again. As soon as I saw him I told him I'd missed him and I wanted to know more about him. It was a bit in his face but he didn't seem to mind. He said he'd tell me later but it was late summer before he trusted me enough.

It turned out that even though he could speak Welsh he wasn't really Welsh. Not only that, he hadn't come from a normal family. I remember clearly what he said and how he said it and how I felt. We were sitting in the den eating our sandwiches when he told me. I'd said to him, 'When are you going to tell me all about yourself?'

He looked hard at me. Then he said, 'I was born in Russia. My mother was single and she had a vivid imagination, she dreamt about leaving Russia and coming to live in the West. She'd learnt English at school and she especially liked English novels. Her favourite writer was Thomas Hardy and she saw herself as a kind of Sue Bridehead.'

I said, 'Who's Sue Bridehead?'

'She's a character from one of his books, it's called *Jude the Obscure* and she wanted to be like her. She wanted to be educated, and study Victorian literature in England, in London. So she found a way to get herself and me to the UK so she could do that.'

'She sounds very clever.'

'Not so clever that she could look after me.'

I didn't know what to say when he said that. I looked at

him but he was staring at the ground. 'What do you mean?'

'She just disappeared. Left me with a neighbour and never returned. That's what I was told.'

'So she left you in London. What happened then?'

'Social Services got involved, I had a social worker and she found new parents for me.'

'Is that how you know what happened, through the social worker?'

'Yes.'

Now I understood why he looked and seemed so different. It was because of his past. It was something about how he looked, and his colouring and his intensity. I leant over and took his hand. I wanted to kiss him like you would a small baby, but I didn't. It would have embarrassed him. I could see he was upset, so all I did was squeeze his hand and say that it had been tough for him. I didn't bring it up again for a while, not until I'd read the Thomas Hardy book.

When I read it, I felt sad. I tried to think what his mum might be like. I didn't understand what had driven her to abandon Ifan, except she must have been unhappy. I saw her as a tragic person, someone who felt out of time and place.

I asked, 'What do you know about your mother?'

'Not much. I can't remember her. I was still a baby when she went so everything I know is from a file in an office... I've got no family of my own.'

'But you have, you have the family who adopted you.'

'It's not the same. They're different from me. They're kind but...'

He didn't finish his sentence.

'Do you have a photo of your mother? If you have, I want to see it.'

He pulled out a photo from a leather wallet and passed it over. It was of a very young woman. She had blonde hair like Ifan and was sitting on a rug by the sea and laughing at who was taking the picture. I looked at it carefully and then at him. 'She's very young. She's pretty and I can see a family

26

resemblance between the two of you. Who do you think took the photo? Could it be your father?'

'I don't know who he is.'

When he said that I was choked. I just didn't know what to say. He was an orphan. Even if he had been adopted and his adopters wanted him, it didn't take away the fact that his own mum left him while he was tiny and his father had abandoned both of them. And none of it was his fault.

He stared at me and said, 'What about you, what about your dad?'

'I'm like you. I don't know my father. My mum won't talk about him, so I don't know what he was like or why he went, or where he is, or anything about him. She gets upset if I ask, so I keep my mouth shut. There's no point. I get on her nerves, and she's said so often I'm difficult, that I believe her now, so I keep out of her way and keep my mouth shut. That way I don't piss her off.'

Ifan said 'So your dad, he's done a runner just like mine.' I must have had a weird expression on my face, because he said, 'It's alright, don't be sad.' I didn't think I was sad, but I didn't say that. He turned his face away so I couldn't see him, then he said, 'We're both the same. We have useless fathers.'

'I suppose so, but my mum said it didn't matter what he was like, because she'd make it up to me.'

Ifan stared. 'Make it up to you? What the fuck does that mean? She's not a man, is she, so how can she be like your father?'

'Oh, I don't know. Who knows what she means and who cares anyway?'

Then I did get upset and Ifan must have noticed because he acted as if he wanted to make it up to me. He grabbed my hand and said, 'Have you finished eating? Because two weeks ago I found something along the river washed up by the tide and I've made a boat out of it. I've been saving it to show you.' I'd been sitting on a log and he pulled me up and said, 'Come on, get up, quick. We need our bikes. We'll have to cycle to get there.'

He led and I followed, and by the time we got our bikes and had cycled along the road and track, we were out of breath and red faced. We came to a stop along a part of the river where it was shallow and he showed me two big, empty drums, which he'd pulled out of the water and on to the grass. They must have floated off one of the boats in the Bristol Channel. He looked proud as he pointed out what he'd made.

'You see this? It's a pontoon and it's based on my research. I went to the big library in Cardiff and looked at different types of boats.'

'It looks like an ordinary boat to me. Or is it a raft?'

'Yes, but it's not ordinary. It's a special type of boat.'

'What's that name on the side?'

'*Baranov 1*. That's my dad's name, he was an engineer and that's what I want to be.'

'Oh,' was all I said. He'd probably made that bit up.

'Look, can you see how it's made? I got the driftwood, lashed them together, then tied them to the two oil drums and then I placed them parallel to each other. They act as floats. Then I connected them with the plank so two people can sit together as it floats down the river. It's a prototype. What do you think?'

I looked at it. As he'd been talking I'd felt my eyes glazing over but in a month of Sundays, I'd never have said that to him. 'I'm impressed, but what next, what are you going to do with it?

It wouldn't have occurred to me what he was about to suggest.

'Well, I thought I'd get some improvised oars, then we could push it on the water, and paddle over to the other side, to England.'

I looked across. England seemed a long way away and the river was a filthy brown colour and running fast. I was doubtful. It looked scary. 'It's dangerous,' I said.

'Echo, you're a spoilsport, I thought you were different from other girls.'

That challenged me. I glared at him. 'Okay, well maybe…
It's a brilliant idea. But what if we fall off and we're swept out
to sea and drown? Then what? Can you swim?

'That won't happen. I can swim,' he said, 'but can you?'

'Yes,' I said, 'I can swim because my mum used to take
me to Hampstead Ladies' Pond.'

Ifan burst out laughing and said, 'Hampstead Ladies'
Pond. Where's that? You're no lady,' and when he said that,
I pushed him in the water. It was only shallow but he got
saturated. He struggled out and said, 'Right, I'm going to
get you, so you'd better run fast.'

I started screaming really loudly, 'Help, help. I'm being
attacked. Somebody, come. I'm going to be killed.' I ran away
through the trees and down the path but I was laughing as
well. He came after me until he caught up with me, then he
dragged me to a shallow part of the river and pushed me in.
I was soaking now, like him. We stood looking at each other.
'Bloody hell,' I said, 'my clothes are clinging to me. They'll
take ages to dry. We'd better go home and change.'

Ifan looked at me but then he said, 'Just take off your
clothes now.'

'And wear what?'

'Nothing.'

'Don't be stupid. Who do you think we are? Adam and
Eve? I'm not doing that. I'm going home now.'

Ifan said, 'Okay, if that's what you want, but are you still
up for the experiment on the raft tomorrow?'

'Yes,' I said, 'but tomorrow I'll wear my bathers underneath, just in case, and so should you.'

'Whatever,' he said, 'and don't forget to look for some
oars, but don't tell anyone. This has to be secret. If they find
out they'll try and stop us.'

I cycled off back to the farm. It was quiet when I got
there. Perhaps they were having a siesta. I had no idea where
everyone was, but I could see Gareth sitting under the trees
in the apple orchard in his favourite ladder-back chair with

29

the rush seat. He'd been drinking cider. I could see that by the empty bottles, but he was also surrounded with pages of writing lying on the grass which he'd weighed down with a stone to stop them blowing away.

I walked over, smiled at him, said, 'Hello,' and asked what he was doing. He said he was writing. I asked what about, and he said, 'Life.'

I didn't know what to say to that so I just said, 'It sounds private.'

'Yes, until I've finished,' he replied. Then he noticed I was wet. 'Why are you wet?'

I didn't tell him. I said I'd fallen in the water at the estuary and had come back to change into dry clothes, and because I could see he wanted to be on his own but was too polite to tell me, I said, 'See you later then,' and went to go in the house.

As I was walking away he called out, 'By the way, where did you fall in?' I turned round and said, 'Along the river. Past the estuary. Know where I mean?' He nodded, so I said, 'Well, it was there.'

He said, 'You should be really careful. Do you know how strong the tidal current is? It sweeps in from the Bristol Channel and it can be dangerous.'

'Thanks, Gareth, yes, I'll be very careful.' He was looking at me doubtfully so I said, 'I'm off for a rest now.'

I went to my bedroom, pulled off my wet clothes, and crawled into bed. I fell asleep straightaway and didn't even wake for supper. No one called me down. Perhaps they thought I'd eaten already but I didn't mind. They must have come in late but that meant in the morning I'd have the kitchen to myself.

I woke early the next day and went down for breakfast. I hadn't expected to find anyone up but Gareth was already sitting at the kitchen table eating scrambled egg on toast and reading a book propped up against the trilby hat he'd taken off the ostrich.

He looked up. 'How you doing, Echo?' he asked.

'Fine, thanks and what about you, how's your magnum opus going?'

He laughed. 'Still working on it. It takes time.' He put a slice of toast in the toaster, and said, 'So what are your plans for the day?'

I was pleased he was interested but I didn't tell him about the pontoon oil drum and our plans. I just said, 'Not much. Meeting a friend and we're going to have a picnic by the river.'

He didn't say any more other than, 'Well, have a good time,' and returned to his reading, which meant I could get on with making the sandwiches without any hindrance.

The fridge was always stuffed with food. I picked some cheese and buttered some thick multi-seeded bread my mum had bought from some trendy bakers who called themselves artisans. Just like London, I thought, everybody has to make up some crap to make themselves exciting and different. I made a huge doorstep for Ifan and me and then put that into a brown paper bag with an apple and banana. Everything fitted into my bike basket.

I said goodbye to Gareth and went outside to see what the weather was like. It was fresh, a little cool but it was going to be another lovely day. I stood wondering if I'd forgotten anything. I'd remembered to put my bathers on and wondered whether to pack a towel too but in the end I decided not to, basically because I couldn't be bothered to go upstairs again.

I fitted my basket on to the front of the bike but as I started to wheel it through the field, I realised I'd forgotten the oars. I didn't know where to look for them and, although I could go back and ask Gareth, he'd want to know why and I didn't want him to know because, as Ifan said, we'd be stopped from going on the river. I thought the best place to start looking would be in one of the outbuildings so I propped my bike against the farm gate and ran back.

I'd been inside this particular outbuilding before and it was full of things: tools, discarded furniture, spare engine

31

parts, horse-riding gear, empty flower pots, gardening tools, but I'd never noticed oars. As I pushed open the massive doors, I saw straight in front a canoe hanging on hooks drilled into the wall and tucked inside were two paddles. I couldn't believe my luck. These would be ideal and far better than anything improvised. I pulled them out, tied them to my bike rack with some rope and set off down the deserted country lanes. It was still early. As I cycled away I stood on my pedals to get up some speed, and I heard Gareth shout 'Ciao.' I looked over my shoulder. He was standing in the kitchen doorway drinking his coffee, watching me.

Ifan was waiting in the den when I got there. As soon as he saw me, he said, 'I've looked at the tide and it's coming in, so we can't be swept out to sea.'

'Ifan, Gareth told me yesterday the river's dangerous. It's the current; it's powerful, he said.'

'You didn't tell him our plans?'

'No, he only said that because he saw I was wet from when you pushed me in.'

'You pushed me first... I know it's dangerous but I've lived here most of my life. We'll be alright. The worst time is when there's a spring tide. It rushes inland from the Bristol Channel, but that's not now.'

He sounded so knowledgeable I didn't like to show my ignorance by asking what a spring tide was. I showed him the paddles I'd got. He was well pleased and said they were 'perfect'.

The plan was to sit next to each other on the raft and paddle across to the other side. I was really excited. We set off towards the river and found the raft. It was still in the same place where we'd hidden it. I took a look at the river. The water was racing past and the other side was a long way away. The reality of what we were about to do hit me. I was getting nervous. If we fell in, we'd have to swim for it but the water was moving so fast, it was scary.

I turned to Ifan and said, 'Did you remember to put your bather on under your clothes?' He nodded but he was staring across to the other side. It looked like he was in a dream. I said, 'Come on then, let's get ready and take our clothes off. You're not scared are you?' He gave me a strange look. I thought maybe he'd forgotten to put them on after all. 'You have got your them on, haven't you?' I asked.

'Yes,' he said, 'have you?'

'Of course I have. I'm waiting for you. You go first.'

He didn't move. I thought he was playing around. I was smiling, he wasn't. He looked deadly serious, standing there just staring at me. I caught hold of his shirt, unbuttoned it, and pulled it off. He stood in his beige shorts. He was still not moving.

'You're like a dummy, Ifan, what's wrong with you?'

He said, 'Nothing. You've taken off my shirt. Now I want you to take off your top.'

That took me by surprise. It was the expression in his eyes. He was looking straight at me and seemed more serious, more intense than I'd ever seen. I wasn't sure what was going on because he'd never spoken to me like that before. I hesitated, then lifting my arms up I slowly pulled off my t-shirt and stood in my bather. It was an ordinary one-piece blue bather, the one I wore at school when we went swimming. Nothing special to look at. He was still staring intensely at me.

'Now your bather and your jeans. Take them off too.'

'But...I'll have nothing on.'

'That's what I want. I want to see you, you know, what you look like underneath. We're friends. Just once, please, Echo.'

I was intrigued. I hesitated for a moment, wondering whether I should, then I did it. I stepped out of my jeans, tugged at my bathers, pulled down the top half, and wriggled out. I stood naked in front of him. I felt the grass under my bare feet and the cool air on my skin. I felt intensely shy. I could see him looking at my breasts and when I looked down at myself, my nipples had become erect. He stood for a moment staring. I watched his eyes looking intently at my face, my mouth, my breasts, my body. No boy had seen me naked before, but seeing myself through his eyes made me self-conscious. I hid myself with my hands.

He moved slowly towards me until he was close. He said, 'You're very beautiful.'

He kissed me.

It was my first proper kiss. It was a French kiss. I'd heard about them from my mates but they hadn't said how it would feel. It was strange. I felt his tongue in my mouth and all kinds of sensations flooded through my body. It was overwhelming. I had had no idea how powerful a kiss could be, but it felt good. Then he pulled away, stood back and stared at me.

'Ifan.' I looked him straight in the eye. 'Don't stop. Kiss me again. Like you just did. Like that.'

He didn't answer. His breathing was fast. He was looking deep into my eyes. He was so close I could feel the heat of his body. He stroked my face, ran his fingers through my hair, touched my breast, my nipples, my body and closing his eyes, took hold of my hand and guided it inside his shorts. As I touched him, he came. But then he turned away and stood with his back to me as if he was ashamed. I sensed he was crying.

For several minutes I didn't know what to do or say but I pulled my bather back on in case someone was watching. I took a quick look round but there was no one.

He said, 'I'm sorry, Echo, I shouldn't have done that.'

I put my arms round him. 'It's okay... I liked it and I like you, and it doesn't matter, because no one will ever know. I won't tell. It's a secret.'

Maybe I loved him, but I couldn't say that. He stood looking at me but suddenly became businesslike. 'We need to get across the river.' He was smiling now.

I was curious, I said, 'Just a minute, before we go, how did you know what to do, how to kiss? You must have done it with someone else before me?'

He was laughing and said, 'No.'

'I don't believe you.'

He looked serious again and looking straight at me, he said, 'No, I haven't. Well, not like that. You're the first. I didn't know that was going to happen. I mean, sorry, that came out wrong, when I saw you this morning, standing by the water, well, it's natural, isn't it?'

He took a step towards me, then stopped himself, so I didn't know what he'd been about to say.

I said, 'I'm your first. You're my first. So, what were you going to say or do?'

'Nothing. I wasn't going to say or do anything. We need to cross the river.'

I said, 'Okay,' but I was disappointed. He was pulling the pontoon closer to the river and as he stood up, he glanced at me. I looked at him and I thought I'll get my own back, catch him by surprise, the way he had me, and when he was least expecting it.

I walked over towards him, all casual like, then I kissed him full on the mouth with my arms wrapped round him and pressed so tight against him, I felt the heat and shape of his body all over again. I also made sure he could feel mine. I had my response. He had a hard-on. He didn't pull away, not straightaway but he looked so startled, I had to laugh.

I said, 'Now you know how I felt. So don't forget, it can work both ways,' and I stuck my tongue out at him. He looked at me in that way of his. That was the moment in my life when I recognised my potential power to get what I wanted or that's what I thought, but all he said was, 'Stop messing around. Let's get the pontoon out.'

He was determined not to give in, I could see that, but it didn't matter. I was happy. Happier than I'd ever been. The feelings that had flooded through my body were new and exciting. I'd always wondered if I was ugly, but Ifan didn't think I was and Ifan was more important to me than anybody. He saw me as beautiful and he wanted to be close and touch me and that made me feel good.

I helped him pull the raft into the water and neither of us said a word. I think he was embarrassed but I wasn't. My mind was still with what had just happened. I kept looking at him but he took no notice. He just said it was time to go and to sit on the raft.

He pushed it away from the river bank, then jumped on it. The raft floated alright. At first we drifted gently along under the trees but then it got caught in a protruding tree root, and we came to a halt. It started spinning, going round in circles – slowly, slowly, slowly, round and round. We looked at each other. We were stuck in an eddy and going nowhere.

Ifan seemed to know what to do. He pushed the paddle with all his strength against the bank until the raft floated free. We began a faltering path towards the middle of the river. It seemed to meander in a diagonal direction until we were halfway across. We took a look around. We were a long way from either bank and surrounded by fast-flowing deep water, but the sky was blue and the sun warm. I smiled; I was looking forward to landing in England.

It was sudden. Unexpected. Violent. An uncontrollable force of water, coming upstream from the Bristol Channel travelling at speed towards us. It hit us. A tidal wave so high and so powerful my paddle was wrenched out of my hands. Powerless, caught in its fury, we could do nothing. Out of control, we were left clinging for our lives on to the raft. We raced past river banks. Its force, its speed, the noise.

I shouted, 'How can we stop?'

'We can't. Hold on tight. It'll be calmer soon.'

I shouted again, 'When, how far will that be?'

'Don't know, we're heading towards Gloucester.'

I was too frightened to ask any more. I closed my eyes. I gripped the plank I was sitting on until my knuckles were white. If we were going to drown, I wanted to be with Ifan. We'd drown together. My mind went haywire. I wondered what it felt like to drown. I imagined my mouth and lungs filling with filthy brown water, not being able to breathe. An image of a baby swimming underwater came to me. She was smiling at the camera and as happy as if she was in her mother's womb. I wanted to be that baby. That made me feel better, but it didn't last because then I imagined the divers underwater, looking for us, and Ifan and me were trapped in dark wrecks with ugly fish swimming around, lurking giant octopuses with long waving arms, and we'd been pulled down, half-eaten and our floating, dead, bloated bodies were caught underwater in the skeleton of a ship and the fish were feeding off us.

I don't know how long that lasted but I still had my eyes closed when the raft shuddered and jerked violently. It stopped, violently tipping me off on to my side. Not in the water, but on wet gravel. I opened my eyes. First one then the other. I sat up. Looked around. The raft had disintegrated. I'd been dumped on a small spit of mud and gravel and I was alone. There was no Ifan. It took me a while to orientate myself. I was alive. Ifan had gone.

I couldn't believe he'd vanished. I stood up. The water was racing past but there was no sign of him. It was unbelievable. I couldn't believe it. He'd gone. Had he drowned? I began wondering how long I'd had my eyes closed. Had he been swept off then? Why hadn't he shouted for me? I sat down and cried. I couldn't stop crying. I asked myself why was I there and he wasn't? But there was no answer. Perhaps he'd been washed ashore. Thinking that perked me up for a while.

But then I realised somehow I had to get off this horrible place and back on to firm land. It was stupid, I know, but I began feeling angry with him. It had been his idea, crossing the river on the pontoon.

I forced myself to look around. The river was wide but I wasn't that far from the shore. I'd been dumped on a long sand bank with shingle disappearing into the water. In the distance I could see one of the drums from the raft had detached. It was bobbing and spinning away, carried along on the current. I watched until it disappeared from view. I never wanted to see that drum again.

I was stranded. The tide was coming in, and the sand-bank would soon disappear under water with me on it. It was obvious I'd have to be rescued or I'd drown. I stood up and gazed towards the shoreline hoping for inspiration.

Should I swim for it? But the tidal current was still running fast and even though it was August and warm, I didn't fancy submerging myself in that filthy water. For one thing, I wasn't such a good swimmer and there was no one to see if I was swept away. Just as I thought this I saw a man walking along the track by the river. He was a way off, walking with long strides but coming in my direction. I stared. He was wearing a shabby brown cord jacket.

It was Gareth. As he got level, I began jumping up and down, waving, screaming and shouting like a mad woman to catch his attention. He heard me because he stopped and looked towards me. He cupped his hands round his mouth, shouted and waved back. I couldn't make out what he was saying, but he put his hand to his ear, as if holding a phone, and pointed at it, as if he was making a call. He held up one hand with five fingers, closed it again, and did that twice more. He waved again. Then he left and ran fast down the track.

I was abandoned. By now I was really scared. I stared again at the muddy torrent racing past. It was full of debris and rising inexorably round me. I was separated from the shoreline by a wide channel. I was alone and about to drown.

I sat down on my haunches like a beggar. I hated that water. I could do nothing to save myself. Second by second I was becoming more resigned to the idea I was going to die. I'd always wondered what it would feel like and I was about to find out. I glanced at a piece of driftwood as it went spinning past at speed. Maybe, I thought, I should have grabbed it so when they found my drowned body at Gloucester it could be prised out of my hand and given to my mother 'as a found object'. She could call it 'In Memoriam' or something like that. This bizarre thought made me giggle, even though it wasn't funny.

The water continued rising insidiously. I wanted Gareth to come back. Just seeing him on land had made me feel better. He had to come quickly. The channel of water between me and the shoreline was growing wider every minute. I walked towards the end of the sand and shingle bank. It wasn't far. I came back. The water was rising so fast, soon I'd be marooned on an even tinier spit of sand and I wouldn't have long on this planet. I was getting colder by the second and I began shivering even though the summer sky was a brilliant blue and it was warm. The reality of what was happening hit me.

I began thinking about the women at the farm. What would they be doing? Would they be laughing at the same time as I was drowning? I thought about my father. I'd never meet him now. Perhaps he'd read about my death and would never know I was his daughter. And Ifan, where was he? Was he already drowned? And Maddy in London. I'd never see her again. Would anyone know that moment I died as I struggled to breathe, my lungs filled with the filthy sedimentary water of the Severn? I began to feel faint and distant from my surroundings. I felt as if I were seeing the river, the trees, the sky through the wrong end of a telescope and colours and sound were fading away until I experienced myself as totally alone in the world. Nothing mattered any more. I didn't care. I was giving up. How long was I there? I had no idea. Time means nothing when you're about to die. I lay down on the muddy, wet sand, my mind empty and waited.

Noise. Lights. Blue lights flashing, deafening sirens, men in uniform shouting at each other, boats, fire engines, an ambulance. One minute alone, about to drown, the next, surrounded by rescue vehicles. I struggled to sit up. An orange powerboat was bouncing towards me. Skimming the waves, it came closer and closer, circled round me, stopped. Three men were inside. They all wore bright yellow buoyancy jackets.

One of them stood up. He shouted above the roar of the engine and the rush of the water, 'Echo, can you swim?'

I shouted back, 'Yes.'

'I'm going to throw you a bag. There's a rope attached. You've got to grab it. When you grab it, don't let it go. D'you understand? Don't let it go.'

'No, I won't.'

The boat veered away, arced in a circle, and with its engine roaring, was manoeuvred so its prow faced the downward flow of current. The man shouted again, 'Are you ready, Echo? I'm going to throw you the rope now. Are you ready?'

'Yes.'

Using overhand and with all his strength he threw across a kind of bag with a rope attached. The three men started shouting, 'Rope, rope, rope, grab it, grab it. Go on, Echo. Grab it. Now.'

I missed it. They hauled it back through the water. He threw it again. I missed it again. By now I was paralysed with fear.

One of them said, 'No worries, Echo. You can do it. We're not leaving you. Just watch the rope.' He gave me the thumbs up. 'Now... Go for it.' It winged across to me. That time I caught it. They cheered.

I watched as one of the men attached himself to the boat by a line. Then as the boat came near to me and into the shallow water, he jumped in and waded towards me. The water wasn't deep but its power and volume was such that he could hardly keep to his feet. When he reached me, he put a belt round my waist so I wouldn't get swept away. There was hardly any shingle left to stand on. He told me to hang on and I was half-dragged, half-carried through the water to the rescue boat. He pushed me into the boat. I was saturated, almost passing out with the cold, barely aware of being wrapped in some kind of foil blanket.

They took off at speed, heading for a place close to the river bank. When I saw Gareth standing by the ambulance I knew I was saved. I stared at him as if I were stupid. My rescuer somehow got me out of the boat and leaning on him, I staggered towards the ambulance. Gareth was smiling and I heard him say, 'How's it going, Echo?' I couldn't answer. I couldn't move my mouth. I was incapable of saying anything to anybody, except thank you to my rescuers. Even now I remember how they answered. It was the man who threw the rope who spoke. He said, 'That's what we do. But we don't want to see you on this river again. You've behaved stupidly. Right? The Severn is dangerous. You could have drowned. You know that now. Get it? You were lucky this time.'

They were scary, unsmiling and like teachers on a bad hair day, except as they went, one of them winked at me.

Two ambulance men helped me into the ambulance and on to the stretcher. It was horrible. It was all white, smelt of disinfectant and full of medical stuff. They said I had to go to hospital to have a check-up. I asked, 'Where's Ifan?' They didn't answer; they took my blood pressure. The last thing I remember was saying, 'Go away. Leave me. I'm fine but I want Ifan,' then I passed out.

Part Two

I woke up in hospital. My mum and Gareth were sitting round my bed staring at me. I sat up. 'How long have I been here?'

My mum answered, 'Not long, you've been asleep since yesterday. It's only Thursday.'

I must have looked blank because she said, 'The day after yesterday.'

I looked around. I'd been put in a side ward of a children's ward. I glanced down. I was no longer wearing my bathing costume but had on some cotton thing with teddy bears printed on it.

'What's this stupid thing I'm wearing? It's open down the back.'

'It's a hospital gown they put on you while they examined you.'

'I don't remember that.' I paused, then I said, 'Where's Ifan?'

Neither of them heard because my mum said, 'Well, how are you feeling now?' It took a while to answer. I felt weird and disconnected from everything. 'Okay. I suppose.' I was staring at her as if I didn't know who she was. She looked as if she was a creature from outer space; perhaps she was.

She said, 'Why are you staring at me like that?'

'You look strange.'

That irritated her, she tutted, 'Well, I'm not. I'm pleased you survived your ordeal but you put a lot of people at risk, as well as yourself. I hope you realise that.'

She didn't look pleased. I didn't want to annoy her further so I said, 'Sorry, it's not like I meant it.' She passed across a plastic box. 'Here's some Florentines you might like.'

I was hungry and began eating one straightaway. I offered one to both of them, but they said they'd not long had breakfast. I looked at Gareth. He hadn't said a word and was sitting on the opposite side of the bed to her.

I said, 'Gareth, you saved my life, but how did you know I was there? It's amazing. You came along at the exact right time.'

'It wasn't me that rescued you, but SARA.'

'SARA. What's that?'

'The Severn Area Rescue Association, they specialise in fast water rescue.'

'Oh. But, they didn't know me...and...they must, well, it was dangerous... I thought I was going to drown. They put their own lives at risk. I want to thank them again.' I turned to my mother and said, 'Shall we give them a donation?'

She gave me a dirty look and said, 'You give them a donation. You got yourself in that mess. They rescued you, not me.'

I thought 'cow' but I didn't say it. My mother was a hard woman, that's for sure.

I turned to Gareth again. I said, 'So how come you were there at just the right time?'

'Pure chance.'

I looked at him in disbelief and said, 'I don't believe you, Gareth, tell me the truth.'

He laughed and said, 'Well, I saw you take the canoe paddles, and bearing in mind you were soaking wet the day before and you'd told me you'd been to the estuary, I put two and two together. I thought I'd check out what you were up to. The river's dangerous.'

I said, 'You're not kidding... What about Philomena, where's she, why isn't she here too?'

'She's going to cook a special meal for you. She sends her love and so does Gaby.'

I said, 'Well, that's nice of her but I'm alright. But what about Ifan? How's he? Can I see him?'

My mother said, 'Ifan. Who's Ifan?'

I said, 'Ifan's my friend. He built the pontoon we were on.'

I remembered then he'd gone. I began to cry. I twisted myself round away from them, pulling the covers over me so they couldn't see my face. Nobody did or said anything for what seemed like ages and then I felt a hand on my shoulder, and I heard Gareth say, 'What's wrong, Echo? Don't cry.'

'Nothing. Go away.'

'We're not going away when you're crying.'

My mother walked over to my side of the bed and pulled the cover away from my face and looked at me in that way she had. 'You'd better say, or for sure, we can't help. Who is he? This Ifan.'

'My best friend.'

'You never talked about him before.'

'My friend at the estuary. I've known him for years.' Then I cried even more. I was struggling for breath and through sobs I said, 'When that wave came and knocked the oars out of my hand, I was so frightened I closed my eyes, and that's when he must have drowned. He was swept away in all that water. I'll never see him again. I loved him.' My voice sounded contorted.

'Don't be silly, what do you know about love? Besides, he was probably picked up further along the river. You survived, didn't you and so will he.'

I looked hopefully at her and Gareth. I said, 'When you were walking along the river before you saw me, did you see someone tall with straight blond hair?'

'No. I'm afraid I didn't, Echo. Maybe he was admitted to hospital and then he might have discharged himself.'

I thought about that and said, 'But he wouldn't be able make that kind of decision for himself, would he? He's only fifteen, after all.'

My mother spoke then. 'Maybe you'd better tell us more

about this boy, since he clearly means a lot to you.' I saw her exchange glances with Gareth.

I glared at her and said, 'He's not a child. He's Ifan and he's my best friend.'

She was looking tetchy and said, 'Well, you never told me about him before, and why didn't you bring him to the farm so we could all meet him?'

I didn't like to tell her the truth – that they embarrassed me with their loud laughter and drinking, their weird paintings, and their strange ideas, so I just said, 'We never had the time.'

At this she laughed and said sarcastically, imitating me as if I was stupid, 'You were so busy.'

As she said this I felt I loathed her and would have liked to smack her one, but instead I sat up, swung my legs over to the floor, pulled my gown across my bare bum and stood up. 'You're stupid,' I said, 'Did you know that? Deeply stupid and you really annoy me.'

She stood up then and said, 'Where do you think you're going?'

'To get my clothes on to go and find Ifan. Since no one knows where he is, or cares, it's up to me. You two are making me feel as if I'm mad. He must be alive and I'll find him.'

Gareth stepped in then and said in his calm way, 'Phoebe, I'll go with Echo. Don't worry, I'll look after her. It's important she finds out about Ifan.'

My mother looked at him suspiciously, as if she thought we were going to get into mischief. She said, 'Fine. That suits me. I'll check with the staff nurse that she can go, then I can get back to my painting. I'll see you both later. But, Gareth, she's a handful.'

I folded my arms across my chest, pursed my lips, rolled my eyes and said, 'And you're so insulting.'

She walked out. It was a typical spat between us. I'd started answering her back, and that had made things worse between us, but her sarcasm wound me up. I suppose she did her best and so did I. It's just we came from different planets.

Gareth sat down and said, 'Why don't you get dressed now and then we'll get off. We can ask hospital records first. I'll wait for you outside.'

I said, 'Okay.'

I picked up the clothes my mother had brought for me. That reminded me of another thing we quarrelled about; what I wore. But this time she'd got it right. She'd brought my favourite jeans, my deep blue, American-style hoodie and pink Adidas trainers. I'd bought the hoodie and trainers in Camden Market and I felt great in them. The blue suited my colouring, dark blonde I'd been told. I pulled the curtains around and got dressed.

I still felt shaky so before we left I checked how I looked in the hospital toilets. That morning I looked alright, but I didn't always. Sometimes I looked ugly. My eyes are dark brown, like my mother's, but whereas her hair was black and wavy, mine is naturally straight, which was fortunate because I don't like cooking my hair in straighteners. Perhaps I looked like my father, but we never talked about him because like I said, he was one of the many taboo subjects, along with sex.

We went to the A&E department. Gareth had told me that was where I first was first brought in, but because I'd fainted they'd kept me in overnight.

'Is that what always happens, or did I nearly die?'

He reassured me. 'You're okay, Echo. You fainted because of exhaustion, cold and the shock of nearly drowning.'

I asked him again about Ifan. 'Are you sure you didn't see Ifan? He wore shorts and when his hair falls into his eyes, he flicks it back. Like this.' I showed him by jerking my head back.

'No', he said, but I could see him looking at me in a peculiar way.

'Was there anything in the papers or on the news?'

'No.'

I said, 'That's strange, where can he be? We were both on the raft.'

'Perhaps he was taken to another hospital,' Gareth said.

I looked at him doubtfully, but I could see that, unlike my mother, he wanted to help. We went to the hospital records department and Gareth asked whether a boy called Ifan had come in, but they weren't able to find his name. The trouble was I didn't have his full name, although in a moment of inspiration I gave them 'Baranov' but there was no one with that surname. Everybody was recorded by their surname, first name, date of birth or post code, but there was nothing. Even date and time of arrival didn't reveal anything. They suggested another hospital but it was miles away and I could never get there.

I was beginning to feel weird again. My name was on the records so I knew I hadn't imagined things and if I'd survived I wanted Ifan to have survived too. I refused to consider that maybe he had drowned. Gareth suggested ringing up the other hospital when we got back which was a good idea. Then he asked what I wanted to do so I said I'd like to go back to the creek to get my bike. We drove there and he parked his car on the road outside the wood. I wanted to show him where it all started so we walked along the path until we reached the river. Looking at the water brought it all back. I thought I was going to pass out but I didn't tell Gareth. I just said this was where we'd pushed the raft into the water but the current caught us and everything got out of control.

Neither did I tell him what we'd done before getting on the pontoon. That was a secret. When I'd first woken up in the hospital I'd dreamt about how exciting it had been when I'd taken off my clothes for him and how touching him made him come. That made him special but made me miss him even more.

But then I got into something weird. Had we nearly drowned as a punishment? When I was little, my mother read me stories about the river gods in Greece. They were really myths but people believed in them. Perhaps they'd been right after all, there were river gods and Ifan had been taken by them. But I said nothing of these thoughts. I acted normal.

'When you were walking along the river and you saw me standing on the sand bank, did you look all around?'

Gareth said, 'You were on your own,' but he gave me a look as if I were mad.

I decided not to ask any more questions ever, or show I was worried, because although I liked Gareth, on this count he'd allied himself with my mother, and so I couldn't trust him. We walked back through the trees until I got to the place where I'd hidden my bike. By then I'd decided not to show him Ifan's den because it was our private place. I told him I was going to hang around for a few more minutes before I cycled back and I promised not to go on the river. I thanked him again and he drove off.

What I actually wanted to do was to check out the den and see what had happened to our picnic which we'd planned to eat when we returned from crossing the river. The brown paper bags were still there with the sandwich, the apple and banana but they were untouched.

My eyes filled with tears. I'd been hoping Ifan would have left me a note if he'd been rescued, but there was nothing.

The den looked the same as always. Minus Ifan. I sat down on a log and contemplated what had happened over the past two days. It was strange for him to disappear like this. I decided when I got back to the farm to write him a note and leave it in the den tomorrow. I'd also phone the other hospital to see whether they had any records of him.

I realised then I didn't know where he lived. I didn't even know for sure his surname, although in the hospital I'd guessed his name might be Baranov, it hadn't helped. It occurred to me that knowing so little about a friend was strange. We'd made the woods and the creek our world and nothing important existed outside of that. But now he was missing I was lost. I tramped all through the woods hoping I'd see him. I called out his name. I listened for his voice but I heard nothing. I gave up and I was close to tears as I cycled back to the farm.

It was late by the time I got back. They wanted to know where I'd been. I'd totally forgotten Philomena and Gaby were making a meal for me and my mother would expect me to be on my best behaviour, but they were alright about me being late. I wasn't told off. We sat down to eat and I told them about the raft and how we nearly drowned. I left Ifan out of it and just said a friend had made the raft. I was beginning to feel something strange was going on and I didn't want to be looked at pityingly all over again.

Everyone was kind, even my mother. She restrained from wise-cracking at my expense. In fact while we were at the farm, I'd noticed she was a nicer woman, possibly because she was doing what she liked best, painting, and with people on the same wave length and she wasn't having to teach the classics to pupils who weren't interested.

I went to bed early that night but before I went to sleep I decided to write the note for Ifan. I'd take it with me tomorrow when I went back to the den. I sat pondering what to say and decided the shorter the better. After all, I didn't want to frighten him off by coming over as a bit strong. I wrote:

Hi Ifan,
I hope you've recovered from the ordeal on the river. I'm alright and I'm looking forward to seeing you again as usual. I plan to come Wednesday.
Your friend, Echo.

I put it in an envelope, sealed it, and put that into a plastic bag to protect it from rain.

That night I had a nightmare. I dreamt I was on the sand spit again and I was about to die. In the dream I was looking across the river at Ifan and as I watched, he faded away. He disappeared in front of my eyes and as he did, the water rose round me and I was swept away. I was struggling to keep my head clear of all the flotsam and jetsam. No rescue vehicles came. I woke up crying. As I lay there I started thinking about Ifan and cried even more.

I remembered a song my mum used to sing to me when I was very little which made me happy. I began humming it quietly. It's called 'The Waters of March'.

I couldn't get back to sleep. Finally I dragged myself out of bed about six and after a quick breakfast I let myself out of the house. No one was up, not even Gareth.

I had to see if Ifan was at the den. The night's dream had left me feeling wobbly, as if there was a catastrophe about to happen. I had to go to the estuary but I was even beginning to doubt if that existed. Nothing seemed real anymore and it felt as if I were awake in a dream.

I cycled down the lanes to the estuary. I left my bike in the usual place and wandered down the path heading towards the river. It was there. It wasn't a dream. I sat down on a fallen tree trunk and watched the sun rise over the water and the light play with the shadows, but my mood was changing. The path through the woods looked sinister, as if it led to another mysterious world, but one that was threatening. I remembered how frightening the river had been. It was as if a hateful river god had been unleashed and had hitched a ride with us, but we had survived; or at least, I had.

I walked slowly back to the den. I almost didn't go inside because I didn't want to face Ifan's absence. I stood looking at the hollowed-out area we'd made in the middle of the bushes. Soon the tendrils of an invading blackberry bush would snake across the grass until all traces of our secret place would be obliterated and it would be possessed by the forest again. I wondered again whether what had happened had been real or if it existed only in my mind, but another part knew it hadn't been imagined.

I searched for somewhere to leave my note and decided on a place under some dense undergrowth. I didn't want to stay any longer. I felt lonely and it reminded me of how I used to feel before I met him. I was close to tears but I forced myself not to cry. I couldn't accept he'd gone and I still believed he'd turn up.

It was lunchtime when I got back and Philomena and Gaby were chatting round the kitchen table. I asked where the others were and Gaby told me Gareth had gone out and my mum was still painting and hadn't wanted to stop. She gestured to me to sit next to her and share lunch. They were drinking Moroccan tagine soup with homemade thick slices of sour dough bread. It was delicious but I didn't feel like talking and neither was I in the mood to listen to their conversation. I was in a world of my own, my mind drifting to thoughts of Ifan.

I heard Gaby ask if I'd recovered from my adventure. I said I had, but I forgot I'd vowed never to speak of Ifan again so I asked Philomena how well she knew the people who lived round there.'

'Pretty well, we've lived here for about twelve years.'

'Have you ever come across a boy with straight blond hair that falls into his eyes?'

'No,' she said, 'who is he?'

'A friend. He was on the pontoon with me but he's disappeared. I thought I'd see him at the creek when I came out of hospital, but he's missing.'

'Sorry, I can't help. I'm sure he'll turn up. Have you rung the hospital?'

'No, but Gareth asked at hospital records. They didn't know.'

'He could live in the mountains on a remote farm. Does he speak Welsh?'

'Yes. Why?'

'Well, knowing that might help. Sorry, I don't know many Welsh-speaking families but the way you describe him, I'd remember him.'

I felt my eyes fill with tears. I left the kitchen before they noticed. Finding him seemed a hopeless task. I stood in the hallway wondering what to do when I heard Philomena speak.

'You know Gareth's worried about Echo. She almost drowned, and he thinks it's been more traumatic than we realise and it's affected her memory. You know, the boy she's just asked about, the one she called Ifan?'

Gaby said, 'What did she tell him?'

'That he disappeared off the raft while she had her eyes closed. He thinks she made him up, but the more he says he didn't see him, the more upset she becomes.'

I stood frozen to the spot and waited to hear what would come next. I didn't like them talking about me.

Gaby spoke. 'Well, she's a lonely child. She's deep too. I wonder sometimes what's going on in her head. It's a shame she and her mother don't get on. I don't know what that's all about. But I like her.'

'Yes, Gareth and I do, but what makes her tick, it's difficult to say. I guess it's her age, coming through puberty in this day and age…it's a tough call. But she lives in her own world and what she does all day, it's hard to know.'

'She reminds me of a boy at the school where I teach. He was a bright child but when he reached adolescence he became more and more withdrawn… We had a meeting about him, and it turned out five years previously his parents had been killed in a car crash and as there were no suitable relatives, he'd been placed with foster parents. It happened before he came to our school, but no one thought to tell us. It turned out he spent his waking hours thinking about an "imaginary friend", one that kept him company and that's why he was withdrawn.'

'Really. So are you saying he created his own world in his mind and that was more real than the real? That's interesting…but sad.'

'Yes, had you heard of this?'

'No, but it's fascinating what children do.'

'Usually, they grow out of it. It's part of growing up for some children.'

Philomena laughed, 'Well, not so different from ourselves.'

I was furious. I didn't like what I'd heard. I knew for

certain Ifan existed and I resented them thinking he was made up and I was mad. I stomped loudly back up the stairs and went to my bedroom. I was in a bad mood all day. From then on I was determined to find Ifan. I'd prove he existed.

I didn't come down for the rest of the day. I put a notice on the door saying I was writing my diary and not to disturb, and ignored them when they knocked and asked me to come down and eat. I wrote down everything I could remember, starting with my mother finding Philomena's notice in the paper, the interview, finding the estuary, meeting Ifan and the river adventure. All I left out was what we did before trying to cross the river because that was private.

In the evening they called me again. I didn't want to go but I had to because my mother came to my bedroom and made such a fuss, saying how unsociable I was, in the end I went. I was pissed off, I didn't feel like talking and was still annoyed by what I'd overheard, so when anyone spoke to me I glowered at them.

My mother said, 'Take no notice of Echo, she's sulking. Just ignore her.'

That really wound me up. I stood up, and snarled, 'Fuck off...what do you know about me? Nothing, so put a sock in it.'

I noisily pushed the chair backwards so it scraped on the tiled floor and left the kitchen. As I walked past the ostrich, I knocked his hat off, caught it, spun it across the table at Gareth, and shouted, 'Quick, catch it, Gareth.' They fell silent and looked at their food with the exception of my mother. She looked daggers at me. I couldn't have cared less. I slammed the door behind me.

I ran up the stairs to my bedroom and lay on my bed. I couldn't stop laughing at the look on their faces when I threw the hat. Ifan would have found it funny, but he'd gone. That made me sad all over again. Maybe, I thought, I should visit the estuary again. Perhaps he'd died or was trapped somewhere and they couldn't tell me. But if he was dead he was sure to be a friendly ghost and would appreciate a visit from me. The more I thought about it the more I wanted to go. I remembered my last visit and the strange atmosphere. It was as if someone was waiting for me. Maybe that was the spirit of Ifan.

I had to go. Soon we'd be returning to London and I'd be back at school and it would be another year until we came to Wales again. I couldn't wait that long. I had to find out before I left. I'd go after they'd drunk a bit and got rowdy, because then they wouldn't notice my absence. First though I'd act normal and tell them I was going to bed early. I'd play the 'mad' card and say I was still upset from nearly drowning. The idea made me laugh. It was the kind of a reverse double bluff that Ifan would have appreciated and would have laughed at too.

I waited until about ten and walked into the kitchen. They were still sitting round the table and on their third bottle. My mother gave me a filthy look. There was no sign of Gareth. I asked where he'd gone. Philomena said she didn't know but he'd gone off somewhere in his car.

'Is he coming back?' I said.

She looked pissed off and whispered, 'I hope so,' and I noticed her look away. I liked her and I could see she was upset. She was looking uncertain, which wasn't like her at all so I winked at her, like she'd winked at me once, and said in a perky way, 'Well, when you see him, tell him I want to ask him something, okay?'

She said, 'Can I help?'

'No,' I said, 'not really. I don't want to be rude. It's him I need to speak to. It doesn't matter. It can wait.'

The truth was I'd noticed Gareth had taken to going out a lot and I wanted to know where he was going all the time. I was curious. He seemed to be out more than he'd ever been and I wondered if he had a lover. If so, and Philomena suspected him, that would explain why she was looking a little down.

Just as I was about to leave the room, I noticed paper

scattered all over the table with writing and drawings on them. 'What are you doing?' I asked.

My mother at that point deigned to speak civilly. She said proudly, 'We're planning an exhibition of our work for next year.'

I said, 'Bloody hell, that's impressive. Here or in London?'

'Here, we thought Wales.'

I asked what kind of exhibition and my mother said, 'It'll have the theme of "Women and Surrealism".'

I said 'Oh,' thought for a while and then said, 'Like that Dorothea Tanning picture? But do you think people will know what that means?' They went quiet. 'I'm only saying that because if I don't know other people won't know.'

No one answered so I finished off by saying, 'I think the title needs changing. It's a bit obscure, if you don't mind my saying.' It was the first time I'd used that word and I felt proud of myself. There was another silence so before anyone could speak I scarpered, and as I left I called out, 'See you in the morning. Work hard.' I didn't care if they were annoyed; after all they'd annoyed me.

I went up to my bedroom and stared moodily out of the window. It was pitch black outside. It didn't look inviting. Maybe I should cancel the trip and just go to bed. Then I thought of Ifan. Perhaps he was waiting for me and I couldn't let him down. I wanted to be faithful to his memory. But it was still a hassle cycling to the estuary and I didn't even know if the bike had lights. I did have a torch though, which I used for going to the loo at night because I didn't like snapping on the lights and waking everyone up.

I got the torch out of the drawer, put on my hoodie and stood at the top of the stairs, listening carefully. I had to be sure the women were busy before I left. They were talking and laughing. They'd recovered. I made my way down the stairs towards the back entrance. The door was rarely locked at night but to make doubly sure I could get back in, I left one of the ground-floor windows open. It was warm that night so it was unlikely anyone would close it.

I wheeled my bike down the gravel path to the lane and cycled towards the estuary. The bike didn't have lights, but there was no traffic and I could see because the moon was bright that night. I was sure I was going to see Ifan. I don't know why I was so sure, but when I did see him I planned to ask if he'd recovered and why he was avoiding me. I cycled so fast it didn't take long to reach the place where I hid my bike.

Looking back, I must have been crazy but people do all kinds of weird stuff when someone disappears. First, I planned to walk to the den and then go to the river. I switched on my torch. Listened. The woods were silent. I couldn't hear a thing. I didn't feel scared. Not until I saw the headlights of a car.

It was being driven slowly along the road, as if the driver wasn't sure of the way. It stopped where there was a gap between the trees, then turned off the road, and bumped along the track. I could see the headlights coming towards me through the trees and that was kind of scary so I moved further into the woods and hid behind a large tree. I was curious and wanted to see who it was. Eventually it stopped and the driver switched off the engine.

No one got out. I could hear music drifting out from the car. It was the type of music my mother plays when she gets involved with someone in what she thinks is a love affair. She had a thing going for Frank Sinatra, but this wasn't Frank Sinatra, it was some drippy female singer playing the piano at the same time. The windows were steaming up, so I guessed the couple inside had the hots for each other and were about to have sex.

I was about to leave when the car side door opened. To my amazement Gareth stepped out from the passenger side. He was followed by a woman I'd never seen before. She'd been the one driving. I had to stay now. I could see her clearly as she stood in front of the car's head lights, smiling up at Gareth. I didn't recognise her or the car, which looked a bit of a wreck.

I took a good look at her. She was sort of bohemian. She was pretty with dark straight hair cut in a short bob with a long fringe. She'd made her eyes up so by comparison her mouth was pale, either because she was wearing very pale lipstick or none at all. I thought she was stylish in an offbeat kind of way. She was wearing the type of thing my mate Maddy liked, like you see on the women working at the book shop in the South Bank. She had on a flowered cotton dress with a calf-length skirt, and a lacy cropped cardigan in a vibrant pink. Although I thought of flowered fabric as usually passé, the design of her dress was modern with colours of burnt orange and fuchsia. The flowers could have been nasturtiums. I liked her outfit. It was kind of vintage looking. I wondered where she'd got her dress from.

I tuned my attention then to Gareth. Unusually for him, he'd made an effort with his clothes. He looked very attractive. I fancied him. Maybe that was because I knew a little more about being turned on after my sexual experience with Ifan. Plus he was a poet. In fact, he suddenly seemed very appealing to me. He was no longer wearing baggy cords but some well-fitting black jeans with a denim shirt and I noticed for the first time that he had a nice body. His clothes showed how well proportioned he was. I stared. After all, he wasn't to know I was staring.

I watched Gareth and the woman move closer to each other. When they were about as close as it was possible to be, they stopped and stood facing each other. They looked serious. Neither of them smiled. Gareth, who was taller, looked down into her eyes, cupped her chin in his hand, gently pulled her towards him and slowly kissed her. It was sure to be a French kiss because it was the kind of kiss you see late at night on television which makes you feel you shouldn't be watching. It was long, smouldering, and it put me in mind of Ifan's kiss and how I'd stood naked in front of Ifan as he watched me. I dragged myself back to the present. I was fascinated. I couldn't tear myself away.

I saw him whisper to her, take a step back before walking back to the car. He switched off the headlights, left on the sidelights, and replaced the female singer with Frank Sinatra. He was singing with the full backing of his orchestra. The silence of the forest broke as 'Let's Face the Music and Dance' flooded through the night air.

They stood opposite each other, moved a little apart. She raised her arms, put her left hand on his shoulder, her right in his hand, and pulled away from him slightly. I watched closely. It was as if they'd danced together forever, they knew each other's rhythm, their timing, how the other moved. They moved as one. They were dancing the quickstep. I knew this because sometimes I'd watch dance programmes with my mum. But this wasn't something you'd expect to see in a forest clearing at midnight. He spun her round, she leaned back, her skirt billowing out. She seemed to fly. After my experience with Ifan I knew what was going on. It was obvious. They had the hots for each other and it was just like watching a film, or having a dream about sex.

A line from the song burnt into my consciousness. It was 'There May be Trouble Ahead' and when I heard that I understood what was going on and why Gareth was absent so much from the farm and why Philomena was upset. She knew Gareth was having an affair and she was jealous. But I was jealous too. I was stirred up, almost tearful, but there was more to come. They hadn't finished with each other yet, they had another song to dance to.

It was Frank Sinatra again, this time 'I've Got You Under My Skin' and like the lyrics of the other song it was about the difficulties of an affair. Compared with the first, this dance was slow and sultry, but even I could tell by the way they looked into each other's eyes and held each other, they were desperate to get it together.

The message was loud and clear and although neither had spoken since they'd got out of the car, they didn't need to because it was obvious why they were there. When the song came to the end, Gareth tore himself away from her, went to the car, brought out a rug, and laid it on the grass. The woman kicked off her sandals and stood on her toes while he kissed her. It was another kiss that seemed to go on for ever. Then she lay on the rug, put her arms up to Gareth and with a slight smile on her face, beckoned to him. He stood over her and watched as she hitched her skirt up. She had nothing on underneath.

I felt myself blush. I was embarrassed. I was an intruder. I shouldn't be watching. It was time to go. As I left, I glanced over my shoulder. I wanted to see how Gareth made love to her. I was fascinated by them, their situation, their passion for each other and curious about how they'd make love. But if I stayed it would be weird and since I didn't want to be a 'perv' I left. I felt sad as I walked away further into the woods.

I'd have to wait now for them to do whatever they were going to do before I could go back and retrieve my bike, so I walked along the track to the river. When I was far enough away, I switched on my torch. What I'd seen unsettled me. I felt angry. The tide was coming in and I stood watching the water race past, wondering how long it takes the average couple to have sex. Five seconds, five minutes, five hours or what? I began imagining what they might be doing, but I stopped myself. What would be the point? I'd get more jealous. My mind returned to Ifan, how he'd asked me to undress and how excited he'd been seeing me naked. Would Gareth desire me in the same way if he saw me naked? I wasn't even sure how I looked without clothes on although Ifan must have thought I looked alright. Even so I still felt ugly, boring and unattractive.

I wanted to be desired like the woman with Gareth and, I thought, if I could have sex with someone like him, I'd feel attractive and worldly. I wanted to become the kind of woman she was. Interesting, sexual, sensual and so beautiful that she could dance with poets at midnight in the forest.

As I thought of Gareth, the woman, her dress, it came to

me, like a flash of lightening, who she was. She had to be the woman in Gareth's love poem; the one I'd read about on our first visit to the farmhouse, the poem he'd left by mistake on the kitchen table, the one he'd called 'The Girl in the Flowered Dress'. The woman I'd seen tonight, had been wearing a flowery dress. It was too much of a coincidence. But why did they meet late at night in the forest to have sex? Was she, like Gareth, betraying someone? Anything seemed possible.

I'd seen Gareth as steady and reliable. Now I saw him as wildly passionate, and I began to think in a crazy way that I wanted to be part of his life or with someone like him. If Ifan hadn't gone, maybe we'd have been just like them, so I walked back to the den and stood outside thinking about Ifan.

I missed him, and his loss came upon with me with such an intensity it was physical, like a sharp pain. I'd been so taken with watching Gareth and his lover, for the moment I'd forgotten about him. My friendship with Ifan had been about playing – until the river. That had changed everything. I pushed my way past the bushes and into his den and sat down on a tree trunk. I remembered how pleased he'd been with his find in the woods and how he'd pulled it along the path and said it was a chair we could both use. That made me tearful. We'd sat on it together and shared my mother's Florentines. But now he'd gone.

I tried imagining him in the hope he'd come back but nothing happened. I was alone. He wasn't coming back, and probably never would. Before long, the bushes and brambles would hide the entrance to his den and be engulfed by the forest.

Had I made up everything? It felt as if I no longer knew what was real and what was imagined. Before Ifan disappeared, I'd thought the only difference between the dreams of the day and the night was time, but now I questioned myself. Gaby's comments to Philomena had put doubts in my mind and I was becoming more uncertain. Had Ifan really existed? Perhaps she'd been right, he had been created by my imagination because if he'd been real, surely after almost drowning, he'd want to know how I was.

I began the walk back to retrieve my bike. I hoped Gareth and his lover had gone. I couldn't bear seeing them. I got to the end of the track. Their car had gone. I picked up my bike and began the walk to the road. Going back to the farmhouse, I found I couldn't cycle fast, my legs felt as if they were shackled and I wobbled all over the road. I was exhausted.

It was 3am when I dragged myself up the stairs to bed. I lay in bed, obsessively going over what I'd seen. I wished I could talk it over with someone but as long as I was at the farm, I couldn't. I liked Gareth and Philomena but I didn't want to betray Gareth, disrupt his love affair, and upset Philomena. If I told my mother, she'd call me mad and accuse me of seeing things. I suddenly felt angry with the lot of them. I didn't want to stay at the farm any more. I wanted to go back to London and see my mates, especially Maddy.

I wasn't ready for what I'd seen. Maybe it was because of the loss of Ifan so soon after my first experience with him of sex. In the space of a few hours, I'd seen the illicit sexual world of the adult and been confronted with Gareth's betrayal of Philomena and his desire for another woman. I was confused. I knew that Gareth and Philomena had an open marriage, but seeing it in operation was something else. I liked Philomena and I knew something had been bothering her and I didn't like to see her hurt. I also liked Gareth. I'd never forget he saved me from drowning. He'd become a father figure but what I'd seen shocked me. 'Up close and personal.' It disturbed and unsettled me. I didn't get to sleep until dawn.

My mother was shaking me, trying to wake me up. I'd slept so heavily, I felt drugged. I glanced at her to check her mood, she looked deadpan but when she saw I was awake she walked over to the windows and noisily dragged the curtains back. Light streamed in. It felt like an assault. I sat up, rubbed my eyes and said, 'And a good morning to you too.' I knew I was being sarcastic but I didn't care.

She turned round and said, 'It's almost midday, time to get up. You've been asleep for hours.'

I mumbled, 'I'll get up when you've left the room.'

She glowered and swept out, banging the door behind her. I'd managed to annoy her in three minutes flat. A record for me.

I was half-dead from the lack of sleep. I hadn't been able to stop thinking about Gareth and his lover, the woman in the flowered dress, and how they fancied each other. But I felt sorry for Philomena. She knew something was up but how much, I didn't know. I could tell her what I'd seen, but that would be mean and besides she might say I was making it up, like they had about Ifan.

Then an idea came to me. I'd find out more about her, the woman in the flowery dress. There were still two weeks to go before we returned to London and with the disappearance of Ifan, I had time on my hands. Becoming an amateur sleuth would take my mind off him and I was interested in what I might discover. Now I had something to do, I felt loads better, so I sprang out of bed, got dressed and ran downstairs to the kitchen.

There was no sign of anyone so I made myself breakfast and ate it quickly. I planned to cycle to the estuary and look for clues in the clearing where I'd seen them dancing. I'd visit Ifan's den and leave a few biscuits in the tin. If I checked every time I went, I could tell if he'd been, because he'd eat them. I'd leave another note with the biscuits sending him my love and ask him to ring me either on the farm number or, if it was later than two weeks, my London number.

But before I left, I had to contact the hospital where Ifan might have been taken after I'd almost drowned. Gareth had found the number for me. I tried ringing off and on for half an hour, but no one answered for ages, and when they did, I was told it was the wrong number, and got passed from one person to another. After fifteen minutes, finally I got through. I was told if I didn't have his full name and date of birth, he couldn't be traced and as they were so busy, I felt bad for asking. I gave up. I wept. It was final. I'd never see him again.

A feeling of boredom came over me. I didn't know what to do with myself. I drifted into the living room, stared vacantly out of the window, sat down, and fell asleep. When I woke up, I felt better. I made a coffee for myself, returned to my chair and looked round for something to read. My eye was caught by a pile of Gareth's poetry books on the floor by one of the settees.

After last night, I was filled with curiosity. I wanted to know more about him and seeing what he read would help. I sat down and began flicking through them. At first I was looking for the poetry he'd written, to see whether there were more references to his lover, but if he had had any published, I couldn't see one. Some of the books were old with yellowing pages stained with brown spots and smelt musty, but Gareth must have liked them because they were marked in the margins with his scribbled handwriting.

There was one book bound in dark green and gold-tooled leather. It looked old but well cared for. I picked it up and opened it. It was full of love poems but one caught my imagination. The poet wrote that he wanted to spread the 'cloths of heaven' at his lover's feet but he had only his dreams. The final line said: 'tread softly because you tread on my dreams'. I was very taken with that and read it several times. It made me think of Ifan and his dreams and of last night, when Gareth had put the rug on the grass and she'd pulled her skirt up for him to make love to her. No dreams there, I thought, only naked lust.

But this was a beautiful poem. I glanced at the author's name, Yeats. I held the book in my hands and started day dreaming about him and wondered what he was like and what his lover had been like, and how she might have responded to a poem like that. Having a poem written for you. That had to be better than your usual present.

I put the book down and picked up another. It was called *Poems of Love* and was by someone by the name of John Donne. Gareth had marked several of his poems and the more I read them, the more interested I became. John Donne was well into lusting after women. It seemed he had the permanent hots and turned all his experiences, which were many, into love poetry. I found him so fascinating that when I got back to London, I decided to ask the English teacher to see if we could study him.

I liked the way he wrote and even though he was writing hundreds of years ago, if his language was updated he could have been writing now. He intrigued me, especially when he wrote lines like:

Full nakedness, all joyes are due to thee
As soules unbodied, bodies uncloth'd must bee
To taste whole joyes.

I wondered if Gareth and his lover felt like that and did the kind of things he wrote about. No wonder Gareth was a poet. Lust and love seemed to be part of the territory of the poet. Had he once wanted Philomena like he did the flowery dress woman? Somehow I thought not. I couldn't imagine Philomena dancing like that and hitching her skirt up for 'full nakedness' for Gareth. She was too down-to-earth and her favourite Birkenstocks would be real passion-killers.

But reading Gareth's poetry books had made me even more curious. Sex was on my mind. What would it feel like to have sex with Gareth? Would he find me a turn on? Well, I thought there was only one way to find out and that would be to come on to him and see what happened. I might be too young now, but next year I'd be a year older.

It was then I came to my big decision. The following year I was going to make love with Gareth. I was determined. I'd be nearly fifteen then. I knew from my mates in London that loads of them already had had sex, even if it was with boys near their own age. They'd said the first time was painful. That's why I wanted it with an older man, and that man had to be Gareth. He'd know what to do and would make sure not to hurt me. He was sensitive, he liked me and perhaps he'd even write a poem for me.

Just then I heard Gareth's car pulling up outside. I jumped up. I didn't want him to know I'd been reading his books but before I could leave, he walked in. He flung his car keys on the side table, smiled and looked straight at me. It was too late. I felt my face colour up. Embarrassment wasn't in it. It was the first time I'd seen him since last night. Had he returned to Philomena's bed and what if she'd wanted him? Then what? I found it difficult to look him in the eye.

'Morning, young lady. What have you been up to?'

'Nothing, nothing much. Just kind of hanging round, and uh...looking at some of the books, your poetry books.'

It didn't register. 'Coffee? I'm about to make some,' he said. He seemed distracted. No doubt thinking of his night of passion.

'Okay.' I acted nonchalant.

We walked into the kitchen.

He put out two mugs. 'Seen anything you like among them?'

I glanced at him, the image of them dancing came into my mind. I hoped he couldn't mind-read because if he could, he'd know I was imagining him having sex with her. I went red again and decided to be upfront.

'Yeah, I did. That poet called John Donne, he tells it, like, well, you know, how it is. I would imagine. Anyway, I wouldn't know, not personally, I wouldn't.'

'Oh, Donne, yes, he's great. One of the most famous and respected Renaissance poets until that is, he converted. 'He was only half-listening. 'But what did you say...something about, not knowing? Perhaps I can help.'

He was looking through the cupboard, his back to me.

I did a double take and I thought, you bet your life you can. Now was my chance.

'Sex, about sex. It's that. What he writes about, like he's very interested in it, don't you think?"

I wondered how he'd respond. Gareth paused, looked straight at me, decided not to say what he was going to say, and turned away to pour out the coffee. He said over his shoulder, 'Why don't you speak to your mum?'

'She doesn't know what to say, she's taken a vow of silence. She spent some time in a convent and never recovered. It affected her.'

This time I had his attention. He stopped what he was doing. He looked at me disapprovingly and said, 'Be serious, Echo. Tell me what you want to know.'

'Okay, sorry, what I meant to say was that...' I was blagging it now, saying whatever came into my head, 'she can't talk, especially about difficult stuff, or if she does she won't say, so I'm left wondering how she came to have me; sometimes I wonder if she did have me, or if really I have another mother who gave me up for adoption. Maybe my real mother is Russian and my father is Welsh.'

He didn't seem fazed by what I was saying and I could see I'd got his total attention because he was looking at me intently. 'What makes you say that?'

'Because I don't seem to belong. Haven't you noticed? She doesn't like me.'

He looked sympathetic. 'Your mum? I'm sure that's not true, but what about your father, Echo? Where's he?'

I sighed, 'And that's another thing, I don't like my name. It's stupid, and as well as that my second name is different from hers.'

'Well, change it.'

I was stunned when he said that and looked at him in amazement. 'Change it? Could I?'

'Why not? You can't change your second but you can your first. I have a pseudonym for my writing.' I must have looked puzzled. 'Pseudonym, a name that conceals my identity.'

'What is it?'

'My pseudonym? You'll have to find out.' He smiled, then said, 'No, I'll tell you, it's Llywellyn ap Dafydd. My book is in Welsh but with an English translation.'

'Oh, that's very Welsh. I like it. It's a good idea choosing my own name. But I can only do that when I know who I want to be. Echo, it's rubbish. Echo, an echo to what, my mum, she wants me to be an echo, that's why I'm called that, but I don't want to be her echo. I refuse. I want to be me. Not like her. She's uptight. Got an attitude problem.'

I looked at him expectantly. He said, 'You still haven't said anything about your father.'

'I haven't said anything because I don't know. That's something else she won't talk about.'

'Why not?'

'Dunno.'

'Would you like to know more?'

'Yeah. I would. Sometimes I wonder if my father abused her so she escaped and took me with her. Maybe her name is a pseudonym too. Phoebe. What a name. Horrible. Then I think, did she have a one-night stand and have me? Who knows? I hate not knowing. Everyone has a father except me. My mate Maddy has a father, and he's great. He's a percussionist. I wish he was my dad.'

'You know that's not true, Echo. Not everyone has a father.' He paused and then said, 'Look, I'm going to North Wales at the end of the week just for the day, to see a friend. Would you like to come?'

I don't know why he asked me but I didn't care. I said straightaway, 'Yes,' and just stopped myself from blurting out, and is your friend the girl in the flowered dress? Instead, I asked who his friend was.

He said it was his publisher, so then I asked how long he'd be, and he said I had a choice. Either I could stay with him, and he'd be about three hours or he'd drop me off at a nearby slate quarry to have a look round. I chose the slate quarry. I'd never been to a slate quarry before.

Gareth's invite cheered me up enough to cycle to the estuary. I left my bike in the usual place and walked down the track to take the tin of biscuits to Ifan's den. Every time I visited I could see there were more brambles and more creeping plants and it was getting harder to find. I stood for a long time thinking about Ifan and the good times we'd had but I had to accept I'd never see him again.

I walked back to the clearing. The enchantment of the wood and the estuary and the excitement of seeing Gareth with his lover had become tainted with losing Ifan. I said to myself, he's dead and you'll never see him again but then I was so overcome with that thought, I lay down on the grass and cried. I felt utterly alone in the world. But when I looked up and saw I was surrounded by tall green trees, I thought of them as my guardian angels, crowding round to protect me. In my mind the clearing had become my sanctuary and gradually I began feeling better and I realised I did have things to look forward to even if Ifan wasn't here. It wasn't the end of the world. But I'd keep Wales, Ifan and the estuary as beautiful memories and I'd never forget him.

I'd looked forward to the trip to North Wales with Gareth. He didn't talk much, but that was alright with me. It gave me time to daydream and look at the passing scenery. The journey seemed to take forever because there's no motorway to North Wales from Chepstow and we had to drive right through mid-Wales.

He told me about his book of poetry. It was coming out soon and they'd prepared a 'mock-up' of the cover. When I heard that, it sounded so interesting, I almost changed my mind about going to the slate quarry. But I'd never been to a slate quarry and I wanted to see what it was like.

I asked him the title of his new book. He said, 'It's called "The Girl in the Flowered Dress".' That stunned me. A wave of anger passed through me. He was shameless. I sat in silence wondering how to react and what Philomena would have said if she knew. She'd be stupid if she didn't put two and two together. But it was obvious he didn't know that I'd been in the forest that night. I stared at him sideways on as he drove, the image of them together dancing floating across my mind's eye.

I said, 'Who is she?'

Gareth said, 'Who do you mean?'

'The girl in the flowered dress.'

'She's an imagined girl.'

'Why write about someone imagined?' I asked.

'Because,' he said, 'I can create her according to my fantasies.'

He was talking bullshit and I knew he was lying. I felt betrayed. I truly had believed in Gareth and wanted him so much to be honest. Either he was lying, or I was mad and what I'd seen in the clearing was all imagined. It was what Gaby had said when she was talking to Philomena, that I'd dreamt up Ifan. They were all at it. Mind games.

'What's her name?'

'The girl?'

I nodded.

'Amy.'

'So what's the poetry about?'

'A love affair.'

I couldn't believe what I was hearing. I knew then with total certainty I had seen him dance with her. He was lying like my mother did about my father, as if I was stupid or just a child and he could say anything because I knew no better. I screwed up my hands into a fist as if I was going to punch him one and stared silently out of the window to gather my thoughts.

A mile or two passed but he hadn't noticed how pissed off I was, so I looked at him and I said, 'And how does Philomena feel about Amy?'

'Echo, she's not real. She's imagined.'

'Don't call me Echo, you know I don't like it.'

'Sorry, what shall I call you then?'

'Nothing. Call me nothing. How much further to the slate quarry?' I was seething by now.

'Another five miles. Shall we stop for a coffee?'

'You can. I'll stay here.'

Gareth turned to look at me. 'What's with the anger?'

I glowered at him. 'Fuck off.'

He suddenly braked and pulled off the road. I was scared then. I'd never seen him angry. I wouldn't have thought he was capable of anger. He didn't look at me but stared straight ahead drumming his fingers against the steering wheel. We sat like that, and with each minute that passed I became more apprehensive. Finally he looked at me. His anger seemed to have gone.

'Tell me,' he said. 'Tell me what's going on. I don't like to see you upset.' He was looking straight at me and looked so caring I thought I'd burst into tears. I just wasn't used to it but I couldn't tell him. I looked down at my hands and mumbled I didn't want to talk.

He said, 'Echo, and I'm going to call you that till you've chosen your new name, I'm not moving from here until you tell me.'

'You'll miss your appointment then.'

'So be it,' he answered. 'Why's it so hard to tell me?'

I took a deep breath and said, 'Because I know you're lying.' He didn't answer. 'Why lie? I hate lies. Don't you know I have to know the truth?'

Gareth said, 'I have no idea what you're talking about,' but when he said that, I went wild. I gave it to him, no holds barred.

'She's not imagined as you say she is. She's real. I saw you. The other night. Screwing her, you were screwing her, in the forest in the middle of the night, I saw you, so don't give me that crap, all that bullshit, about love and poetry. You have the hots for her, you were fucking her, end of story.'

That shut him up. I had his full and undivided attention. I was about to get out of the car and run before he murdered me, but he retorted. 'So what's it to you? You should have been in bed not roaming through the woods.' I didn't answer. He continued, 'Has it occurred to you that I might love her and I wasn't screwing her as you so delicately put it.'

'Delicate. Don't make me laugh. There was nothing delicate about it.'

We sat glaring at each other.

'Maybe not, but you need to know something, Echo. Love isn't all romance and prettiness, it's about passion, desire, and really wanting someone, to possess them, to be as one with them. Real life. Get it. Are you on message?'

I looked at him as if I wanted to kill him, which actually I felt like doing. I said nothing. But he hadn't finished.

'Why's it so disturbing? Why so upset? You live in London. Aren't you supposed to be cool? Know what life's about. It all happens there. What's the problem? Eh? What's so shocking? A man and woman having sex?'

'You lied to me, and that's what pisses me off. And what about Philomena? Have you thought about her? How upset she'll be?'

'Philomena and I are good. We know each other.'

'Well, if it's so good, why are you still fucking married to her, when you're screwing someone else? Jeez, I can't do with the hypocrisy. You're a bastard, like all men.'

'Leave her out of it. What am I supposed to do? Tell her I love someone else?'

'Why not, it'd be more honest.'

'Life's just a little more complicated. Has it occurred to you saying that would be hurtful?'

I shouted at him then, 'She's hurt already, haven't you noticed? Fuck-wit.'

He was breathing heavily. He looked at me as if he wanted to shoot me. He started the engine and pulled away, but he was so angry he wasn't looking and pulled in front of a car. The driver had to brake hard to avoid him and honked his horn enough to wake the dead. I smiled. I'd got right under his skin. Serve him right, I thought. Neither of us spoke. He drove fast. Once he looked at me as if I was a piece of shit, but that didn't trouble me. The fact he was so worked up made me feel powerful. I'd begun experiencing the fruits of sweet revenge.

I knew I was right. I was on the side of Philomena and I hated to see her hurt and I hated him bullshitting and I didn't believe all that stuff about being in love and writing poetry. He was like that poet, John Donne. I couldn't stop myself then. I became a verbal assassin. I couldn't keep my mouth shut.

'John Donne. Role model. Sounds good, doesn't it? Like an epitaph on your gravestone. 'He couldn't keep his trousers on or his hands to himself.' Yes, the spirit of John Donne Esquire passes down through the centuries. A prototype for the many who followed. Read, listen, learn, you too can become just like him.'

In that moment I loathed all men and in particular Gareth. I didn't resist saying what came next. 'Having sex with her, Amy. Whatever she's called. It must give you inspiration. Your next poetry book. A sequel? The subject? Betrayal. What do you think?'

He didn't answer. I wondered if he'd heard or if he'd hit me when we stopped. I'd run if he did. He was slowing down, indicating right and turned into a side road, then he stopped. 'Here's where you get out. Follow the track up into the hills and you'll get to the slate quarry. I'll pick you up here. In three hours. You've got my mobile number. Do you have money?'

He wasn't looking at me, he sounded normal if cold, but it might have been an act. 'Yes. See you then.' I got out.

He didn't reply and noisily accelerated off. I didn't need to be a genius to see how angry he was, but I didn't care. It crossed my mind he might not come back and pretend his car had broken down, but that would be a dumb thing to do and also childish. In any case I had money on me and somehow I'd find my way back to the farmhouse.

I began looking round me. I hadn't any expectations about what a slate quarry might look like, but I didn't like what I saw. I'd been dumped in the middle of a remote mountain range with sheep as company. The landscape was bleak with a biting cold wind, the grey sky lying low and heavy over the bare, flat moorland cluttered with huge piles of discarded slate. I had no idea what to do next and wondered if this was Gareth's revenge; it felt a bit like being sent to Siberia for speaking out; that's what they did with mouthy people in Russia. But I didn't care. He was full of bullshit like all adults. I had liked him, but now I didn't.

I began walking up a path and the further away from the road I got, the better I felt. I didn't care about the bitter wind. I was wearing the right clothes. I'd been coming to Wales long enough to know all about the weather, especially in the mountains where, even in the summer, someone told me, the temperature can change in a second from scorching sun to so cold you were at risk of hypothermia.

I picked my way over rough grassland. I passed a pile of slate and picked a piece up. I loved its colour. It was dark-blue-grey and when I banged a flat piece with a stone, it made a satisfying 'tinging' noise. My mum had a posh friend in Islington with slate tiles on her kitchen floor and I'd always admired them. The tiles were classy, a muted matt blue, and they'd been cut and laid in both oblong and square shapes and arranged in a geometric pattern. Now I come to think about it, Patricia (her name) told me they'd come from Wales and that Welsh slate was the best in the world. I'd asked my mum if we could have them on our kitchen floor. She said they were too expensive. Typical.

All around were scattered heaps of slate, which set me wondering how they came to be here. I looked around. The path continued up and round the side of the hill so I decided to follow it and see where it took me. Looking down the mountainside, the road looked tiny with toy cars moving along it.

I walked for almost an hour. The path meandered up and past more piles of slate. Looking up to the skyline, there were actual outcrops of slate rock far ahead, and a row of very rough, single-storey dwellings. It looked as if someone might have lived in them but now they'd been abandoned to the elements. I decided to walk to them, then stop and have some of the chocolate I'd brought with me, but I discovered then I'd forgotten to bring any water.

I was about five hundred metres off when I saw a man in an orange Gore-Tex jacket coming out of one of the buildings. I hesitated and wondered whether to continue. After all it was a lonely spot, a long way from the road, and he might have been a weirdo but then I saw he had camera equipment and was very preoccupied with taking photos so I thought I'd take a risk. I carried on walking until I reached the buildings. I wanted to see what they were.

He was crouching down taking a photo of a chimney opening in one of the rooms when I came up behind him. 'Hello,' I said. 'What are you doing?'

He jumped. He turned round, saw me and stood up. I could see he was young. He looked totally normal but serious. He said, 'I didn't see you or hear you, where did you come from?'

I gestured down the mountain and said, 'From the road. Is there another way?'

He didn't smile. 'No.'

'What are you doing?'

'I'm a research student. I'm doing a PhD on the Welsh slate industries.'

I said, 'Oh. A student. From where?'

'Post-grad. London.'

'That's where I live. London.'

'So what are you doing here?' He was as direct as me.

'I'm on holiday.'

'But why are you here?
'In this slate quarry?'
'Yes.'
'I'm waiting for somebody.'
'What do you think of it?'
'It's interesting. But I don't know enough about it.'
'I can tell you,' he said. I looked at him in amazement.
'What do you want to know? Go on, ask me.' He must have
been desperate to talk to me. It turned out he knew loads and
was so enthusiastic about his subject he captured my attention.
He told me about the geology of slate, the different types of
quarry scattered over North Wales, how slate was 'dressed'
and 'split', and about the hard and dangerous lives of the
quarry men. I found that the most interesting. He said there
was an underground slate quarry in Llechwedd in Snowdonia
where visitors could go underground. He recommended that,
told me I'd be fascinated. It was hard to stop him.

Finally I interrupted him by saying, 'So, you're a historian?'

'No,' he said as if I should wash my mouth out. 'I'm not
a historian. I'm an industrial archaeologist.'

I didn't dare ask what the difference was because we'd
be there forever, but I did ask why he'd chosen slate quarries
as his subject. He said he'd discovered that on his father's side
going back to the early and mid-nineteenth century some of
them had been quarry men and he'd got interested in tracing
their lives. He said, 'I'm a descendant of the quarry men, and
they were tough.'

I asked him his name. It was Kieran Lloyd. I noticed
he hadn't asked for my name and I didn't offer to tell him
because I was getting more and more sick of people's reaction
to my first name. I looked at my watch and said I'd best be
off as I had to meet someone down the bottom and it was
a long way down.

He was still on his mission to inform. 'Before you go,
don't you want to know about these buildings?'

'Yes, go ahead.' In for a penny, I thought, in for a pound.

He told me they were called 'barracks' and were built by the mine owners for the quarry men. Some of them had to travel so far to get to the mines, they'd have a five-mile walk up into the mountains so they'd stay for the week; four men in each unit, with minimal facilities.

I said, 'That's awful, they must have been freezing, open to the cold and rain, how did they survive?'

'Well,' he said, 'they had a strong sense of camaraderie and each quarry had a meeting place for the men, called a "Caban". They'd discuss politics, work, and their lives and in one quarry the men got together to write and produce a magazine which they called "The Caban". It was read all over North Wales. They were highly literate, you know.'

I stared at him, '"Caban". That's sounds familiar. I've seen that magazine somewhere.'

That got his total attention and just for a change he was listening to me. He waited while I searched through my mind until I got there.

'My uncle lives in Liverpool and he's got connections with Wales. We visited him when I was little, he's got a load of stuff in his house that he hangs on to because he's got OCD. He's my mum's older brother but they fell out. He's got copies of that magazine, but they're in Welsh.'

He looked at me as if I was now the most interesting person on the planet. He said, 'Can you contact him? I have to see them. I'd be so grateful. They'd be fantastic. For my research. I'd walk my Viva.'

I thought he was going to swoon and although I didn't know what a Viva was, I wasn't about to ask otherwise we'd be there until darkness fell.

'Well, I probably could, but do you speak Welsh? They're in Welsh.'

'No problem. I'll get them translated.'

I looked at the time. It was getting late. 'I have to go.'

'Give me your number and promise you'll contact me? I'll make it worth your while.'

'How?' I was immediately interested.

'I don't know, but I will, what's your name?'

'Echo Morgan.' I waited for the inevitable but none came. He went up in my estimation. I gave Kieran my number, took his, and flew down the mountain. It was quicker going down than going up.

Gareth was already there, sitting in his car, listening to music, waiting for me. I'd half-expected him not to be, because that would be true to my experience. I'd got the idea that although men may come and go, in my case, it was mainly go. I asked if he'd been waiting long. He said about fifteen minutes.

He added, 'I was just about to get out and start looking for you.'

I was astonished. 'Aren't you still mad at me? Don't you want to kill me?'

'I did but not now. Negative emotions are a waste of time and energy. Besides you're entitled to your view even if it's hard for me to hear.'

He looked serious. No one had ever been so reasonable and respectful of me. My mother always spoke to me as if she was the Pope's emissary and treated me like a sinner about to be cast into hell. In fact I was so shocked I was stunned into silence. He started the car and drove off. Then he said, 'I'm going to stop for tea in a minute. I'd like you to come with me.' I replied, 'Of course.'

I was all sweetness and light now. After a few miles, he pulled off the road into one of those farm outlets with a café attached and led the way in. We sat down. I asked how his day had gone and whether he'd been pleased with the 'mock up'. I noticed he looked rather apprehensively at me but must have decided it was a straight question. 'I'm very pleased,' he said.

'So what's it look like? Will you show me?' I paused before saying, 'I promise I won't sound off at you.'

He had a black canvas courier bag which he opened. He passed over the artist's design. I looked at it carefully. Painted in strong colours, it showed a picture of a young woman on a swing wearing a dress like the one I'd seen Amy wearing in the forest the other night, the one with the full skirt. She was leaning back to get momentum as she swung away and her skirt was billowing out. Standing behind her ready to catch her and then push her was a man. Gareth, I presumed. I looked at it for a long time. I wanted to understand what the picture meant and what was going on between them.

'I like it very much. It's beautiful. She's beautiful. Is that your lover, the one I saw you with?'

'It's not her.'

'But it could be. Couldn't it?' I looked in his eyes, searching for the tell-tale signs of evasion, the avoidance of direct eye contact.

'I suppose it could. I wanted the artist to capture her.' He stopped.

I knew he was wondering how much he could say, so to encourage him, I said, 'Capture what?'

He said, 'Her erotic innocence.'

Gareth certainly had a way with words, but then he was a protégé of John Donne. I didn't reply because I didn't know what it meant. Perhaps it meant what it said. But still I couldn't understand. Erotic innocence. Was that how I'd felt for Ifan by the river? I filed it away at the back of mind for future reference. For some reason it made me feel sad but I don't know why. I thanked him for showing me and carefully handed it back to him.

Gareth picked up my mood. He asked what I was thinking but I couldn't say. He said again, 'She doesn't exist, she's not real, you know.'

I think now that as far he was concerned, she had the most mystical and imagined qualities of the most beautiful woman in the world but at the time I didn't understand that. I wasn't going to fight anymore. Once I understood that, I knew why I was sad. It was like what they'd said that about Ifan, that I'd made him up but if I believed them, it meant I didn't know what was real and what wasn't. It felt as if I was being driven mad.

Gareth cut across my reverie. 'How did you find the slate quarry?' I looked at him for a split second and almost began playing head games with him about what was real and what wasn't, but it wouldn't have been fair on Gareth. He was trying his best.

'It was good, once I found it, but why did you just dump me? You left me in the middle of nowhere!'

'I'm sorry. I was angry. But I've thought about what you said and it's true. But it is a very difficult situation. I'll make it up to you.'

I said, 'That's the second time someone's said that to me today. I met a student at the quarry called Kieran, an industrial archaeologist and he was a mine of information.' I looked at him to see if he got it. He had.

'Okay, Echo, very funny, tell me what you found out.'

I told him. He seemed genuinely interested and it was like how it used to be before the river and before the forest and when life seemed more straightforward.

By the time we got back it was late. Gareth said he had work to do and as soon as he parked, he disappeared without even saying hello to the others. I planned to go straight to my room but I had to pass through the kitchen.

The three women were sitting round the table but there was somebody new, a man I hadn't seen before. As usual they were very noisy and looked and sounded like they were enjoying themselves. Philomena asked if we'd had a good day and what I'd done. She always made me feel welcome. I briefly told them about the slate quarry and Kieran, but I left out the row with Gareth and how he'd dumped me on the mountain.

It seemed nobody was going to introduce me to the man so I smiled at him and when he saw that he sprang up, walked round the kitchen table and stretched out his hand to me. He said, 'Forgive me, my name's Tarquin.'

I couldn't believe anyone could have a name like that or speak like that. It was like being in some kind of radio drama or listening to the news about the Tories' latest escapade. His name was almost as stupid as mine. I choked back a quip.

He was sophisticated looking with an olive complexion and gorgeous honey-brown eyes. Dressed in black; black cords, black polo sweater, black leather jacket which he'd carefully hung over the back of his chair. His dark hair was long and swept back from his face. Maybe he was Welsh or he could have been French or Italian but he had a deep voice and a Welsh accent. I suddenly felt shy. He wasn't the usual type I saw at the farm.

I said imitating his ultra-polite manner, 'So good to meet you, my name's Echo.' With a name like Tarquin there was no way he'd think my name strange and I was right. It didn't register with him.

My mother asked if I wanted some supper. I said I did but I'd take it to my room. I wanted to finish reading my book. She went to the fridge, got some lasagne out, heated it in the microwave and put it on a tray. Then she said, 'Remember to put some parmesan on your lasagne, Echo, before you go up.' I knew she was putting on a show of the caring mother probably for the benefit of Tarquin and I wondered if she fancied him. I could have told her, forget it, he's gay, you're wasting your time.

The next day I came down for breakfast, expecting and hoping to see Gareth, but he wasn't there. Gaby appeared. She sat down next to me to eat her cereal and I found out from her who Tarquin was and why he was there. She told me he was the curator of Chepstow Art Gallery and they'd been planning a forthcoming exhibition together. The one they called 'Women and Surrealism'. I was interested and wanted to know more and I asked lots of questions.

Gaby told me. For fifteen minutes I couldn't get a word in. Her enthusiasm reminded me of Kieran in the slate quarry. All teachers have this tendency; they never stop talking. They assume the listener is hanging on to their every word. It's like someone has wound them up and there's no stop button. After ten minutes I felt my eyes glaze over and my attention wander.

She said they wanted an art exhibition that would show women's experiences of the world and subvert the familiar male-dominated notions of femininity and sexuality as well as conventional ideas of art. That's how she put it. I said to her, 'What's that mean?'

To this Gaby said, 'When the exhibition opens you'll understand.' It wasn't just the work of the three of them, because Tarquin was arranging to borrow other surrealist works from private collections and art galleries.

Gaby showed me some post cards of an artist's work called Frida Kahlo who'd lived in Mexico. When I saw her paintings I was knocked out by the colours. Some were self-portraits, showing how she dressed, everything in vivid pinks, vibrant oranges, electrifying blues. Her black hair was pulled back from her face and she had deep brown eyes under heavy eyebrows which stared out at me. She was beautiful but her face showed suffering.

I asked, 'Will you be going to Chepstow to meet Tarquin again?'

'We're going tomorrow. You're welcome to come.'

'Is Gareth coming, and my mum?'

'Gareth's too busy but yes, your mum's coming, and Philomena...but does that matter to you, your mum coming?'

I pretended I hadn't heard but she knew I was avoiding answering and carried on with what she would have said, if I had answered.

'Echo, I've noticed you and your mum don't get on. What's that about?'

I laughed gaily as if it was a preposterous idea. I had no intention of talking to Gaby. I'd noticed how friendly she was with my mother so if I talked, it would all be fed back to her. So she dropped the subject and said to be ready first thing tomorrow.

The following day, as we were going to Chepstow Art Gallery, I thought I'd make an effort with what I wore. Tarquin had made an impression on me and I wanted to be cool like him. I contemplated whether to wear a skirt for a change but I only had one. It was stone-washed denim and very short. I'd got it cheap on eBay but it was an original 'Fat Face' and a bargain.

I tried it on and looked critically at myself in the mirror. The magazines say you should know what are your worst and your best features so I gave myself a thorough going over. The skirt showed off my legs. They weren't bad, but I wished they were longer, browner, more rounded. They were skinny. Like a young girl's legs. I liked my face, it was oval shaped and my eyes deep brown. I took a hand mirror and brought it close to look at my mouth. I decided my mouth was my best feature. I think it's what a poet would call sensuous, full and well shaped. My hair was thick, glossy and straight. I practised swinging my head round so it swished, like that woman in the ad but I decided against that because I'd look stupid.

I took off my top and looked at my breasts. Even if Ifan had liked them, I didn't. They were a girl's breasts. Too small. Maybe they were the right size for the rest of my body, but I just didn't like them. I wanted the full breasts of a woman. I wondered if Gareth would think the same if he ever saw me naked.

I stood and pondered. Should I cover up my small size with something slouchy or should I show them off with something tight, or should I wear something in between? I just didn't know. I got them all out, every top I'd brought to Ffridd and lined them up on my bed in colour order, and then I tried them on. Eventually I came across one I'd forgotten about. I'd begged my mother to buy it. I'd gone on and on at her and in the end she'd bought it. But I'd never worn it. I liked it too much. It was too good to wear. It had a hood, was over large, had widely spaced pale blue stripes but the logo across the front was fab. It said, 'Let's find a beautiful place and get lost'. I decided that had to be the one. It was perfect because that's what I'd like to do with Gareth.

I lay on my bed and began daydreaming about him. How

he'd rescued me, watching him dance, seeing him in the forest, driving to North Wales with him. He was my number one and, for the moment, had usurped Ifan. Did I feel bad about that? Not really, because Gareth was here and Ifan wasn't.

But thinking that wasn't so cool. A flame of anger surged through me. Ifan had abandoned me. He wasn't dead, I just knew, and, I thought, Gareth knew more than he was letting on. That's why he was so nice to me.

Maybe, if I got him on his own he'd tell me. I wished he was coming to Chepstow and we could go somewhere else and leave the rest. Perhaps he wasn't coming because there were four of us. He was a poet after all and interested in passion, sex and love, not an artist like the rest of them, fascinated with surrealism.

I made my way downstairs to the kitchen. It was nine o'clock and as I walked into the room I noticed my mother giving me the once over. Her eyes raked over me. I waited for the 'put down'. She'd choke rather than pay me a compliment but she restrained herself that morning. She just said, 'I haven't seen you wear that for a long time.' She must have been looking forward to seeing Tarquin.

It wasn't far to Chepstow. Gaby drove. We found the car park near the art gallery and bundled out. Even Philomena had made an effort that morning; she was wearing an outfit I'd not seen her in before. She'd discarded her baggy trousers and her Birkenstocks and wore some well-cut linen trousers in dark red with a vintage-style white blouse, and beautiful drop earrings art deco style. But she still had her favourite dark pink paisley scarf wrapped round her hair. She looked suitably arty and interesting. When she saw me looking at her, she smiled and said, 'Alright then, Echo?' I nodded and told her I liked her outfit. Then we climbed up the stone steps to the Art Gallery.

As we entered Tarquin came forward to greet us. Everything about him was style, including his office. It was large, painted white with a few modern abstract paintings on the wall. It was minimally furnished and had a stunning view of the River Wye. In the middle of the room was a huge mahogany table with varying sizes of paper placed along its length. He said, 'Do sit down,' and with an expansive gesture indicated where he wanted us to sit.

He began talking immediately, first about his difficulties in getting funding for the exhibition. Despite this, he said he'd managed to track down a little-known foundation which financially supported the development of new surrealist artists. He proposed to change the name of the exhibition from 'Women and Surrealism' to 'Women Surrealists: Then and Now'. I glanced at the women. They looked transfixed. Nobody objected or said anything.

He turned to the paper placed on the big table. These represented the art work, how they'd be arranged on the walls. The various forms of sculpture, including 'found objects' were to be displayed in a separate gallery. He asked for questions and comments and everybody became very animated, and started cutting across each other as they spoke. He held up his hand in an imperious way as if quelling an unruly mob of toddlers fighting for the last piece of chocolate and announced in a loud voice, that his assistant had been working on themes and after coffee she would talk us through 'her thinking'.

A woman brought in a tray of coffee and biscuits. No one spoke to her except me. I thanked her. I felt intimidated and not part of it. I began moodily looking out of the window at the river. When they'd finished commenting on the display and drinking their coffee we sat down again.

Tarquin spoke into an intercom and said, 'Chloe, do you mind coming in now and talk us through "themes".' She walked in. I did a double take. She was instantly recognisable. It was the woman in the forest. The one who'd lifted her skirt for Gareth. The one he'd called Amy in his poem 'Girl in the Flowered Dress' except this time she didn't wear a flowery dress because like Tarquin, she was dressed in black. Black must be some kind of uniform for their type of work.

I was transfixed. She wore black wide-leg trousers, a matching short cropped tight jacket, pearl earrings and just about the reddest lipstick I'd ever seen. It drew attention to the paleness of her complexion, her mouth and its shape. Even in day light she was mega attractive. She looked round the room and flashed a smile. She seemed totally unfazed.

My mother had a look on her face of extreme disapproval. Sometimes she described women as looking like they'd been round the block a few times and probably she was thinking that now. When I heard it the first time, I'd laughed. My mother had meant it negatively, but I'd taken it positively. For me it meant urban, sophisticated, worldly wise and attractive to men. All the qualities I wanted.

But, now I knew now why Gareth wasn't here. Chloe aka Amy, was involved with this project and it would have been excruciating for him to be in the same room as her and his wife. I couldn't take my eyes off her, my mind kept drifting away to the forest when she'd been with Gareth.

But it was him I'd become obsessed with. He'd saved my life, but his wildness, his way with words, his affairs, his craziness, like dancing at midnight in the forest before making love; all this was deeply romantic. There was no other man like him. Tarquin interrupted my thoughts. He was introducing Chloe. If she recognised any of our names, she kept it hidden. She was cool and professional in her manner and it was difficult to reconcile what I now saw, with what I'd seen the other night, her naked desire for Gareth. I dragged myself into the present.

She was setting up PowerPoint and explaining how she'd organised the exhibition into various themes. She spoke about how the Surrealist Movement had begun, the influence of psychoanalysis, the disillusionment with the establishment after the First World War, and how the surrealists challenged the accepted ethos. She spoke of women's contribution and how their work was a radical protest and a refusal to be categorised by the male hegemony. I nearly fell off my chair when she said hegemony. It was a word I'd heard only once before and that was by a boy in my class who saw himself as a swot and planned to go to Oxford. He should be so lucky. They don't take kids from Housing Associations, but I didn't say that to him.

I took out my notebook and wrote down everything she said, including 'hegemony' intending to look it up later. I felt hypnotised just listening to her. It was like being back at school with Mr Harris, my favourite teacher. He taught media studies and just before the summer break we'd been looking at theories of culture and it was the kind of word he'd use.

I decided to ask Chloe if she could tell me more about why they didn't like 'male hegemony' and how their art was different. She looked directly at me and said I'd asked a very important question. I caught my mother's eye. She was glowering at me but for once I didn't care. Chloe said she'd be brief but they objected to being seen as passive, dependent and defined through their relationship with men, whether in the kitchen or the bedroom. Their art was a critique of that and they saw themselves as agents of their own lives. However, she said, like the male surrealists they drew on the developing knowledge and interest in the concept of the unconscious.

Then she stopped and said, 'Echo, if you like I can recommend some books you might be interested in, but it'll have to be later as I'm concerned with the passage of time and how much we have to get through. Would that be alright with you?' She smiled at me and I noticed her voice was soft with a very slight South Wales accent and a rhythmic lilt.

I was so pleased she'd remembered my name and was interested in me that I answered her politely. In fact, I was so polite, I surprised myself. I was becoming more mannered by the minute and I felt as if I was turning into a version of Chloe and Tarquin. I said, 'Thank you so much, Chloe and yes, I'd very much welcome your recommendations,' and then I smiled sweetly at my mother to annoy her. She didn't like me feeling pleased with myself. I felt sure Chloe knew who I was, because of the way she spoke to me and it could only be Gareth who'd told her. I hoped he hadn't told her about our row.

Chloe now was explaining how she'd organise their art work. I heard certain phrases she used, phrases like 'narrative fantasy', 'female earth', 'women's muse', 'the depiction of the female form' and as I listened these ideas entered my mind and took on a life of their own. I was becoming more and more fascinated with these women. Their ideas of freedom, their rejection of convention, the support they gave each other, their lifestyle, and their weird art. It was no wonder Philomena was so interested.

For a mad moment I contemplated whether, when Chloe gave me the book references, I'd tell her that I'd seen her and Gareth making love in the forest. I wanted to shock her, shake her out of her self-assurance and make an impression on her so she wouldn't forget me. The reality was, I didn't do that. For everyone's sake, everything had to be kept a secret.

After her talk, Chloe left the room. I thought she'd give me the references before she left but she didn't. I was devastated. She was just a bull-shitter, I thought but I was wrong. Just as we were about to leave she returned and gave me a list of books and a book about surrealism and women artists.

'Echo,' she said, 'I thought you might like this book. I can only lend it to you, but you might find it of interest and when you've finished will you bring it back? I'll need it soon, but you know where I am.' Then smiling, she looking me straight in the eye and said, 'And we can go out for coffee.'

I was pleased. I could hardly believe how nice she was. I took it out of her hands and carefully turned over the pages. The book was called *Women Artists and the Surrealist Movement* and it had photographs of their art and photography and, even more interesting, of themselves. She'd underlined some chapters and told me these were ones she especially recommended. There was even a section on Dorothea Tanning, the one who'd painted that weird picture my mother liked. When I came to a picture of Frida Kahlo, I almost burst into tears. She'd painted a picture of herself trussed up in bandages. She looked in terrible pain. It was awful.

I looked at Chloe, my eyes full of tears. She could see I was upset and she said, 'I'll tell you about her sometime. She was injured in a terrible street accident when she was a child. But don't let things get to you, Echo. She turned her pain into art. Life's full of good and beautiful things as well as the bad. That's just how it is.'

It was a beautiful book and she was beautiful too. She made such an impression on me that I was almost ready to forgive her for her relationship with Gareth. I understood now why they were in love with one another. They were good people. I closed the book and told her I'd take good care of it. She gave me her card with her contact details on it and I put it in my blue-and-purple Welsh canvas bag with 'Celf' written on it.

When we got back I showed the book to my mum. Even she was interested, particularly in Dorothea Tanning, but she wanted to read it before me. She said I could have it back in the morning.

The next morning, before I got up, I lay in bed and thought about the past five weeks. There were only a few days left before we returned to London, which didn't leave much time to read Chloe's book or to put my plan into action, but I must have had bad dreams because when I woke up I felt moody and pissed off. Everything that summer had been difficult; almost drowning in the river, losing Ifan, being told I'd imagined him, seeing Gareth and Chloe dance and have sex in the forest, being abandoned in the Welsh Mountains.

I concluded the adult world was full of lies and rightly or wrongly I couldn't trust anyone. I would have liked to talk to someone about everything but there was no one I could think of and even if I waited until I got back to London, my friends wouldn't understand.

As I lay there I heard my mother laughing loudly outside in the gardens. I got up and looked out of my bedroom window to see what was going on. She was with Gareth and they were taking a shortcut across the grass to where he'd parked his car. She was looking up at him and laughing at something he'd said. She was such a flirt. I suddenly hated her. I knew she wouldn't be interested in helping me make sense of how upset I was by Ifan's disappearance and how I felt about Gareth.

The more I thought about her, the angrier I felt. Her top priority was always herself and what she wanted. She didn't really care about me beyond feeding and clothing me and doing what seemed right. I felt lonely. I wanted to be close and special to someone like I'd felt with Ifan. We'd understood and looked out for each other. It was still hard to accept he'd gone. Surely people didn't just disappear in this country? It wasn't exactly a police state. I couldn't even talk with Gareth because he'd say I'd imagined it, and then I'd begin to feel crazy. It seemed like I was destined forever to be left with feelings of loss.

My mother was standing by Gareth's car as he searched for his keys. He must have forgotten them because he started walking back to the house while she stood and waited. I watched her. She bent down and looked at herself in the car's wing mirror. She smiled at herself and fluffed up her hair, then seeing her reflection in the car window she stood sideways, pulled in her stomach and observed herself with simpering satisfaction.

'Putting on a show.' That was something my mother did. For her, life was one big performance. Maybe it was because she was a teacher. I'd read that some of the best teachers were great actors, that's how they got the attention of their pupils. But who was the real Phoebe? I didn't know. She never talked about herself or why she'd become a teacher of classics. She could be a stranger I passed in the street. As for her choice of classics. It was the type of subject people were taught at posh schools before they went on to Oxbridge, yet she worked in a North London comprehensive. It was a good one, admittedly. She wanted me to teach too, but I didn't want that. I wanted to do something in my life that she couldn't or wouldn't want to do, so she couldn't compete with me or take it from me.

I wasn't sure what, but I'd find something. I wanted to be different. I felt and looked different from her. Maybe I was like my father. Whoever or wherever he was.

I couldn't stop myself. I suddenly flung open the window and shouted out 'Oy. You. Yeah. You, you look great, doncha think.'

My mother looked up towards the house and when she saw me, she started to wave. I joined in the act and waved back just as if we both got on. I moved away from the window, went to her bedroom and retrieved the book Chloe had given me. If she asked for it back, I'd refuse. I planned to spend the day reading and tomorrow I'd go to Chepstow and return it to Chloe.

The next day I got up early and went down to the kitchen. No one was around as I ate my breakfast. I was glad, because I wasn't up to being sociable but I'd decided that before I returned the book, I'd phone Chloe to make sure she'd be there.

She wasn't there. Apparently she didn't arrive at the office until about midday. I asked the woman who answered if I could see her tomorrow afternoon. She said she'd speak to her and get back to me later. That meant I could look at Chloe's book at the estuary. It would be my last visit before we left for London. I put the book in my 'Celf' bag and cycled slowly through the back lanes. The tracks through the trees leading down to the water's edge were alive with memories of Ifan. 'Gone but not forgotten,' I'd read once on a grave stone, but I didn't even know if he was dead.

I made my way towards the river and in case anyone was walking around and interrupted me, I searched for a place to hide. Eventually I found one in the base of a tree, formed by the hollow of its root. I opened the book. On the inside front cover, written in a large sprawling hand were the words, 'To my darling Chloe. Love you always. Huw.' It was dated three months ago.

I took a deep breath. Held the book tight in my hands. Stared at the page. So…she was with someone else, as well as

Gareth. I was shocked. I said to myself, it wasn't my business. After all why should I care but it was more of the same. Every time I thought highly of a person they turned out to be two-timing. I'd assumed Chloe was a free agent. She behaved like one. It's true it had vaguely crossed my mind she might be married but I hadn't known for sure. Now I did. Someone who wrote 'for always' must be married. Chloe's passion for Gareth, his love for her, his indifference to Philomena's feelings was bad enough, but now there was someone else. Someone by the name of Huw. This put me even more in a bad mood.

To distract myself, I began turning the pages of the book. It was beautifully illustrated. Surrealist art is stunning, mysterious and enigmatic whether photography or paintings, but it needs decoding, like dreams.

I was more interested in the women's lives. They were free agents and some might say they were mad, but they were no madder than the men they hung around with and no one called them mad. To me they were wild by nature and the idea of being so rebellious and fighting convention through art and lifestyle appealed to me mightily. It didn't occur to me that perhaps Chloe might also be influenced by the surrealists hence her refusal to be trapped in marriage.

I wanted to know more about her so whatever happened tomorrow, and whether she was available or not, I planned to go to Chepstow to return the book and hopefully have a coffee with her. But I'd still have to organise a lift.

I cycled back to the farmhouse and walked into the kitchen. Philomena was sitting at the table, reading. I asked if she knew if anyone was going to Chepstow the next day. She said Gareth was, but he was out. I wondered if she'd noticed how much he went to Chepstow, but if she had, she said nothing and neither did I. I was learning to keep my mouth shut so I left a note asking for a lift, in case I wasn't around when he got back. All that afternoon I waited for a call from Chloe's secretary but none came. There must have been a good reason why she didn't ring, but I'd promised to return the book and I'd keep that promise.

I got my lift to Chepstow from Gareth. Throughout the journey neither of us said much. He seemed preoccupied with his thoughts and didn't react even when I told him I was returning a book to Chloe. I wondered what he was thinking but sensed we were on dangerous territory and I had to be careful with what I said. I was beginning to recognise I had considerable power knowing about their affair.

He dropped me off near Chloe's office and said he'd pick me up at 4pm He didn't say where he was going and I didn't ask. As soon as he'd gone I went to the art gallery to see if Chloe was there. She wasn't. Her secretary said she had the day off unexpectedly, but she'd asked her to give me her apologies that she was unable to see me. She promised to take me for a coffee when next we met. That cheered me up. She hadn't forgotten me.

I had three hours to kill so not having anything very exciting to do, I began exploring the centre of Chepstow. It's old, medieval in fact, with a castle and has a history because it stands between Wales and England, but I was more interested in the charity shops. I wasn't looking for anything in particular, just browsing for bargains. But nothing appealed and as I hadn't brought a book with me I decided to visit a coffee shop down a back street. It was old fashioned with tiny square windows and inside were bare wooden tables and benches. The floor was tiled. The walls plain white.

It was a good choice. I sat at a table in the window drinking my coffee, eating a delicious homemade chocolate brownie. I picked up some local leaflets left scattered around. There were loads of them and after I'd read a few I came to the conclusion the people who lived in Chepstow spent their time going to folk concerts, singing lessons, aromatherapists, yoga classes, massage therapists, poetry readings, and generally having fun. A leaflet advertising 'The Two Rivers Festival' caught my eye. It was out of date.

Just as I finished my coffee, I looked up. Gareth was passing the window. He still looked preoccupied, but I noticed at that point how well dressed he was. Something I'd missed when he drove me here. He was wearing his tight black jeans, the ones he'd worn when he met Chloe in the forest. This time with a white shirt. He looked extremely attractive. I knew he wouldn't welcome me rushing out to greet him, but I also was curious about what he was doing and where he was going. But then it came to me, and it was obvious – he was about to meet Chloe and that's why she'd cancelled and taken the day off. I was filled with anger. I'd been discarded. I wasn't important.

I stood up from the table, left the coffee shop and began following him. It was easy to conceal myself, as there were lots of tourists and it was a market day. I began trailing him. I kept as close as possible and always kept him in sight. He didn't stop or look over his shoulder, which made it easier, but walked quickly, every now and again looking at his watch. Eventually he reached a hotel. It was old, covered in ivy, with hanging baskets of geraniums around the entrance, the kind you rarely see in central London. He walked straight in through the entrance. This left me with a dilemma. I wasn't sure how to follow him without being noticed, so I hung around outside for a moment and then peeped inside.

It looked very classy and was probably expensive. The reception desk was across the room facing the door. I could see Gareth. He had his back to me and was talking to the receptionist. Fortunately for me the leaded windows, the oak panelling, the deep red plush carpet and the brass side lights made it dark inside. There were quite a few visitors milling around, so without being noticed I could hide behind one of the oak pillars.

Keeping my eyes on Gareth I walked in and looked around for the toilet. If I was stopped and asked what I was doing, I'd say I wanted the toilet and if it was Gareth who saw me, I'd express surprise at seeing him, smile sweetly, say I wasn't well and was on the way to the loo. There were lots of nooks and crannies but straightaway I saw the sign saying 'ladies powder room' and having located that, I sat at the furthest part behind a pillar. I was well away from the reception area but I could still see Gareth.

I picked up one of the fancy magazines scattered around and began flicking through the pages as I watched him. He was leaning over the desk and the receptionist was looking up at him and talking. She stood up and gave him a key. He signed the visitor's book, walked over and sat in a chair where he could see the entrance.

I just knew he was there for Chloe. I wondered how long he'd have to wait. It wasn't long. I looked at the time. She came within ten minutes. He stood up. She walked right past him, sat in one of the armchairs, cursorily greeted him. They behaved as if they barely knew one another. Gareth nodded, then left, making his way up the wide staircase. To the bedrooms I supposed. Chloe remained where she was but she was looking round.

I kept my head down, shrank back into the chair and put the magazine close to my eyes as if I was short-sighted. I started giggling. I was thinking to cut some holes through the magazine so I could hold it up to my face, but still see what was going on. Instead I put my sun glasses on.

If she did see me, she didn't let on. She'd left her flowery dress at home. Maybe that was for special occasions, like when she and Gareth planned to have it away in the forest, whereas in a hotel bedroom she could be in 'full nakedness', as John Donne would have said. I studied her clothes. Today she wore a knee-length, sea-blue shift dress, outsize round white earrings and carried a cane basket with a tan leather trim. As usual she looked stunning. For some reason I wondered if she wore perfume when they made love. I decided she probably would. She was the glamorous type after all. I didn't imagine either she or Gareth carried their jim-jams around with them for these occasions, but that thought amused me too. There was nothing ordinary about either of them.

After a short time Chloe stood up and without looking round her, made her way upstairs. I looked at my watch again. They wouldn't have much time, but presumably it would be long enough. A really passionate affair, I thought, and again a wave of jealousy passed over me but it was mixed with disapproval. These feelings always came together for me. I wondered how much Philomena knew and how hurt or angry she felt. There was also this Huw person. Did he know about Chloe's lover?

As I sat thinking, a man entered the reception area. He stood looking round, his eyes scanning the reception area. There was something intense about him. He was in his mid-thirties, with short, curly, black hair, a sallow complexion and he was wearing a dark suit. He looked like a professional of some sort, maybe a solicitor or a manager because of his confident manner. He had a muscular neck and athletic build, like a rugby player but as I looked at him, he noticed me. I looked away. It had to be Huw looking for Chloe. Perhaps he'd called the art gallery and had been told, like me, she'd taken the day off.

He was staring at me almost as if he knew me but when he began to walk towards me, it was time to scarper. I sprang up, walked briskly to the loo and stayed there for ten minutes. By the time I came out, he'd gone. I left the hotel. I didn't want to be there when Gareth and Chloe returned downstairs. I walked back to the coffee house and ordered a carrot and ginger juice. I had ten minutes before I was due to meet Gareth.

I wondered if Gareth and Chloe would ever leave their partners and I came to the conclusion that Gareth would probably stay, no matter how much he fancied Chloe. He'd been with Philomena so long and the farmhouse was important to them. The farmhouse was their baby, they'd created it together, but it was strange to me that couples stay together just for security and material reasons. I thought about the man who'd stared at me in the hotel. I was sure it was Huw and he knew who I was. If I'd stayed any longer he might have asked me if I'd seen them, and I wouldn't have known whether to tell him the truth or not.

I began thinking about my own father. Had he left my mother because he'd been involved with someone else? If so, unlike Gareth, he'd dumped her and I was dumped along with her. Why he'd do that was a big mystery to me. Maybe he thought he wasn't my father, but whatever the reason, without knowing anything about him, I felt weird. I felt I had no roots and I didn't know who I took after and I wanted to know.

I decided to break the vow of silence my mother had placed on me. 'Never speak of your father.' She hadn't actually said that but if I asked questions or showed any interest in knowing about him, I felt as if I'd burn in hell. Maybe Kieran would help, the archaeologist I'd met at the slate quarry. He was a researcher, so he'd know what to do and how to find out so, after I was back in London, I'd ask him. It was time I knew.

Part Three

After spending our summers in Wales, I'd always been pleased to get back into London, but even more so that year. I'd missed the buzz, the noise, the crowds, the red buses, and even the noisy, crowded, filthy tube. I straightaway met up with my friends and gave them an edited version of the summer's events, but I didn't tell them about Ifan because I got upset if I spoke about him. I'd wanted us to be like those ancient wrinkled couples I'd seen in the paper, holding hands and celebrating seventy happy years together. I couldn't accept he'd disappeared and what had happened lay hidden at the back of my mind. I couldn't talk about it but it was all there.

Life was no longer predictable and people were not always as they appeared. I'd glimpsed how the adult world operated and the fragility of life and relationships. The river incident, the loss of Ifan, and the realisation that Gareth was infatuated with someone else and didn't love Philomena, or not in the way I'd thought or expected, had affected me greatly.

Back at school I told my favourite teacher, Mr Harris, about the Surrealists' exhibition my mother and her arty friends were putting on, and I asked the English teacher, Ms Spencer if we could study John Donne. She asked why the sudden interest and laughed when I told her, but she agreed to it.

I liked them both and being with my mates cheered me up and things improved for a while. The world seemed a safer place, but the feeling was temporary. Now we were back in London, me and my mum started sparring with each other. I don't know why we got under each other's skin. I'd try my best not to wind her up but we'd only have to be in each other's company for a few hours and we'd start sniping. She watched me like a hawk and always found something to criticise. Usually it was about how I looked and what I was wearing but it could be anything, like how I spoke or what mood I might be in, or why I was so bad tempered.

One Saturday morning she kicked off big time, but this time I gave as good as I got and said things I'd never have dared say before. I was eating my breakfast when she started on at me.

'You're not going out like that, are you? You look ridiculous.'

I glanced at her and retorted, 'Give me a break, what I wear is my own business.'

'That's what you think. Look at you. A total mess.' I took no notice but when she said, 'Why do I have to put up with your bad manners?' that really got under my skin.

I shouted, 'Bad manners...what do you think it's like living with you? Under surveillance. Like I'm in an effing boot camp. That's why I'm out all the time and why I'm with my mates.'

She walked over to me and, folding her arms, bent her face so close it was an inch away from mine and hissed, 'I'm your mother and I have a right to know what you're up to.'

I raised my eyebrows and said, 'Really, when we were at Ffridd, you didn't give a shit what I was up to. I was left alone.'

'Isn't that what you want?' She sneered as she said this.

'Yeah, so get out of my face.' We were eyeballing each other and she was looking daggers at me. I stood up.

'Where are you going?'

'To the sink. To wash my stuff up. It's allowed, isn't it?'

'Give it to me.' She tried to snatch it out of my hand. 'I'll do it.'

I gave her a look and passed my bowl across. She grabbed

it but as she did, it slipped out of her hand and smashed on the floor. I laughed. I knew it would wind her up even more but I couldn't stop myself. 'See,' I said. 'See what happens; you should be more careful. That comes with being so uptight.' I walked to the door and said over my shoulder, 'I'm going out.'

'Where to?'

'Maddy's.'

'No, you're not. I want you here. I want you to do some shopping for me.'

'Sorry, otherwise engaged.'

She glowered. 'You have no sense of responsibility.'

I fell on my knees, put my hands together as if praying, 'Please God, help me to be a better person, so I can shop, cook, clean, for my dear mother. And make me a better daughter, make my mother a better mother and please, please bring a little sunshine into our darkness.'

She almost ran at me. She was about to slap me but I was up and away before she had time. I shouted, 'I'm going now, but you know what...I'm sick of you telling me what to do, you're a control freak. I'm not you and I don't want to be like you. I'm different and the sooner you get that, the better for both of us.' I didn't stop there, 'And why did you call me Echo, it's stupid...and I'll be at Maddy's if you need me.'

She looked shocked. 'Yes, go to Maddy's. Much good she'll do you.'

'Fuck off.'

She made another lunge towards me but I ran into the hall, raced for the front door, and shouted, 'I'll be back, when you've calmed down.' I slammed the door behind me. I knew she'd try and stop me but she wasn't dressed, so by the time she'd have flung on her clothes, I'd have disappeared down the street. She just wasn't quick enough.

Madeleine had been my best friend for as long as I could remember. I called her Maddy for short. She was great. She was wise, clever, funny and observant. She was in my class at school and liked the same things and the same teachers as me, but she was good at maths and I wasn't. She and I used to talk about what we'd do when we left school. She knew already what she wanted to be, an architect. I really wanted that for her, because life for her and her family had been tough. Maddy told me that when she was an architect she planned to design a house for her family and close friends. She'd build it in the Scottish mountains overlooking a loch. It would have massive windows looking east and west so wherever you were, you could watch the sunrise and the sunset. She'd told me she felt cramped where she lived. It was too close to the neighbours. I knew what she meant.

Her dad came from Brazil and he was a talented musician. Every time I went to her place, there was music playing. He was a freelance percussionist and he was always laughing. I think it was the music that made him happy. He said it was good for you and better than any medicine. His name was Roberto, but he answered to Berto and he'd met Madeleine's mum when she worked in one of the jazz clubs in the West End.

Madeleine's mum was called Grace and she was a real Londoner. She'd been brought up in Hoxton near the flower market along the Columbia Road and she was the polar opposite to my mum. Whereas my mum was uptight and rarely smiled, Grace was smiley, easy going and liked to sing. She could make me laugh too. Nothing seemed to get to her. Two years after the birth of Madeleine, they had a baby boy. Berto wanted him to be called Antonius after a famous Brazilian musician, but every one called him Tony.

It looked like he was going to take after his dad as well as his namesake. He was always playing his guitar, not rock music but the bossa nova music of Brazil and he played it beautifully. Sometimes he'd play and sing 'The Waters of March' in Portuguese. I loved it when he did that and it reminded me of happier times when my mum sang it to me.

Grace and Berto got on really well even though they didn't have much money. At one time or another all of them had been racially attacked, even Madeleine's mum, just for marrying a Brazilian, but they seemed able to ride life's problems; not like me, or my mum.

They lived in a flat off Green Lanes and I lived in a garden flat in Stroud Green so I'd cut across Finsbury Park when I went to see her. I wasn't allowed to ride a bike in London. My mum said I'd get knocked off so I had to walk, bus, or go by tube everywhere. That makes it sound like she cared but I didn't think so. The way I looked at it, she did everything to annoy me but after that row with her, I got in a strange mood, and I'm going to write about it the way it happened so you know how I felt.

So I'm walking across the park to get to Maddy's. There'd been a music festival the previous night and some council workers were clearing away rubbish and litter, another lot were dismantling a stage. I stopped to watch them. There's always a big clear-up after a music festival in the park. My mind went over the row. I knew I'd been lippy with my mother but when she started, it was like there were no holds barred for either of us. Then I think about the farmhouse in Ffridd and how when I was fed up I'd get on my bike and cycle to the estuary.

I missed it and I missed Philomena and Gareth and I'm wondering what's going on between him and Chloe and whether he's still involved with her. It's like I'm obsessed and I keep thinking about them dancing in the forest at night, and how incredible it had been. But most of all I think of Ifan and how much I miss him.

I'm beginning to feel weird. I'm feeling as if I'm spaced out. I'm thinking I've imagined it, that nothing happened, there hadn't been an Ifan, he didn't disappear because he'd never existed and I'm feeling more and more strange, and kind of floaty, as if I was on some kind of acid trip. I was on that spit of sand again, in the middle of the river. I'm about to die. I no longer know what's real and what isn't. I look around me.

Focus. Stare. The workmen. The noise. The shouts. The metal bars banging. I hear the roar, the rush of the river, Ifan, the cool air on my naked body, he's smiling, I touch him, he comes.

A workman. He shouts. I stare at him. 'Cheer up love, it may never 'appen.' He's in my head. What if it has? It has happened. He's already dead.

I'm walking now towards Green Lanes. I hadn't said anything to anybody. I have to talk Maddy because she's a good person and she'll listen.

I cross the park and reach the top of Green Lanes. I look around. Start walking. It's familiar. I'm feeling in the world again. Not totally, but a little. It's early and it's buzzy. Just the same as I remembered it. Life as normal. North London. I'm back. I'm here. In Green Lanes, among the Greek and Turkish Cypriots.

I walk down Green Lanes. They've brought their culture with them. On the dreariest of days they get up early. Some of them have a siesta in the afternoon as if they still live on an island in the Aegean. It's a moment in time. I love it here. I'm beginning to feel normal again. I love the vibrancy and colour. The greengrocers with their boxes of fruit and veg spilling out of the shops on to the pavement. The contents piled high, geometrically straight, or carelessly disorganised. A kaleidoscope of clashing colours, the vivid oranges, the purple shiny aubergines, the yellow melons, the crimson tomatoes, the crisp green lettuces. The colours of the Aegean brought to the greyness of London's streets. And jammed between the travel agents selling cheap flights to Cyprus, the hardware shops, the dazzling lighting shops with ornate displays of curling gilt and shining glass, the bread and pastry shops and the neon lit coffee shops. Inside, the men, complexions darkened and lined by lives in the sun, spend their days and nights playing board games, gossiping, talking, smoking.

I cut down a side street parked up with cars packed together so tight you couldn't get a playing card between them, reach Maddy's block of flats and climb the stone steps up to the first floor. There's no lifts but unlike some London blocks this is an okay place. It feels safe. I can tell that because the stairs don't stink of urine and they're free of needles and contraceptives, and there's pots of geraniums and other plants outside some of the flats, and no one's nicked them or smashed them.

I ring the front door bell. I can hear the chime from outside. Berto had downloaded 'One Note Samba' on to the front door bell and hearing it again makes me feel happy. I look at the door viewer, wave and blow a kiss because I know Maddy will check to see who's there. She opens the door straight away. I can tell she's pleased to see me.

She smiles broadly, says hello and asks whether I want a coffee or tea. I say a coffee. I sit down in the same chair in the lounge I always do. Maddy disappears into the kitchen.

Maddy rarely called me Echo because she knows I hate the name, so she'd christened me with her own choice – Annie. Her grandmother on her mother's side loved old films, especially the music of *Annie Get Your Gun* and they'd often watched it together. Her Gran told Maddy that I reminded her of Annie in that film and that me and my mum were like the song 'Anything You Can Do I Can Do Better'. After that, I got hold of a copy. I laughed when I saw it. I didn't mind being called Annie and I liked the main character in the film. She was feisty.

She comes back in and says, 'How you doing?' and hands me a mug of coffee. She's still in her pyjamas. She's sitting opposite me with her legs curled underneath her.

I look around. 'I'm fine,' I said, 'But where is everyone?'

'Gone to see my gran. I didn't want to go. I saw her recently. They're going to Brick Lane for a curry this lunchtime.'

'Bit early to be out and about on a Saturday.'

'That's how they are. My dad's working late tonight so he wanted to sleep later.'

Maddy was looking at me. She says, 'You're upset. Quarrel with your mum?'

'Yeah, nothing's new.'

'What about?'

'What do you think? The usual. Everything, anything and nothing.'

Maddy sighed. 'The trouble is, the two of you are so different.'

'That's the problem. We're different. But she wants me to be her. To think like her. To have the same opinions as her. To do what she wants, and, by the way, she'll choose my friends. As if we're Tweedledum and Tweedledee and I'm a clone. She gets on my bleeding nerves.'

Maddy was silent and continued drinking her coffee. She looked thoughtful. 'It's not going to get any better, is it, not until you move out.'

'Don't say that. It's depressing. That's years off. I'll need a job first. I've got no money.'

Maddy looked at me, then she said, 'You haven't told me about Ifan this time. Did you see him? What did you do? Was it enjoyable?'

'Well. I wouldn't say so. Not this year. It's been different. I've grown up. Things happened. It's been hard. I did want to tell you, but now I don't. I don't want to spoil your day. Besides. You're too nice.'

'Don't talk bollocks, Annie. I'm your best mate and you know I'm not nice. Go on. Tell me.'

I didn't know what to say or how to say it. For a long time I just sit and then bits come to my mind but they were all jumbled up. Images, feelings, words, nothing made sense, and nothing joined up. Words come out but everything was muddled.

'It's weird. I don't know where he is. Is he dead? Maybe. Yes. Hiding? Maybe I imagined it. She said that. The river. I, I liked it. And the dancing. The two of them. That's odd… with me standing there. They didn't know. That's how it was and you can never be sure. They're having an affair. I do know that. I have proof. I've made a decision. About sex. Have you had sex, Maddy? You will say, won't you?'

That bit came out loud and I was looking at her but her face was making me laugh. It was like a clown's face and her mouth was in the shape of a big O.

'Annie, stop it.'

Her voice came through my confusion. I stared at her. 'Stop what?'

'You're strange. You've never been like this before. You're frightening me.'

She was looking straight into my eyes. 'Shall I make you some camomile tea?'

That made me laugh too. I switched to a cockney accent. 'What! Camomile tea. Why camomile tea? Is it 'erbs man, 'erbs. I don't smoke 'erbs, nah never, I drink 'erbs, and I don't eat 'em eiver so doncha give me 'erb cake neiver – cos I don't do it, I'm a gal who ain't 'ad sex but after me birfday, I'm gonna get me a man and 'ave it off wiv 'im. Hey, wacha staring at me for? I'm yer best mate. Nah. Coffee will do, coffee will do fine, just fine, just fine, coffee will do.'

Then I laughed. Maddy was staring at me. She was wide eyed. She wasn't smiling. I looked at her. I'd scared her. She got up and put some music on. She didn't say anything and neither did I. We sat and listened. It was a woman singing and playing the guitar with a soothing and gentle voice.

I said, 'Who's this?'

'Souad Massi. She's Algerian.'

'She has a beautiful voice.'

'Yes. I thought you'd like her.'

The music brought me back from the dark place I had been in a few minutes ago. I felt bad that I'd frightened her. I said, 'I'm sorry, Maddy. Just joking. I didn't mean to scare you but it's too much, you know to talk about. I will tell you, one day. I want to find out about sex. Do you mind telling me, have you ever, you know, had it?'

She looked amazed, 'What's this about? What's going on for you? I have, but it's private. Why do you want to know?'

That put me on the spot. I felt embarrassed and Maddy

could see that. She said, 'Come on. Nothing you say will shock me. Have you met a guy? Is that what it's all about?'

'Not exactly. Let's put it this way. Something did happen. With Ifan. But I'm not going to talk about it. It's strange because almost straight after, I saw...and I'd thought of him in a kind of fatherly way, and he was with this beautiful woman, but he's having an affair because he's married, and I was watching them dancing at night in the forest, then he screwed her. I didn't watch though. How pervy would that have been?'

Maddy had an expression of disbelief on her face. I carried on.

'Well it happens. You walk in the woods and all kinds of things are going on. It's not about just the birds and the bees, anyway they were about to have it away, I thought...time to go. Maybe it was a turn on, but Ifan, you know my friend, he's gone, who knows where, so after seeing that, I decided I wanted to have sex with him. The other one, the rescuer. Gareth's his name. I fancy him.'

'But Ifan, what's happened to him?'

'I'm not talking about him. I told you.'

'Annie. You look as if you're going to burst into tears.'

'I'm talking about Gareth now, that's who I want to tell you about.'

'How old is he?'

'Dunno, thirties, forties. I don't care how old he is.'

'But why?'

'Why what?'

'Why him? Why not a guy your own age? How old's Ifan?'

'Ifan's disappeared. I keep telling you, I'm not talking about him.'

Maddy looked at me as if she didn't know what was going on but she knew me well enough not to press me further, so she said again, 'Okay, so why not someone younger?'

'Boring. I want someone exciting, like him.'

'Exciting! How is he exciting?'

'He's a poet. He likes John Donne.'

'Who the fuck is John Donne?'

I sighed. 'Another poet, dead now, but that's what he was into. Fucking women.'

'John Donne?'

'Yeah. He wrote all about it, who he fancied and what he did and how he did it and I want a bit of it.'

Maddy was still looking at me as if she couldn't believe what I was saying. Then she laughed. I asked what was so funny but she just said, 'You, you make me laugh. It's the way you talk. You don't read or watch porn. It's poetry that turns you on... Tell me about Gareth and how you think you're going to come on to him. You'll have to look different.'

'What do you mean? I'll have to look different? What's wrong with the way I look? I'm not fat and I'm not skinny. Do you think I'm ugly? I'm not that bad, am I? Anyways, how come you've already had sex and I haven't? Come on, tell me. What's it like?'

'What do you want to know?'

'How it happened? So I know what to expect.'

'That's the point. It's unpredictable. It just happens.'

I looked at her in disbelief. 'You mean, like,' and I was thinking then about Ifan asking me to remove my clothes, 'a guy is overcome with passion and the girl wants it too, and they just make out? That's not chance, is it? Is it? They must think about it, want it, you know, before it happens, what it might feel like and what you do and what he might do.'

I could see I was making Maddy uncomfortable, but I could also see she wasn't going to tell me. She was looking at me as if she was deciding what to say.

She said, 'The difference between you and me, is I know him well. He's my age. I trusted him and it was good. I don't regret it. Whereas,' she paused, 'whereas with you, Annie, what you're thinking of is you'll have it away with an older man who's married and who's already having an affair. Not exactly a recipe for happiness is it? More of a disaster waiting to happen, I'd say. I know you, Annie. You'll fall in love with him, or think you have. He'll have sex with you and then dump you. Older men like to be the first ones. It's a national pastime with a certain type.'

'The first ones. What do you mean?'

'To have sex with a girl who hasn't had it before.'

'It was Theo, wasn't it?'

'Yes.'

'Does your mum know?'

'Yes.'

'What she say?'

'Not to get pregnant and not to get hurt.'

'I wish I had a mum like yours.'

'I'm saying the same to you, Annie. When she said to me, "Don't get pregnant and don't get hurt," it means, choose your guy, choose your own age, not an older married man, because sure as hell, it won't work out.'

She was getting through. I stood up and idly walked across to look at a framed photo of her dad playing the drums with her brother on guitar. I picked it up. I said, 'This is a nice piccie. Tony and Berto. I wish I had a dad.' Maddy wasn't saying anything. 'I met a guy in the mountains in Wales. I want him to help me find my dad. A researcher, researching slate quarries.'

'Weird thing to study.'

'It's not. It's interesting. He was interesting.'

'How old?'

'Twenties – early.'

'More your age. Why don't you go for him?'

'No spark.'

'I suppose not. You prefer wild Welsh men who're married, who write poetry and have sex in the woods with beautiful women.'

'Woman. Maddy, not women. There was only one. She's not a random woman.'

'As far as you know. Anyway you want to add yourself to his list. "Women I have screwed."'

I gave her a filthy look.

She said, 'Listen to me, won't you. Don't do it. Keep away from him.'

I said I would but I had no intention of following her advice. I listened. I ignored it. I had to find out in my own way.

'I'm going to get dressed, I won't be long,' she said, and disappeared into her bedroom.

When she returned she asked whether I'd like to go to Camden Market with her and I said I would, so we caught a bus to Camden Town. We planned to meet our mates in our usual coffee bar and check out what was new but when we got there, no one was there. Maybe we were too early so we decided to go straight to the market.

We walked up Camden High Street. It was packed. Full of tourists, cars and buses nose to tail. We could hear the noise and smell the different street foods way before we got there. The place buzzed. The music jammed. Camden Market. Shoppers of the world unite. A feeding and buying frenzy. Something for everybody. By the time we got there it was already teeming with people but we knew our way around and where to go. It was always worse Saturday afternoons but we were earlier than that, so it was just about bearable although we still had to push and shove to make our way through.

We both had our favourite stalls. Maddy always made a bee line for the one selling Latin music. The guy running that stall loved his music. He'd rigged up a sound system. Each side of his stall was flanked with huge amplifiers and cables running from them. They looped and ran all along the back and the top of his brightly lit stall. You could hear his music a mile away. He didn't do restraint. He did noise. He did rhythm. He believed in hitting his customers with the music of the world. Samba, bossa nova, mambo, salsa, tango, calypso, music from Cuba, music from Brazil, music from Africa, music from the Caribbean, music from South America; he had them all. He was like his music, exuberant and extravert, and when particular tracks came on that he found irresistible, he'd just take off and dance in front of his stall.

Tourists loved him and he loved them, especially the young, petite and pretty Japanese. If they made the mistake of hesitating as they passed his stall, he shouted out a greeting as if they were his long-lost best mates. Then he'd ask if they'd like to dance but before they could answer, he'd grabbed them. He'd stand in front of them clicking his fingers in time to the music, gyrating his hips, spinning round, begging them to dance. Mostly they giggled but one took up his offer. She must have been a professional dancer, she was so good. He couldn't believe his luck. Together they were crowd stoppers. Her friends and passersby took photos of them, and afterwards clustered round his stall like locusts. He was totally uninhibited and had to be seen to be believed. I found him embarrassing and tried to avoid catching his eye but Maddy didn't care because she was always on the lookout for music for her dad and brother. She told me to ignore him.

The stall I liked specialised in vintage-style clothing. I'd been there so often that Jen, the woman who ran it, recognised me. She knew what I liked and as soon as she saw me she told me she'd got in a new line. Fifties style tops, in loads of different colours. She looked at me, picked out a red one and held it against me. It had three-quarter length sleeves and was made out of some sort of stretchy material and I could see even before trying it that it was tight and cut low. I turned to Maddy and asked what she thought, and she said, 'Go for it.' Jen asked if I wanted to try it on but I didn't because there was no proper place for trying on clothes and I'd either have to queue to get in the public toilets or use a makeshift place at the back of her stall. There was a mirror propped against some boxes but you couldn't see yourself properly. Jen said if I bought it, I could try it on at home and if it didn't fit, I could bring it back.

I kept looking at it. It wasn't the kind of top I usually wore but I did like it. Finally I decided against it, basically because I didn't have enough money but then Maddy offered to lend me some. At first I wouldn't accept her offer, but she went on at me for so long, in the end I agreed. She said if her family wasn't back I could try the top on at her place. She wanted to see me in it and she was determined.

When we got back to her flat, she put on her new CD, a funky compilation of Brazilian music. She insisted I try on the new top, so I went to her bedroom and pulled it on. It was really tight. I looked critically at myself in her full-length mirror and I couldn't decide whether it was me or not so I walked into the lounge to see what she'd say. As soon as she saw me she said, 'Wow,' and asked me to turn round.

'Annie, your figure is fab.'

'Fab? How do you mean?'

'You look hot and guys are going to fancy you if you wear that.'

'Why would they?'

'Don't be dumb. Look at yourself. Go on. There's a mirror there, have a look-see.'

She pointed to a mirror over the sideboard, I walked over. I could see her reflection, she was sitting behind me and smiling. I switched my attention to myself. I still wasn't sure. Maddy came over, stood in front of me and pulled the top down even lower than it was already. The material was stretchy, but because it was cheap it was cut small and in a deep v, front and back. You could see my boobs.

I said, 'Don't do that. It's too revealing.'

'That's the point, Annie. You want it, so you said, so give 'em it, the green light.'

'You're taking the "p", Maddy. Give me a break. It's too much, what about my mum?' I was feeling apprehensive about what she'd say and I knew she'd be horrible if she saw me in this. She was the mistress of the put down.

'It's not for your mum, it's for you, stupid. Are you going to live your life for your mum? She's older than you, she's your mum and she's had it.'

I said, 'You're right.'

I looked at my reflection. I was always critical of myself

but this time I could see what Maddy meant and why Jen at the market had picked out this top. It reminded me of glamorous stars in fifties' films. It was almost off my shoulders and the deep 'v' swooped down and drew attention to my breasts. The red was a good contrast with my dark blonde colouring.

But in my mind I was back in Ffridd to the time when I hadn't known what to wear, and how, when I'd seen myself in the mirror, I wasn't sure whether I was looking at an adolescent girl or a young woman. I turned to Maddy and asked, 'What shall I wear with it?'

'Skinnies and wedge heels. I can see you in them.'

I could see myself in them as well. 'Mmmm,' I said, 'but.'

'But what?'

'What colour?'

'Orange, pink?'

'Christ.'

'You can carry it off. You know I wouldn't say that if it wasn't true.'

I looked at her doubtfully and then I said, 'I'm gonna have to save up.'

The next time I went to Camden Market I bought some pink skinnies and some wedgies. They were about as high as you can get without getting altitude sickness. When I tried them on and looked at myself in the mirror I could see I'd changed, not just physically, but emotionally. I was a little more self-confident so I could wear jeans that were so tight I had to lie on the floor to pull the zip up. The wedge heels made my legs look long. My breasts had got bigger. All of a sudden. Weird or what? Maybe that was because of a push-up bra that Maddy recommended.

I began cutting my own hair. Maddy did too. Her mum said our hair looked like we'd just rolled out of bed and the rats had been at it while we slept. That was the point. We did cool, the urchin look was in and going to a hairdresser wasn't cool.

Looking like this I attracted attention from the guys.

Lots. They found me a turn-on and I liked that but I remained aloof from them. They were too young. I was still set on Gareth. I never showed my mum my new outfit because I knew she'd go crazy if she saw how I was dressed. I'd leave my clothes with Maddy and when we went out I'd get ready at her place.

Maddy had her own style. She was different from me. She was subtle and she liked black. She reminded me of Chloe. I could see her as an architect already. She was arty, stylish and beginning to look the part of a creative. I thought she was beautiful with her Latin looks. She had dark skin and almost black eyes but she had a self-confidence that came from her mum's approval and care for her. She didn't have to work on it as I did. She was easy on herself and she loved her fella, Theo. She told me he turned her on and she liked sex with him but she wouldn't tell me more.

Meanwhile, I was developing my own plans but I didn't tell anyone what they were. I was totally obsessed with Gareth which meant I forgot Ifan for most of the time. He wasn't around but Gareth was. Besides I was pissed off with Ifan. I didn't think he was dead. He should have contacted me and his absence made it alright for me to write to Gareth. I asked him how his poetry book was going. I also sent my love to Philomena because I felt for her having to live with a two-timing husband. She'd always been good to me, but there was a disconnect between that thought and what I was up to with Gareth. I didn't see it at the time, but when you think of it, that's like most of the population so I'm no different. I'm not making excuses though.

I asked Gareth if he'd visit me if he came to London. He wrote back to say he would. He said when his new book came out he'd been asked by the Poetry Library on the South Bank to give a reading. He didn't have a date yet but when he did, he said I'd get a personal invite.

I was over the moon when I read that but the more I thought about him, the more determined I was to seduce him.

I felt different from girls my own age and I wanted to make out with a man, not a boy. I wanted to be seen as beautiful, womanly and irresistible. I'd wear the outfit; the skinny pink jeans, the tight red top, the red wedges. They were tried and tested for their pulling power. The question was, when and how it would happen. It needed careful planning, like a military manoeuvre.

I came to the conclusion the best time would be when he came to London for his poetry reading or when we returned to Ffridd next year. I had to get him on his own and that could be London or Wales. The exact place wasn't important, as long as it happened. Maybe we could go into the mountains and visit the slate quarry. They were remote, isolated and anything and everything could happen, but then reality intervened. Even I couldn't walk in wedgies and skinnies into the mountains. I'd look stupid so it had to be somewhere else.

I forgot Maddy's warning about the possible conse-quences; that he already had a lover and a wife. I focused on the fact that he and Philomena had agreed to an open marriage and in my mind that made it alright. Meanwhile I checked out the scene round Camden Town but 'I was just looking'. I wasn't going to put myself about. Gareth was and had to be my first lover and that was mightily appealing to me.

The beginning of October I got a text from Kieran Lloyd, the guy I'd met at the slate quarry. He wanted to remind me of our meeting at the slate quarry and my promise to help him. Actually, I didn't think I'd promised him but it didn't matter because I had my proposal to put to him. He was back in London and asked if we could 'progress it' as he put it. I suggested we meet in Camden and he agreed to that.

We arrived at the same time. He'd chosen the place. It was called 'Reason to Eat'. I'd never been there before and he led the way. It was a bit posh compared to where I usually hung out. We sat opposite each other and I could see him looking at me intently. I told him without his Gore-Tex he

114

looked different, but he didn't respond. He had no small talk. He was shy and it was only when he was talking about his research that he got animated, and then it was difficult to stop him. I hoped that would change if we got to know each other, because I wasn't into a crash course on industrial archaeology on a Saturday morning in Camden.

He was different from the guys I knew. There was something quite sweet about him. He wasn't smart, cool or mouthy, but kind of intense. Not in a deep way like Gareth, but in a focused, one thing at a time, kind of way. Maybe he was like that because he'd been brought up in Cardiff and that's how people are there.

He asked me if I wanted something to eat. I looked across to the front counter and I could see a pile of almond croissants. I adore almond croissants so I said I'd have one of them. He bought one for himself too. As soon as our coffee turned up he began talking about his research. He got to the point fast. Like I say, there was no small talk, no hanging around.

He wanted me to contact my uncle and check out how many copies he had of *The Caban*, and what the publication dates were. He'd made enquiries at his department at University College and there was a small fund to buy them and get them translated.

I said, 'What if they're no use?', but he seemed sure they'd be worth reading. 'Was there anything special you're looking for?' I asked, and he said, 'Yes, anything referring to the conflict between the quarry men and the owners during the "Penrhyn lockout" between 1900 and 1903.'

I'd never heard of a 'lockout' before so I asked him about that. His knowledge was impressive. Then he said, 'You have no idea how exciting it was to meet you.' That made me wonder whether he was coming on to me, but one look at his face put me right. He was in love with his work, that's what turned him on, and not me or anybody else. That made things easier, that there was no possibility of complications. But he'd given me an opening.

I told him I'd do everything I could to help him but I'd have to talk to my mum first and I didn't know how she'd take it. She was moody and unpredictable, and she'd have to get back in touch with my uncle and I didn't know if they got on. Kieran asked if there was anything he could do to move along the process.

'Actually,' I said, 'there is. I'd like to look for my father. You're a researcher. Do you know how to go about it?'

He looked blank. He said, 'Find your father?' He began stirring his coffee, and didn't say anything for a while. Eventually he said, 'It's not the type of research I do. Family history. That's not what I'm trained for, but I'll do my best. When did you last see him?'

'I've never seen him.'

He made no comment. I was picking up he didn't do personal. 'Well,' he said, 'What do you know of him?'

'Not much.'

'Name, date of birth, last known residence?'

'Zilch.'

'I do need something to go on. Will your mother tell you?'

'I think I was a virgin birth.' I smiled so he knew I was joking.

I could see he was thinking. Then he came up with an idea and it was a good one. 'Your uncle, the one in Liverpool, would he know anything about your father?'

It was my turn to be excited. I said, 'I never thought of that, but that's brilliant. He might, mightn't he? He's my mother's brother, even if they have fallen out.'

He actually looked pleased but I wasn't born yesterday. I knew what I'd asked would benefit him too. I was right. He said, 'When you meet him and ask about *The Caban*, you could ask about your father too.'

'Or the other way round.'

'Exactly, and your fare to Liverpool, I wouldn't expect you to pay, I've got a grant for research costs.'

'You're on.'

He wanted to make a definite date for our next meeting, so we made one in six weeks time and in the meantime he said I could contact him anytime. He paid for the coffee and the croissants, then he went. He had a meeting to attend, he said. I got the impression he didn't want to hang around for long, maybe because he didn't know what to say.

I sat and thought for a while about what to do next and how to play it with my mum. I'd tell her about Kieran and his research, but I wouldn't say anything about my father because she'd only go into one. I was about to break the habit of a lifetime by becoming a family sleuth so how she responded was important. I didn't want her interfering, or stopping me.

As soon as I got home I began my plan of action. My mother was in a good mood. Maureen was visiting. She taught at the same school as my mum and I knew she liked me because she always spoke to me and laughed at my jokes. She asked how I was, but she didn't ask about Ffridd which made me think my mum had already said something. I said fine, but the summer had been difficult, finishing with 'As my mother probably told you.' She nodded her head sympathetically so I knew I was right. Maureen's presence would sweeten her up and stop her being so snippy.

I turned to my mother and said, 'Mum, I don't think I mentioned to you before, that when I went to North Wales with Gareth, and he was at his publisher's, I went to a slate quarry up in the mountains, and I met a guy there, an industrial archaeologist. Do you know what they do?'

'Of course I do. Why wouldn't I?'

She glared at me. Bingo, I'd annoyed her already. It didn't take much. I pressed on. 'His name's Kieran and he's really nice. He told me about what he was doing, researching slate quarries, and I happened to mention Uncle Harry had loads of old magazines about the quarries, so to cut a long story short, he'd like to see them. Apparently they're hard to come by, so I offered to find out more. Kieran is so pleased, he's going to pay my fare up to Liverpool.'

She didn't reply. I ploughed on. 'So, I just saw Kieran in Camden for a coffee and he's asked me to find out more.' I waited for a response.

Maureen spoke. 'Does he want you as his unpaid research assistant, because you shouldn't work for nothing.'

I said, 'No, it's not like that. I'm interested too, and besides, I'd like to meet Harry.'

My mother was silent for a moment and then she said, 'How old is he?' She meant Kieran, but I knew where she was coming from then.

'Like I said, he's not interested in me, only in his research and he wants to see copies of *The Caban*. They're by the slate quarry men and I want to help him. I could meet Uncle Harry as well. Come on, Mum, what's wrong with that? I thought you were all for education.' I looked at her with what I hoped was an appealing expression on my face.

My mum looked unimpressed but eventually she did say, 'Well, when do you want to go?'

'As soon as possible.'

'Well, as long as you keep me in the picture, you can.'

For the rest of the day I made sure to be really helpful and polite, but she hardly noticed. I didn't mind, because I'd got what I wanted. After Maureen had gone, I asked my mum why they'd fallen out but all she'd say was there was a personality difference and she'd never got on with him. She said he could be difficult. I didn't say it must run in the family, but I thought it. She didn't even have a photo of him. She'd totally cut him out of her life, in the same way she'd done with my father.

Knowing this made it difficult. I felt apprehensive about contacting him as he might be a weirdo so it took me a while to psyche myself up to ring him. Then I changed my mind and decided to write. It would give him time to think about whether he wanted me to visit.

Getting his address turned out to be difficult. My mum had to look through her papers and it put her in a bad mood.

She'd last seen him years ago when she'd gone to some distant cousin's wedding and stayed with him. She'd taken me with her but after that visit she'd decided to 'terminate contact', that's how she put it, but what led her to do this, she wouldn't say.

My memories of his house were vague. I remember going up the stairs to a room full of boxes and a trunk. I could hear my mum and Harry arguing downstairs and I wanted to get away from them. That's when I came across the magazines. I'd opened the lid of the trunk and saw neat piles of them tied up with string. I took one downstairs to look at them. I was intrigued by the black-and-white photos. It showed men dressed in suits with flat caps on and they were arranged in lines, with the tallest at the back and the ones in the front crouching down. They all looked poor, tired and care worn. Behind them were the mountains. I showed them to Harry. He said the slate was hacked out by these men working in tunnels under the mountains and it was dangerous.

After several tries I managed to compose a letter to Harry asking if I could visit. I even showed my mother because I wanted to keep her on board as long as possible. In the letter I introduced myself as Phoebe's daughter and said I had a friend studying the Welsh Slate industries and I'd promised to help him and could I come to see him as I understood he had a connection with some slate quarries. I put my mobile number on the letter.

He didn't ring but wrote back within the week saying he'd be happy to meet me and I could stay with him. He came across as quite sad and lonely. He mentioned time passing and perhaps he wanted to make amends, but whatever it was I was about to find out. His phone number was on the letter so I rang him and we made an arrangement for the weekend.

Two weeks later I stepped off the train at Lime Street Station. Harry said he'd meet me at the station and he'd asked for a photo so I'd sent one of me and Maddy laughing together in a photo booth. I'd marked who I was with an arrow. He told me he'd be wearing a dark green Gore-Tex jacket and carrying a copy of *The Independent*. I liked him as soon as I saw him, primarily because he reminded me of Mr Harris at school. In fact he could have been a teacher but he wasn't. He'd been a mining engineer but no longer worked because, from what he said, he was on long-term sick, but he wanted to get back eventually. I was amazed at how open he was. It seemed he wanted to confide in me and was different from how my mum described him, but I'd already decided I wasn't going to bad mouth her and take sides, even though I felt like it.

Harry lived in Allerton and it was late afternoon by the time we arrived, but when we got to his house he became nervous and began stammering. I don't know why. First he showed me my room and the bathroom and when I was ready, he said to come back down for a cup of tea. After he'd gone downstairs, I looked around. It was full of dark furniture and smelt musty as if it hadn't been used for a long time. The walls were bare, and must have been painted a long time ago because they were a yellowing white and there were no pictures at all, which was strange. I wasn't used to bare walls. By the bed was an old Bible. I picked it up and wondered whether he expected me to read it. Maybe he was a Christian and thought I was one too. There was a marble washstand in front of the window with a vase of freshly picked pink roses. I liked them.

I looked out at the garden. It was beautiful. Harry might not be interested in the house but he loved his garden and that's where he must have got the flowers for my room. I went downstairs. Harry was waiting. I told him his garden was stunning and he brightened up and said he'd show me round later. He was really making an effort. We sat down for tea.

There were three types of cakes on the table and he said he'd bought them from a shop that baked their own. I looked at them. They all looked delicious. I really like home-made cakes and I didn't know whether to choose the chocolate brownie, the carrot cake or the lemon polenta. I chose carrot cake and Harry had cream to go with it. I had some of that too.

We had tea in cups with saucers, not mugs, and I began to think everything about Harry was a bit weird because I'd never met a man who drank tea out of cups and saucers and had a Bible. He's the type I hadn't come across in London but I liked him and I could see he liked me too, but he wasn't sure how to take me. I told him I liked the cakes but I didn't want to get fat because I'd recently bought some tight pink jeans. He looked at me as if I'd come off a different planet, which when you think of it, I had, compared to him.

He asked me how my mother was and I said she worked in a secondary school teaching classics but she didn't like it because the school kids weren't interested and they didn't see it as relevant. I told him she saw herself as more of an artist and that for the past five years she'd taken me with her to a place along the Welsh borders, and that she was part of a group of artists who wanted to keep the spirit of surrealism alive. He didn't know anything about surrealism and I said very few people did. As I spoke I could see he was weighing me up, but I was doing the same with him and wondering when I could ask him about my father.

He said then, 'Shall I show you the garden?' We walked into the garden and he pointed out the names of the plants. Not so interesting, I thought, but I kept my mouth shut.

I said, 'We live in a ground-floor flat. It's biggish and it's got a garden but my mum doesn't do gardening, so you couldn't really call the grass outside a lawn.'

'And what's the area like?' he asked.

'It's Stroud Green in North London and near Finsbury Park tube. You can easily get anywhere you like from there. Finsbury Park has a park and it's okay, it's not posh like some London parks but around the tube it's a dump. If you didn't live there you'd say it was interesting. But it's rundown, with loads of small shops selling stuff no one in their right mind would buy, unless you're poor and desperate. You have to watch your back, especially at night. The druggies are out in force after ten, hassling, begging but where we live it's okay.

The street's got big houses, some are dilapidated and others done up, like ours, but they're all flats. When a football match on, it's mayhem. I hate footie people and I keep asking my mum if we can move somewhere else, like Highbury, but she says it's too expensive.'

When I looked at him, his eyes were glued on his garden so maybe I'd said too much. To break the silence, I said, 'You must have spent weeks designing your garden. It's beautiful.'

He looked pleased, 'You think so?' he said.

We reached his patio. 'Wow,' I said. I stood admiring it. It was made out of old bricks and paving and it had an enclosed area with a table and chairs and was surrounded with flowering climbing plants growing up a wooden framework.

'You like my loggia?'

'Is that what's it's called? Do I like it? You bet I like it. What about sitting outside later and eating there. Would that be possible?'

'We can, if the weather's good.' Then he asked what I wanted to do the next day and whether there was anywhere in particular in Liverpool I wanted to visit.

'I dunno. Why don't you choose?'

In the end he took me on a tour. We went to Chinatown, visited John Lennon's house, walked round the refurbished docks, popped into Tate Liverpool and finished the day's sightseeing with a walk by the River Mersey. We parked near the shops. I told him I liked clothes and was working to save up for more. I was surprised when he said he'd buy me a new pair of skinnies and a t-shirt from H&M, but there was a condition. I had to wear them that night.

At the time I thought nothing of it because compared with my mother, he was easy to be with. He didn't snipe at me and I even made him laugh once or twice, and because he was so nice and generous I was on my best behaviour, but all the time I was thinking how I was going to ask him about my father.

He said I could choose what kind of food we'd eat so

I decided on a Chinese takeaway and I put on my new jeans and the t-shirt, as he'd asked. Everything was black because I wanted to look cool like Tarquin and Chloe. They were tight, especially the top but not as tight as the Camden one.

He said 'They fit perfectly. Turn round. What's it like from the back?' I turned round. 'Yes,' he said, 'very nice indeed.'

I'd never had this kind of attention before and his interest made me feel good. We sat down for the meal. He was drinking a beer. He'd given me one too, but I didn't like it, so he changed it to a spritzer made with lemonade. We'd already eaten when I began with my questions. It seemed the right time, now or never.

'Harry, I expect you're wondering why I rang you.' He looked up but didn't say anything but I'd got his attention, 'You know my mum. She doesn't talk to me. It pisses me off, but there's some things I want to know, things you might know.' He was looking at me but didn't say anything. 'Some things I think I should know, like everybody else, I have a right to know, so I wondered, whether you'd tell me?'

I was gabbling but he didn't seem to mind.

'What do you want to know?'

'About my father, I don't know anything about him. Do you, or did you know anything about him?'

'You don't know about him?' He sounded surprised.

'No, I don't, I don't, that's why I'm asking you.'

He didn't speak for a long time or that's what it seemed, and then he said, 'I'm sorry Phoebe hasn't told you what happened. I'd have thought she'd have got over it.'

'Got over it? Got over what?'

'Your father. What happened.'

He stopped then. I could see him weighing me up and wondering whether to continue but by this time I was busting to know so I said, 'Please, Harry, tell me.'

'I'm wondering whether I should, if she hasn't told you.'

'I can cope with most things, living with my mother gives me a good start.'

He didn't laugh, looked at me directly, blurted out, 'Your father was married to someone else.'

That was an angle I hadn't thought of. I was shocked into silence. The thought of my mother having sex with a married man was beyond anything I'd have imagined of her. It put her in the category of a femme fatale and like Chloe and Gareth. I couldn't get my head round it. She was always so uptight and judgemental and behaved as if I'd been the virgin conception. He continued. I was glued to every word.

'Of course, she didn't know he was married. She'd been deceived and it was terrible for her when she found out. She'd been crazy about him. She never stopped talking about him, what he'd said, where they'd been, where he was going to take her.'

I managed to ask a question, although I was still reeling. 'How long did she go out with him?'

'Over four months. She said they were soul mates, that's what he told her… Do you want to know more?'

'Yes. As much as you know.'

'He'd left his wife but he hadn't told Phoebe he was still married. They'd met at a concert and they got talking in the bar and started going out. They shared a passion for opera and when she got pregnant, she'd thought they'd marry because he'd said he was in love with her.' He paused and looked away from me before continuing the story. 'When she said she was expecting, he told her he was married already and that he and his wife were having a trial separation. Phoebe was devastated. She never saw him again. All she had was his name and an address, but when she went to look for him, he'd left and there was no forwarding address.'

'What about his work? Couldn't she find him that way?'

'He'd told her he worked for the BBC, but no one knew of him.'

'What was his name?'

'Tomos Morgan.'

'So that's the Welsh connection. Morgan. She's given me

his name. I'd always wondered why I had a different name.'

'She said he was the father and you should have his name. I think she hoped he'd come back one day.'

I was stunned into silence. For once, I felt sorry for my mother. No wonder she never spoke of him. He'd well and truly shafted her. Maybe that's why she disliked me. Maybe she even blamed me for him leaving her because if it hadn't been for me, he might have hung around. But what a two-timing wimp. An arsehole of the first order.

I said, 'Do you know where he might be? I'm thinking of shooting him.'

'I wouldn't do that. No. I don't. Sorry.'

'Don't worry. I'm joking. I don't care.' I was beginning to feel upset. 'I don't suppose you've got any photos of him?'

'No.'

'Do you think that was his real name, Tomos Morgan?'

'Who knows? It could be but it doesn't necessarily mean anything. It's possible he made it up. Along with the story he spun her.'

'Wanker.' I paused, he was giving me such a look, I added, 'Not you, him.'

Neither of us spoke for a long time.

'I want to be on my own.' I stood up and walked away to the end of the garden where I couldn't be seen. It was dark. I was tearful. I didn't want to say any more to him because I might cry and he'd be embarrassed.

I'd hoped by meeting him I'd get to know more about my father. Then I could track him down, and I'd feel less alone, but the opposite had happened. I did know more, but now I wished I didn't. To have a father like that, a man capable of deceiving and betraying a pregnant woman carrying his baby, who happened to be me; the more I thought about it, the worse I felt. I was damaged goods. I felt like shit and so bad I didn't know what to do with myself.

I looked up. Harry was coming along the path towards me. He put his arm round me and said, 'It's late, come back, you haven't finished your meal.'

I did what he asked but sat staring into space. I didn't want to eat. I was trying to keep myself together.

'Echo, stop. Please. Stop. Your foot's banging my chair.'

I felt a flash of anger. 'So what?' I looked daggers at him as if it was his fault, but it wasn't. 'Sorry, I didn't know I was doing that, swinging my leg. But don't call me Echo. I hate it.'

I glanced at him. He looked sympathetic, but intense. He caught my glance and gazed directly into my eyes. That brought me up sharp. There was something about his expression that reminded me of Ifan. He would have totally understood, after all he'd had a similar experience.

'I had a boyfriend once.' I looked at Harry. 'Did you ever had a girlfriend?' He didn't answer but he looked uncomfortable so I backed off. 'His name was Ifan and I met him in Wales. I miss him now. You know, times like this. We told each other everything.'

I stared at the garden. The lights from the house next door lit up the roses and they were smelling strong and sweet. 'But something happened. Do you want to know what that was?'

Harry shot up out of his chair, 'It's dark. I'm going inside.' He walked into the house. I followed him.

'Listen, don't walk off. I want to tell you about Ifan because it upsets me. He's gone. That's what I was going to tell you. We were crossing the river and I nearly drowned. That's when he vanished. They said I was imagining him. But it's not true, he was real, he was the best friend I'd ever had... I'm not mad. You don't think so, do you? You don't, do you?' My eyes were filling with tears.

He sat down. He was silent. He was looking past me as if I wasn't there but then he switched his gaze to look directly at me. He wasn't smiling. There was something about him I didn't like. He was watching me. I knew where I'd seen that look before. A man in the park. I was eight and on my own and I'd had to run.

I watched his every move, every gesture, every flicker

126

of his eyelid. He was tall and sitting in one of those old-fashioned, long, low armchairs. He yawned, lifted up his arms, sprawled back, his legs wide. He patted his thigh. 'Come here, sweetheart. You're upset, you need a cuddle.'

I saw what was going on. It was obvious. It was obscene. 'I'm going.' I almost ran towards the door, but before I could leave, he'd leapt up, strode across the room and put his arms round me. He pulled me towards him. He had a strong body odour which disgusted me.

'Don't go. I was going to make some tea.'

I pulled away from him but he wouldn't let me go, so I had to struggle. I felt his hands on my breasts as I pushed him away. I tried to pretend everything was normal and said in a gasping voice, 'No. Water's fine, there's some in my room. I'm tired.' I backed away from him, left the room, pulled the door shut behind me and galloped up the stairs.

I got to my bedroom. I locked the door. I thought he'd been kind because he liked me. How stupid can you get? I looked at myself in the mirror. I hated myself. I must look like a tart, because that's how he made me feel. Did he think I'd let him touch me up? Couldn't he see how upset I was when he'd told me about my father?

I began to cry, hot tears flowing down my face. I pulled off the new jeans and the top he'd bought and stuffed them into the rubbish bin. I put my own clothes back on. I looked out of the window; I had to go, leave without him knowing.

The door knob rattled. He was standing outside my room. 'Echo, let me in. I'm sorry you're upset. I won't hurt you.'

I didn't answer. I was so frightened and I wondered what I'd do if he forced the door open. I looked around for something to hit him with but there was only the vase with the roses in, but that was better than nothing. He went away eventually. I packed my case. Hours later, after he'd gone to bed, I crept downstairs, silently opened the front door, walked to the main road and caught a cab to the station.

The night train was about to leave for London. I arrived

back in the early hours. I never told my mother that he'd come on to me. What would be the point? She'd only say she told me so. It made it easier. I vowed I'd never see Harry again and the next day I texted Kieran with his name and address. I said it was better that he follow up *The Caban* himself. Months later he got in touch thanking me. He asked to meet up again but I didn't want to, so I never saw him again either. It was like he was associated with finding about my father and the kind of bloke Harry was. Irrational, I know, but that's how I felt. I knew the truth now about my father and that was bad enough but how Harry had been, was something I wanted to forget.

After the visit to Liverpool, I felt really low about everything and everybody and it got so bad, I didn't want to leave my bedroom. I'd get up, get dressed, go to school, come back, do my homework, watch television, read, go to bed. I lived in my own bubble and looked out at the world from inside that bubble.

My mother noticed. She said, 'Since you saw my brother, you've changed. What's got into you?'

'Do you really want to know?'

'That's why I'm asking you,' she said.

I paused, then I said, 'If I tell you, promise you won't go on about it.' She didn't answer, so I took the risk and told her, not about Harry but my father.

We were standing in the kitchen and she was leaning against the kitchen units. 'I wanted to find out about my father, but because you won't talk about him, I asked Harry.'

There was an ominous silence. I ploughed right on. 'I know about him now... He let you down, didn't he, and you were left with me, and you never saw him again after you told him you were pregnant.' She looked shocked and stared at me. I said, 'Aren't you going to say anything?'

Eventually she said, 'What is there to say?'

She turned away and started putting clothes into the

washing machine. I felt sorry for her. I saw her as human now, rather than an evil mother.

'Well, I wanted to know the truth and now I do.'

She still didn't say anything so in desperation, because I wanted some kind of reaction from her, I said, 'Look, it's not just about you. You had a lover who betrayed you but I have a father who abandoned me. We share the same man. He doesn't give a shit about either of us.'

'That's enough. I prefer you don't speak of him again.'

She walked out of the kitchen and within a minute she was speaking to Maureen on the phone, making an arrangement to see her. That was it. I was left to deal with the emotional backwash on my own. I felt no better.

As for Harry, I'd thought, hoped, he was a regular guy, reliable and trustworthy. I wanted him as an uncle just as I wanted my father. I'd thought he could be a friend, but he had other ideas and he'd made it plain what he wanted. He'd conned me with his niceness, while all the time he had dirty little fantasies about me. What did he expect me to do? Give him a hand job? I wasn't up for sex, not with him, I wasn't. He was family. My uncle, my mother's brother, amongst other considerations. I didn't like it, and I didn't like seeing him with a hard-on. He knew I was upset about Ifan and my father, but he'd ignored that and tried it on. I didn't exist for him. Not as a real person. I hated him. He was repulsive, gross and repellent.

I felt so angry with him, with her, with Gareth, with Chloe, the whole fucking lot of them, that I decided to tell Maddy. She'd already noticed I was withdrawn because I'd stopped going out, but unlike my mother she reached out to me. She came round to my flat one evening when my mum wasn't there and insisted I tell her what was going on. I cried when I told her. She put her arms round me and hugged me.

She said, 'All men lead with their trousers,' and 'Sex is never far from their thoughts.' That's what her mum had told her, and she'd said we should feel sorry for them because they were victims of their testosterone. Maddy had a badge at home which when she found, she gave to me. It had a bright red apple on it and it said, 'Eve was framed'. It had belonged to her mum because when she was young, she'd been part of the women's movement. Maddy made me promise never to throw it away.

She made me laugh that night and I began feeling better. She wanted me to go out with her over the weekend, but I wouldn't say if I would or not. Just as she was about to leave, she turned round and said, 'And, Annie, keep away from older men, and that includes Gareth.'

'Gareth?' I was surprised she'd remembered.

'Gareth. Yes. You know who I mean. What's going on? I know you, Annie. Your silence means something.' She sat down again. 'I want to know.' She was staring at me and I knew she wouldn't go until I told her.

I said, 'He's coming to London for his book launch. I haven't a date yet but it'll be at the South Bank. He agreed to meet me.' I was bullshitting because I didn't know for sure, but that's what I hoped.

'Nice one, I'll come too.'

'You don't like poetry.'

'A small detail.'

We sat staring at each other. She said, 'You told me he was exciting, that he read John Donne, that he made love to beautiful women in the forest, and you were going to seduce him. It's so vivid it's burnt a hole in my brain.'

'Maddy, I told you before. Not women. Woman. One woman. Chloe.'

'All the rest I've said is right. Right? So?'

'What's that mean? So?'

'Is that still what you're going to do? If so, where and when? Let me think, I'm you. I've got a plan. A plan of seduction and my target is a male by the name of Gareth and he's about to hit town. We arrange to meet in a hotel room. I'm interested in him, in poetry, his in particular. But I get

pissed. I'm scared. It's my first time. I dress in a way designed
to attract him. Nothing obvious. Nothing crude. Poets go for
subtlety. He doesn't want your breasts falling out. I leave the
balcony bra at home. "Au naturel" is what turns him on. He's
a man of feeling, of imagination, of romance, love, passion
and sincerity – that's what he wants. You plan to give it to
him. Right, Annie?'

I look at her. I burst out laughing. I couldn't stop.

'Shut up. What's so funny?'

'You are. You're funny, Maddy.'

'You think that's funny. I don't think so. It's the truth.
But, what if it goes wrong?'

'How can it go wrong?'

'You're not stupid. Loads of ways. Then you'll be upset.
Like you are with your uncle.'

'No comparison. Gareth's good. He's not a relation.'

'But you want to seduce a married man. More than
double your age. What if you succeed? Not too good, is it?
Screwing a young girl.'

'Fuck off.'

'I will. I plan to see Theo.'

Maddy stood up. We eyeballed each other.

'I keep telling you. Stick to your own age. It's safer.'

I sighed deeply and said, 'I wish I was as sensible as you.'

'Don't take the piss, Annie. I'm trying to get you to look
after yourself. But you're like Sisyphus.'

'Great. You've just reminded me of my mum. Every time
she says that, I say, like pushing shit uphill? It drives her mad.'

'I'm going now. Think about it. I'll see you Friday.'

What Maddy had said was interesting. Interesting but
irrelevant. It was a kind of abstraction to me. I was as determined as ever to follow through with my plan but what I didn't
realise at the time, a kind of self-destructive wildness had taken
hold of me.

Part Four

After Easter, my mother began planning the summer visit to Ffridd. She gave me a choice; I could stay in London if I wanted. She'd noticed how bored I got in Wales and I was old enough now to look after myself, she said. I thought the real reason was she didn't want me with her because it was the year of the exhibition in Chepstow, the one they'd called 'Women Surrealists: Then and Now'. I would have been interested in that but I knew her tolerance level would be zilch, and I'd rather put my head in a lion's mouth than share the time with her.

Besides, going back to Ffridd would bring back memories of Ifan's disappearance, and that still hurt. I wasn't sure, so I told her I'd think about it. For years I'd loved those holidays, but now I was older, I didn't want to leave London. It's true I liked Wales, but not every summer. London to the Welsh Borders, they were always in my head but not my heart. I lived in both, but belonged to neither. But – I wanted to see Gareth. Desperately. Time was passing and the longer I waited, the more I wanted to see him.

One night, I was by myself at home and bored. My mother was out and I'd been idly trawling through eBay and I saw a bag that I had to have.

You probably know about eBay. It's a world of its own, a market inside a computer and the buyers and sellers call themselves ebayers, but you need to wise up if you use eBay.

It's a tricky place to do business and when I bought that bag, I was still under the influence of surrealism and I could have a weird take on things. Why was that? Who knows, but life is full of wackos and weirdos as well as the normal and the nice, and you have to be careful. I wasn't so careful, or at least that's one way of looking at it. It's the way I prefer because, even now, I think there are forces beyond our comprehension. Even scientists know that. Bridges fall down, planes crash, and boats sink, despite the engineers' mathematical equations. What does it all mean, I ask myself. You can call it magic, god, angels, the devil, nature, imagination, the spirit world, or the unconscious. You choose. But whatever you choose, for me it was the bag and with that bag I wreaked havoc.

Before the bag, things were normal. After the bag, they definitely were not. Before the bag, I was a child. After the bag, I became a woman. It was like eBay was a kind of fairy godmother. It took a while before I realised what was going on but I was young then. Now when I look at it, I just see a bag, but I'll never throw it away. It got me through a bad patch so it's still special in my eyes.

When I first saw it, it was like falling in love. I stared at it. It was perfect. It had been used but was described 'as new' and in 'vintage style' but something about it captured me. It was up for auction but the bidding was about to end so I put in a really high bid. I sat over my computer for two hours. I was prepared to snipe to get that bag, although, generally speaking, I don't approve of snipers. But it was worth it. I won it and when that happened I was pleased as a cat thrown a fresh sardine.

I could hardly wait to hold it in my hands. I looked for the postman everyday and when it arrived, I opened the parcel straight away. I unwrapped the bag from its tissue paper and I knew I'd made the right decision as soon as I saw it. It was the most beautiful bag I'd ever seen. It was large, pouchy, and made of soft squashy leather the colour of the night sky and it was lined in emerald green, watered silk. It described itself as a catwalk tote bag. The colour, the look, the feel and the enigmatic smell of perfume drifting out as I opened it, was wonderful. I'll never forget that moment.

Holding it in my arms I danced round the room. It was beautiful, it was classy, it was stylish and it was called Anya. I knew that because her name was in brass on a separate little leather tag attached to one of the plaited handles. It said 'Made by Anya'.

I stared at her name and the bag. I remembered Gareth telling me I could change my name. My name was Echo but with this bag I was about to transform into Anya. I felt an affinity with Anya even though I'd never met her. I wanted to be her. Someone who could make a bag like that, a bag with attitude, must be special. It sulked, it pouted, it wanted to go places with me. That bag and its enigmatic fragrance seemed real and it had more meaning to me than anything or anybody. At the time, it seemed normal that I should think like that but that was because of my summers in Wales. I'd been told that the bizarre and myths were part of us all.

I became obsessed with this bag. I looked at it all the time and I began thinking it came from a spirit world and the fragrance from the bag was a way of communicating with me. I decided that Anya, the woman who'd made the bag, liked this perfume because it expressed her personality, or putting it another way, Anya is the perfume, the perfume is Anya and I wanted to be Anya. I became more and more fascinated with what the perfume meant and the more I thought about it, the more I thought it was an escaped wild female spirit. It got so every time I opened the bag, it felt like I was letting Anya out.

I had to know more about this fragrance and eventually I did, though it took a while. I'd been walking down Bond Street one afternoon, escaping the crowds along Oxford Street and as I passed a French perfumery, I thought I'd go in and ask. Someone might know. The French after all are known for their sophistication.

I walked inside and was almost blinded. There was enough light bouncing off the glass display cabinets to make me feel the second coming was imminent, but I didn't let that put me off. I walked over to the nearest sales assistant, opened my bag, and asked if he recognised the perfume. He saw my question as a challenge to his profession as a perfumier and to him as a man. You know how some men pretend they know even if they don't, but in this case he did know.

I was intrigued by his accent, the way he talked, his gestures, the way he looked. He had dark hair, a deep tan, a well-cut suit, a French accent and a theatrical manner. He took the bag, turned it round in his hands. He had quite a supercilious manner, it has to be said. He put it to his nose. He looked up towards the lights as if for inspiration. He drummed his fingers on his lips and, after a long pause, he said it was chypre with an undertone of sandalwood and bergamot. I was impressed. Then he pulled open a drawer and started showing me perfumes. He said I might like them because they were in the same fragrance category.

Neat, I thought. Nothing comes free, but I'd been captivated by his performance. It was better than watching Kenneth Branagh doing a takeoff of Laurence Olivier.

An hour later I walked out having bought an expensive bottle of 'Coco Mademoiselle' and from that moment on, for very special occasions I began to wear 'Coco'. It was my perfume of choice for what became my special missions. It was perfect because it was pervasive and a powerful reminder after I'd gone. My presence was still there.

I was ready now to change my name too. It was something I'd thought about for a long time so, inspired by the bag, I began calling myself Anya and told everybody I knew to call me by that name.

Six months later, I was still waiting for Gareth. Every now and again I'd drop him a line to ask how things were going at Ffridd and what he was doing. He always wrote back although it took him a while. I wondered whether he and Chloe were still lovers, but I didn't ask. I didn't want Philomena seeing my letter and after the row with him on the way to the slate quarry, it was still a no-go area.

I was still obsessed with him. I used to imagine him making love to me and for this occasion I planned to wear a vintage outfit. I'd got that idea from eBay too and, although I wasn't sure what it would look like, when I saw it, I'd know it was right.

Eventually he wrote to say he'd got the date for his book launch in London. It would be in the middle of August and he was coming on his own. He enclosed an invite, asking if I'd like to attend and hear him read, but after thinking about it, I thought not. I'd feel shy on my own amongst all those poets and publishers, and although Maddy had offered to come with me, I wasn't going to ask her, not after she'd gone on about avoiding married older men. Gareth scored on both these counts, but unlike Maddy, when it came to Gareth, for me, an older married man was a turn on.

The upshot of all this was that I told my mother I'd stay in London. She was pleased. She arranged for Maureen to keep an eye on me while she was away. I didn't mind Maureen as long as she kept out of my face, so with my mother out of the way doing her thing in Wales, I concentrated on making plans for seeing Gareth.

August arrived and I was alone in the flat. Maureen either rang or dropped by to check out everything was okay. She was no trouble. I did exactly what I liked and that suited me just fine. I kept the flat clean and tidy and put in extra hours working in the supermarket in Kentish Town. Buying 'Coco Mademoiselle' had set me back a bit but Gareth's event would provide the perfect opportunity to try out its powers.

I was prepared to find a hotel for Gareth, but when I mentioned this, he said his publisher had already booked him into a bed and breakfast – but I still went to check it. Just in case. I wanted him to stay somewhere smart. It was smart. It wasn't an ordinary B&B but a beautiful, large, white house down an exclusive quiet side street in Chelsea. The garden was full of shrubs with different-coloured leaves and shapes, all untidily tumbling across the paved entrance to the front door. The windows had white shutters. There were carriage lamps each side of the door. The owners must have been millionaires. I liked the look of it very much.

I phoned Gareth to tell him I'd seen where he was going to stay. I told him the house was beautiful from the outside and I was wondering what it looked like inside. It was a casual aside but he picked up on it and asked whether after his poetry reading, I'd like to come back with him, have coffee and catch up, as he put it. You can imagine how pleased I was. It would make my plans of seduction easier, but the feeling didn't last.

His suggestion might have been innocent but it made me anxious. What if, I thought, Gareth came on to me, like the 'perv' Uncle Harry? I didn't want any more surprises. If I was going to be alone with a man, I wanted to do the coming on but the more I thought about it, the more apprehensive I became. Something was driving me though. I couldn't stop myself. Eventually I decided not to think anymore about it, and with the exception of planning what I'd wear, I'd just see what happened.

I started with my underwear. I needed some new stuff anyway including a bra. Maddy's comment about 'balcony bras' intrigued me. I didn't know what they were so I looked them up and having seen them on line, I decided against them. Not my scene at all. I didn't need more uplift and my boobs were full already. I didn't want them in his face.

I decided to pay a visit to Marks & Spencer, the one in Marble Arch. I planned to spend an afternoon looking at underwear, but it turned out not to be such a good idea. There were too many and I got totally confused with the choice, the colours and the designs.

There was a woman there called a bra fitter and she took my measurements to get the right size. I was a 'full cup' she said. She brought out five different ones for me to try on and said, 'Take your time to choose.' I did.

One hour, ten bras later and I was still in the changing room. She stood by the cubicle door with the bras hanging over her arm. I'd just tried on a white and lilac flowery one with lace insets and matching pants, but I didn't try the pants on.

She said, 'That looks very feminine. Is it for a special occasion?'

I looked at her and wondered how to respond. She was getting on a bit but she had twinkly eyes. I asked her if she had children.

'Why yes,' she said. 'Why do you ask?' I noticed then she had an Irish accent.

'Do you remember your first time? You know, when you made out?' I could see she was taken aback but she made a quick recovery. 'It's a long time ago now, but yes, I do. It was quite memorable.' She looked away with a slight smile on her face, but I didn't follow through by asking her any more. I said, 'Well, I'm planning for my first time.'

'That's nice. Someone at school, your first boyfriend?'

'No, an older man. He's a poet.'

'A poet. How much older?'

'Quite a bit. But I don't mind. To me, age doesn't matter.' I smiled at her and said, 'He doesn't know I'm buying underwear for him. I want it to be a surprise.'

'Have you talked about this with your mother?'

'My mother? No way. She knows him. But she doesn't know my plans.'

'Wouldn't it be a good idea to tell her?'

'You don't know my mother. She's not like ordinary mothers. She lives in her own world. She paints. We don't talk. She doesn't like any of that stuff. Besides, she might tell him.'

'So he doesn't know either…it sounds like you want to seduce him.' She seemed incredulous.

I laughed. 'That's right. You're spot on. You see, I want to be irresistible. I want him to be overtaken with passion, his breath hot on my neck, his hands all over my body. Know what I mean?' I was winding her up. I winked at her.

She gave me a faint smile and was clearly struggling to work out what was going on but she must have given up because she said in a disapproving voice, 'Well, I hope it goes well for you.' Then, 'Are you any nearer to making a decision? Not that I'm putting pressure on you.'

'I don't know which one's the best? What do you advise?'

'These all fit you.' And she pointed to the small pile I'd put in the corner, 'And you have a pretty figure, but it depends how you want to look.'

'Like I said, womanly, desirable, voluptuous. Not pretty, so nothing with flowers on them. I want to look older than I am.'

She gave me a look, pursed her lips and said, 'Wear the black mesh then, the ones with the polka dots.'

I picked them up. 'But they're not padded.'

'You don't need your bra padded, your figure doesn't need any further help.' She was exasperated, but I pressed on.

'Do you have a set like this, only padded?'

'Yes, but it's a balcony style and you said that's what you didn't want. What about a push-up bra? You might like those.'

'I want one like this in red or black lace with matching pants, and padded. Do they come as push-up?'

'They're expensive.'

'I don't care. I'll work longer hours.'

'I hope he's worth it.'

'He is worth it.'

She disappeared, returning with a stunning matching black lace and mesh bra and pants. When I put on the bra it covered only half my breasts, pushed them together and up. I had cleavage and they looked even bigger than they were. There was nothing subtle about them. I stood staring at myself in the mirror. I hardly recognised my body.

'What do you think of those? We sell a lot to burlesque dancers.'

I glanced at her. 'I don't know what a burlesque dancer is.'

'Dancers who entice men with humour and style. They don't strip off but look as if they might. They tease. Some men like that kind of thing. Is that what you want?' She said this as if she expected me to say no, how vulgar, but what I said was, 'That's exactly what I want.'

I took the bra off and handed it to her. 'I like this. I'll have it with the matching pants. This is how I want to look.' We stood looking at each other. 'Thank you for all your help.'

'That's alright. I hope it goes well because...' She stopped.

'Because what?'

'It's strange to me, a pretty young girl like you going after an older man, but it takes all sorts. He must have something but I hope it's not his money. You look after yourself. It's a shame you have a mother who doesn't talk to you. About life and men.' She turned away picking up the bra debris, avoiding my eyes.

I thanked her again and said, 'It's not money because he doesn't have any. I don't know what it is. Sex probably. Strange, isn't it? Or maybe love? It's a mystery to me.' By now I was kidding her. 'As for my mother, I was a virgin birth. She still doesn't know what caused it. Pregnancy. It was a shock to her. Such a shame. She's a bit simple.'

She gave me a look. I don't think she got me. She was too serious. Did she think I was a sex worker? If she did, that didn't make me feel good at all. I walked out with my set of black lacy lingerie. I couldn't wait to try them on when I got back home.

When I did, I liked how I looked. I was transformed from a girl into a woman and she was right, I did have a good fig-ure. When Maddy had told me that, I hadn't believed her. My self-confidence was inching up despite my mother's constant negative comments, or so I thought. I turned my attention to what dress I should wear. It had to be something bought for the occasion, and something grown up. The kind of thing that Gareth would like. When I'd first seen Chloe, she was wearing a vintage-style dress. I wanted something like that. I began combing Camden Lock and Camden High Street, but nothing appealed. Once more, I turned to eBay.

There were hundreds of dresses to choose from in the vintage category, all conveniently labelled with their style so you'd know when to wear them; rockabilly, swing party, 'boho', ditsy floral, tea dance, land girl and so on. A blast from the past, their names made me smile and set my imagination going.

The one I chose was called 'vintage tea dance'. It wasn't an original but a copy but I just loved that dress. It was duck-egg blue with sprigs of tiny darker blue, yellow and white flowers scattered over it. It had cap sleeves, a fitted bodice, a V neck back and front which showed off my cleavage, and a full skirt. It was made from polyester, not cotton, and was cut on the cross so it hung right. It fitted as if it was made for me. I put it on a hanger so as soon as I woke up I could see it. It was pretty and feminine and the style clashed with my burlesque black lace and mesh bra and pants, but I didn't care. I liked them both.

Now I had my dress I wanted a bag that matched but that put me in a quandary. My Anya bag, strictly speaking, didn't match the 'tea dance dress' so after a lot of thought I decided not to take it. That was a big mistake.

Every time I thought about meeting Gareth I felt nervous. I was still suspicious and apprehensive about why he'd asked me to his B&B. I didn't want a repeat of Harry, who, a month after the Liverpool trip had written to say he was sorry I'd left so suddenly and he hoped there hadn't been a misunderstanding, but apologised if he'd upset me. I hadn't replied. I'd heard that crap before, the denials, the implication I'd got something wrong; it was like when Ifan had disappeared and I'd almost been called mad to my face.

A week before I was to meet Gareth I had a dress rehearsal in the flat. I wanted to look absolutely right. I put on my new underwear, my tea dance dress and the retro style shoes I'd bought off a stall in Camden Market. I loved them as much as my dress. They were pale green with a block heel and they did up with a bow. Dressed in my new outfit I pirouetted around the kitchen. Then I stopped and imagined Gareth making love to me. That was a real turn on.

The day of his book launch came and the weather was glorious; he'd arrived in London the night before and rang to tell me he loved his B&B and that his host and hostess were interesting, gracious and well travelled. The man had been a film editor and on location all over the world.

My mother sent her love from Wales but Gareth didn't mention Philomena, and although I'd assumed she wasn't coming, I asked where she was. There was a long silence. He said they weren't getting on too well so I guessed she was pissed off about his affair with Chloe. I kept my mouth shut.

He asked whether I was sure I wasn't going to come to the launch. I said, 'What will you do there?'

'Read from *Girl in the Flowered Dress*, answer questions, sign my book, things like that.'

When I heard that I was so embarrassed, I thought I'd pass out. My dress was flowered and people might think he was writing about me. It just hadn't occurred to me. Maybe no one would notice, wouldn't put two and two together, but I couldn't be sure and that meant I'd have to keep away from them.

So I said, 'I tell you what, I'll be down in the café, level two, and I'll wait there for you.'

He accepted that. So I got to the South Bank, went to the café and sat and waited for him. It was packed, noisy, but no one gave me a second glance. I didn't get there until ten but he didn't pitch up until almost eleven. I was reading my book, listening to music and on my second drink, when he tapped me on the shoulder. I hadn't seen him for a year and I was shy.

He looked good in his denim shirt, black cords. Cool, I thought. He took my hand, pulled me gently out of the chair, kissed me lightly on the cheek and holding me at arm's length studied me. 'Good God,' he said, 'you've grown up,' and then, 'Your outfit suits you. Quite the young lady.' I thought about my black lingerie underwear – when he saw that, he wouldn't say I was a lady. 'How did your reading go?' I asked.

'Well. Very well, they liked it, interesting people and good questions by and large. Book sales went well too.'

He sat down and for the next five minutes talked about the launch of his book. I wasn't listening. I was thinking about going with him to his B&B and wondering about why he might be interested in me. I knew why I was interested in him.

I interrupted him, 'Shall we go? It's late.'

'Of course, you're right.' He stood up and said, 'We'll get a cab.'

We went down in the lift, got to the ground floor, walked towards the exit, when three middle-aged women rushed towards him. They stood blocking his way.

'Gareth,' one of them gushed as if she knew him really well, 'we were hoping to catch you to sign copies of your book.'

They pushed copies of his poetry book forward. I could see the picture of a woman on a swing on the front cover. I didn't want to be reminded of Chloe. It upset me but I was about to feel worse. As Gareth signed their books, one of the women turned to look at me and smiling sweetly, she said, 'Is this your "girl", the girl in the "flowered dress"?'

Gareth turned and looked at me. His face was blank. I eyeballed the woman. I felt like smacking her one. Gareth was taken aback, I could see that. He blushed, glanced at me again, then at the floor and said, 'This is my niece.' He took hold of my arm, and muttered under his breath, 'Goodbye and thank you for coming, we have to go, it's late.'

He smiled at her, propelling me towards the door but once out of earshot he muttered through clenched teeth, 'Bitch.'

He looked grim. I kept my mouth shut. I didn't want to say anything, but he was right to be angry. The woman was a wind-up merchant. As for myself I was mortified. I didn't want his yearning for Chloe associated with me. I wasn't her and I wasn't a substitute. That's how I saw it. My mood had plummeted. We walked in silence to the back of the Royal Festival Hall. Once we reached the street, he said, 'Are you sure you want to come? It's late. I'll accompany you back to Stroud Green if you need to get back.'

There was a line of black cabs waiting. It was now or never. The moment I'd prepared for. I took a deep breath. 'No, I want to see where you're staying. You said I could. Let's get a cab.'

He shrugged his shoulders, looked resigned, then smiled. 'Okay, I shouldn't let these comments get to me. They're bad for the soul.' He pulled the cab door open, did a mock bow, said, 'Ladies first,' and leaned over to give the address to the cabbie.

Once we'd left the South Bank, he relaxed and became chatty. I could tell the evening had been successful by how happy he was. He looked good and very fanciable but I was getting more nervous the nearer we got to where he was staying. The cab pulled up, Gareth paid and we walked up the path to the house. He had a key to the front door. We walked into the hall. I was hoping everyone was out. I didn't want a repeat of the kind of comment we'd heard earlier. I was edgy and wanted to get to his room before we were seen. The house was quiet. Everybody must have been asleep in bed, or out. We walked up the stairs. The hall was lined with paintings and prints, but I didn't look at them.

He unlocked the door and led the way into his suite. It was a large room, the double bed placed near the window. One corner of the white duvet was pulled across. The room was decorated in shades of off-white, gold and yellow, including the Roman blinds which were made of linen printed with massive, deep yellow, shaggy chrysanthemums.

I avoided looking at the bed. I was feeling slightly intimidated. On the mahogany side table someone had placed bouquets of flowers in glass vases. Gareth walked across and looked at the cards attached to the cellophane wrapping. He read them in silence.

'Who sent you those?'

'Chloe, my wife, my publisher, and two anonymous.'

'That's nice.'

It wasn't really, not the one from Chloe, but I couldn't tell him the truth. Gareth sat down in one of the velvet chairs and looked at me. Not in a horrible way but in a kind of bemused way, as if he couldn't make out what was going on and didn't know what to say. I sat down opposite. I felt awkward.

'Well, that's it. I'm glad it's over.' He paused. 'It's good of you to come.'

'Anya. Not Echo.'

'I wasn't going to call you Echo.'

'No?'

'No. What have you been up to?'

By that time, I was really edgy. I jumped up and blurted out, 'Do you have anything to drink?'

He got up. 'What would you like? Coffee, tea, hot chocolate, Perrier water?'

'None of those. Haven't you got anything stronger?'

He folded his arms, looked disapprovingly at me. 'Yes, I have, but should you have anything stronger?'

'I'm...don't be patronising. I'm almost sixteen. I've had wine and I've been drunk.'

'Not such a good idea.'

I ignored that. 'Do you have a mini bar?'

He looked exasperated, walked across the room and opening a cupboard, which concealed a bar, said without looking at me, 'What would you like?'

'Is anyone else here?'

'Don't know. What would you like?'

'Wine. White.'

'A spritzer? With lemonade?'

'Okay.'

He started to mix one but didn't finish it because his mobile was ringing. He looked to see who was calling, then he said, 'Sorry, Anya, I won't be long. I need to take this.' He walked into the dressing room, shutting the door behind him.

I was on my own. I looked round the room, walked across to the flowers, picked up a card. It said, 'Darling, congratulations. So sorry I'm not there with you. Hope it went well, all my love. "The girl in the flowered dress".' It was from Chloe.

Another said, 'From your wife, Philomena. Remember me?'

I couldn't be bothered to read the others. So far, so predictable. I wondered how long Gareth would be.

I sat down, waiting for him to return. I felt nervous and at a loose end. I finished mixing the spritzer and drank it without tasting it. I peered out of the window into the night. I couldn't see a thing. I went back to the mini bar. I poured myself another wine, this time leaving out the lemonade. It was a large one. I downed it quickly. He was taking a long time. I walked to the bed and lay down on top of the duvet. I almost fell asleep until I imagined Gareth kissing me. That kept me awake. I didn't want it to end.

Gareth's raised voice interrupted me. He was saying, 'Don't be ridiculous. I told you she's not here.' I got off the bed, put my ear to the door and listened.

His voice was muffled, 'Look, I have Anya here. Echo, yes. She's changed her name. You knew that. She's got a right to do that. No, I'm not getting her to the phone. Yes, yes, yes. I know that already. I need to get her home soon.'

There was silence. I could hear Philomena ranting even through the door so he must have been holding the phone away from him.

The wine was getting to me. I walked unsteadily across to the mini bar. There was no wine left. I turned my attention to a row of small cans of cocktails. I didn't know any of them.

I picked one at random called 'French Kiss'. It was okay but not wonderful. I tried a 'Mojito'.

That was better. I liked it. I was about to have another when waves of sickness pulsed through me. I tried to focus. The pattern on the carpet came up and hit me in the face. I was going to vomit. I lurched into the bathroom.

The loo was covered with cling film. I ripped it off and knelt with my head over the bowl. I tried to be sick but I couldn't, even when I pushed my fingers down my throat. Eventually the nausea passed and I got back on my feet. There was a huge mirror over the bath. I looked at my reflection and began to wobble. I looked weird and felt dizzy. I thought I might collapse and fall on to the edge of the bath, so I steadied myself by holding on to the basin. I noticed a tumbler with plastic over it, so I tore it off, filled it with water and drank it but it didn't stop the effects of the alcohol. That was hitting me big time. I could hardly stand. I had to lie down before I fell over.

I staggered back into the bedroom, pulled off my dress and threw it on to a chair. I stood for a moment swaying in my new black lace bra and pants. I looked down at my new shoes, then I kicked them off one at a time so they swung through the air, landed across the room and on to the bed. I thought that was very funny. There was a full-length mirror by the side table and I stood admiring myself, practising seductive poses. That made me laugh as well, especially when I wobbled. With my back to the mirror, my hands on my hips and my legs apart, I looked over my shoulder and winked at myself. Maybe I could become a burlesque dancer if I was ever out of work.

After I got tired of posing, I needed to go to the loo and lurched across the room to the bathroom again. I didn't bother shutting the door. Gareth was still talking in the next room.

I made my way back to the bed, carefully negotiating all the obstacles. I fell over once and banged against a table piled with books. They flew off, including one of Gareth's poetry books. I picked it up and carefully placed it back on the table. I expected Gareth to open the door but he didn't. He was so into his row with Philomena, he didn't hear. I got into the bed, pulled the duvet over me and fell into a drunken sleep.

I was woken by Gareth. He was shouting, 'I find that extremely offensive.' It went quiet. I drifted off back to sleep, but not for long.

I was roused again. Gareth was shaking my shoulder and standing over me. I opened my eyes. Even through the alcoholic haze, I could see he didn't look pleased. 'What the hell are you playing at?'

'Gareth...sssh...be quiet...I'm asleep...don't... A Mojito. It's that. I've. Had. Drunk too much. It's. Your. Fault. It's your...'

I was falling asleep between each word and my speech was slurred. I tried sitting up but the room spun round on its axis. I lay back feeling sick as a pig, and drifted off. When I woke, he'd moved across the room and was sitting in a chair. He looked angry. I tried to apologise, but no proper words came out. I was speaking gibberish.

He banged his fist against his forehead and said, 'This is all I bloody need. A drunken teenager in my bed.' He was glowering with rage. He stood up. Started pacing the room. Back and forth. Back and forth. He was making me feel worse. He glanced at me, saw I was waking up. I struggled to sit up. 'I'm thirsty, Gareth.'

'I'm getting you some water.' He went to the bathroom, filled a glass and stood over me. 'Here. Take this. Drink it.' I drank it. He gave me another, then moved across the room and sat in an armchair, watching me as I drank.

I slowly put my finger to my lips. 'Sssh, Gareth, you must be quiet, you'll wake people up. Come here and don't be angry.' I patted the bed, pulled the duvet back. 'Look. I've got nothing on. Look. Wouldn't you like to see me without clothes?'

He was silent. His eyes transmitted hate, hostility, dislike. I, on the other hand, was on a mission. 'Did you hear me, Gareth? Gareth. Gareth.' My voice became slower, more seductive each time I pronounced his name. 'You don't believe me? Do you?'

I pulled the duvet right down, undid my bra, swung my legs out of the bed and stood up.

'Oh no, you don't. You're drunk.'

With just my pants on, I lurched towards him. He jumped up as if scalded and, turning his back on me, moved fast towards the bathroom, slammed the door shut and locked it. That was funny. So funny. Everything made me laugh now. He was frightened of me. I rattled the door knob. 'Let me in.' There was no response. I remembered what that bra fitter had said about burlesque dancers. They tease. I spoke sweetly outside the door.

'Gareth, I've got nothing on. I'm waiting for you to make love to me. You know, like you do with Chloe. I saw you. I want you to do to me what you do with her. Gareth.'

It was cruel, I know. He'd gone quiet. I went across and put on a dressing gown lying across a chair. Then I returned to sit outside the bathroom door like a cat waiting for a mouse. Eventually I fell asleep on the floor and when I woke up, he'd come out of the bathroom and was asleep in a chair. I felt mean.

I slowly walked across towards him but he heard me because he opened his eyes and looked at me as if I was a cockroach crawling out from underneath a door.

'I'm sorry, Gareth, I was drunk, but I don't feel so bad now.'

He was wary. 'You're still drunk.' As he said this my dressing gown fell open. He recoiled, 'Don't come any nearer and do up that dressing gown.'

I pulled it across. 'I wasn't going to do anything, anyway.'

'Behave yourself, because if you don't, I'll leave and go elsewhere.'

'You're horrible to me. Gareth. What time is it?'

He looked at his watch. 'Three twenty-five.'

'I want a cup of tea. Will you make me one?'

He sighed, but got up and silently made one. He put it on the floor by me. 'Don't spill it.' The atmosphere was tense.

'Don't you want one?' I said, as if everything was normal.

He didn't answer, went back to the chair and sat watching me. He shook his head as if he couldn't make out what was going on.

'Why didn't you make love to me?'

He didn't answer.

'I wanted you to. You could have been the first.'

'Give me a break, Echo.'

'Anya. I keep telling you. I'm Anya. Why? I want to know why.'

After a long time he said, 'Why do you think?'

'Because I'm ugly?'

'Is that what you really believe?'

'Dunno. Maybe you find me repulsive.'

'No. I don't find you repulsive.'

'Well, what is it?'

He sighed. 'Maybe it's because you're still below the age of consent. Maybe it's because you're very drunk. Maybe it's because I have a wife and I'm in love with another woman. Maybe it's because I'm already in a mess. Are those enough reasons to be going along with? Do you understand?'

I looked down at my tea. 'I've finished my drink. I want to go home.'

'Now? Is anyone there?'

'No. My mother's with your wife in Wales.'

'Yes, I know that. But are you on your own?'

'Yes.'

'You're staying here the rest of tonight. Until you can look after yourself.'

I looked at him and began to cry. He didn't say a word but neither did he come over to me. He sat looking at me.

'You're horrible. But I know what you're thinking, you're thinking my mother's right, I'm out of control. Like she said to you in the hospital. You're against me like the rest of them. I miss Ifan. He was my best friend and I didn't make him up. I wish he was here now. He never rejected me, not like you. He loved me – I feel like shit.'

He said nothing at first. Then he said, 'Anya, I haven't rejected you. Can't you see I'm looking after you? I don't want to hurt you... I'm old enough to be your father.'

'My father. Don't talk about him. I don't give a shit about him. Fathers.'

'You haven't found him then.'

'No. I know nothing. Where he is, who he is, what he is, except he's a bastard and he left me and my mum. He didn't care, like the rest of you. Always screwing around.'

He didn't respond to the last bit. 'Are you still looking for him?'

'I've given up. I'll never know and he'll never know about me either, so that's equal, isn't it? We're quits. In the long run, we're all dead.'

I threw myself on to the sofa, hid my face in a cushion and cried. This time he came over to me. He pulled the dressing gown round me, put me in his bed and sat in a chair by me until I fell asleep.

When I woke he'd fallen asleep on the sofa. It was still early. I went into the bathroom to get dressed and by the time I'd finished, he was awake. He made me a coffee but neither of us said much. He called for a cab and came back with me to Stroud Green. He waited outside to make sure everything was alright. He wouldn't come in. I was glad he didn't. I was humiliated and I needed to be on my own. He told me he wasn't going to tell anyone about that night. He gave me a signed copy of his new book of poems. I was polite, thanked him, but it was the final insult. I felt like throwing it across the room.

I hated him. Whatever he'd said, I didn't believe. My self-confidence had been shattered. I was ugly, I was sure of that and I vowed I'd never get involved with men again. I'd had enough of them; my father, Ifan, Harry and now Gareth.

I made a promise to myself. I wouldn't go to Ffridd again or have anything to do with men for the rest of my life. For five years I kept that promise. Then I started to see a therapist, a male therapist, and my troubles started all over.

Part Five

I didn't speak to Gareth about what happened that night. I didn't visit Ffridd. I didn't respond when he wrote. I didn't open his poetry book. The picture of Chloe on the front got to me. Every time I thought of them making love, it felt so unbearable I hid his book, so I didn't have to look at it. I didn't tell my mother about it either. She'd only say I'd got myself to blame.

Maddy guessed something had happened because I'd gone quiet. When she asked, I said I'd met Gareth after his book launch but nothing more. She questioned whether I'd slept with him and I said no. So she wanted to know what happened. I told her I didn't want to talk about it. She took one look at my face and never raised it again.

My mother came back from Wales. The Surrealist exhibition had gone well and there were plans to show a version of it in one of the art galleries in Hoxton. She told me it looked as if Philomena and Gareth were about to split up because he was involved with Chloe, the woman who worked in Chepstow. It was serious. Gareth wanted to marry her, but her husband was refusing to divorce her. I kept my mouth shut.

I was depressed. Men finding me attractive didn't help how I felt about myself. I didn't go out with any of them, no matter how fanciable they were. Men were big trouble and I kept them at arm's length. More than once, I was called a 'prick tease' but I didn't care. It amused me. It was my version of the burlesque dancer and was a good way to pay them back.

Maddy eventually split up with Theo and for a year or two we were inseparable, until she met someone else. He was Italian and called Beppe, short for Giuseppe and he was nice, like Theo. They looked as if they belonged together, both good looking, both a laugh. She seemed to have this knack of picking the right ones, or they picked her. Her boyfriends were always regular kind of guys and she told me she only split with Theo because they'd got together too young. She was sensible and I wished I was, but being sensible was an unknown quality for me.

Even so, we both did well at school and we had no trouble getting into the right Uni. Maddy chose UCL to study architecture which is what she'd always wanted and I went on to the London School of Fashion and Design to study 'Innovations in Recycling and Global Marketing'.

None of my eBay research had been wasted. I'd become more and more interested in recycling clothes so I knew what I was going to do when I left school. I planned to set up a business recycling clothes. I hadn't decided on its name but something along the lines of 'Re-vamp Designs' although that wasn't too exciting, but it could always be changed. I made a portfolio which I called 'Fashion as Art' with the help of one of the lecturers. Knowing about surrealism contributed to the development of my ideas, so I had my mother to thank for that. I found the colours and style of Frida Kahlo's dresses and her paintings inspirational. Ethnic styles, colours that shouted – shocking pink, scarlet and vermilion – appealed and although they didn't always do much for me, they would for others.

My degree was a mixture of art, politics, and economics and suited me very well because I was taught how to integrate all these aspects. I wanted eventually to start a Cooperative and work with designers with a social and political conscience using colours, fabrics and ideas from other cultures. I wasn't interested in the status and competitiveness of high fashion, but on a day-to-day level wanted to work with those who weren't affluent and brighten up their lives.

I loved my course even though being in London meant I still had to live with my mother. But the older I got, the less she bothered me. We lived in parallel worlds, although to be fair to her, she did take an interest in my work at the School. I worked hard and by the end of the second year I was on track for a first. That depended on how I did at the 'End of the Course' show.

I started planning for the show months before and the closer the day came, the more excited I became. It was important because all kinds of influential and creative people would come, and if I impressed them they'd help my future career.

My theme was to be Vintage Fashion, but updated. There'd been lots of discussion on our course about climate change, recycling, the conservation of materials and I wanted to use that knowledge in my designs. Once again I searched eBay for ideas, fabric and designs.

We only had ten minutes each to show our work and the idea was the models would come down a catwalk and strut their stuff in front of the audience. But that's not how I wanted to play it. I didn't like the politics of the catwalk, the elitism, the snobbery, the arrogance. What I wanted was a colourful, ironic burst of high energy and that's how it turned out. Every detail and the timing was planned minutely. My models weren't pale and anorexic, but toned, fit and healthy. They looked as if they loved life.

I'd asked my mother, my friends, my art teacher, and my English teacher to the show and that's when I pondered whether to invite Gareth. As time passed, I was more ready to forgive him. That's how I saw it anyway. My mother told me he regularly asked how I was and when I was going to come to Ffridd. He still lived with Philomena but I didn't know any more. Asking about him and Chloe wasn't the kind of thing I'd ask my mother. But I knew if I invited Gareth, he'd come.

In the end I didn't. It was all too complicated and I wanted to keep focused.

I was the last student of the evening to show my designs. I figured the audience would need livening up by then so the performance had to explode with high energy.

I called my show 'Johnny's got a Boom-Boom' after the song by Imelda May. The music was fast, rhythmic and a fusion between rockabilly and electro-swing. I'd recruited some dancers from a dance school to wear my clothes and demonstrate the versatility of the fabric and designs. The clothes were made for movement as much as visual impact.

The first couple leapt on to the stage, jived down the centre of the cat walk, and were followed by more couples who jitterbugged into the audience. In the final scenario the dancers jumped on the stage and did acrobatic versions of the lindy hop to a version of 'Peas and Rice'. Everyone loved it; the dancers, the audience, my tutors. They were all smiling and the audience stood up to give us a standing ovation. I cried, especially when I was given three bouquets. One from Maddy, one from my mum, and there was one really beautiful one but it didn't say who'd sent it. The flowers were in my favourite colours, pink, blue and purple. I was so excited I didn't think much about that. After the excitement, the congratulations, and the networking, we planned to go for a meal in Soho. My mum was going to meet a new fella she'd met on an internet dating site so she wasn't coming, but I'd asked Maddy. We were walking along Oxford Street in the general direction of Soho, when someone tapped me on the shoulder. I swung round. I expected to see one of my friends. I froze.

He was standing right behind me and really close. Instinctively I took a couple of steps back. 'Congratulations. You're good. Impressive,' he said. His voice had deepened. He was tall, well built, wearing a grey, short-sleeved t-shirt and black jeans but his hair was still blonde and straight. I stared at him. I didn't smile.

I looked at Maddy. 'You go on, I'll catch you up.'

She was puzzled but could see something was up. 'Are you sure? I can wait.'

'No, go ahead.' I took a long hard look at him. I could say nothing. My brain had stopped working and my mouth wouldn't open.

'Aren't you going to speak? Echo. You know who I am.'

I glanced back. They were way ahead. I began walking to catch them up. He called after me. I increased my pace. So did he. The faster I walked, the faster he did. He overtook me and we both came to a halt. He was standing right in front of me, blocking my path.

It was then I spoke. 'Go away.' I glared at him. 'Why are you here? I didn't invite you.' I couldn't get past him. 'I don't want you. I don't want to see you.'

It was his turn to be silent. It reminded me of when we first met at the estuary only this time it was me running from him.

'Why won't you speak to me?'

'You're supposed to be dead.'

'Well, I'm not dead. You can see I'm here.'

'Why? Why? You left me. Why should I? Why should I talk to you? I don't need you. I've got along without you. It's too late, Ifan.'

I side-stepped round him and slipped past. He didn't stop me at first but then he caught up and took hold of my arm, so I had to stop. He held on to me tightly. 'I'd like to tell you what happened. If you'll let me.'

'Let go of me. You're hurting me. Do you think I'm interested?' I twisted my arm away.

'We were good friends. Weren't we?'

I stared at him. 'Fuck off.'

'Okay. But before you wipe me out. Think about what we had. Ring me. Whenever you like. Please, Echo.' He gave me his number scribbled on a piece of paper.

I took it. Looked hard into his eyes, 'You don't seem to understand. What happened and how it affected me.' He didn't answer. I said again, 'I'm going.' He stood staring at me.

I began walking, then I looked back at him over my shoulder. 'By the way, my name isn't Echo anymore. I've changed it. My name's Anya.'

I heard him shout, 'I know,' but I didn't stop. I was really stirred up. When I reached the restaurant I stood outside trying to get my head together. I wanted to tear up the paper with his number, but I couldn't. I put it into my bag. I felt all over the place. I walked inside and went to sit by Maddy. The place was buzzing, hot and noisy. I was disorientated.

'You look as if you've seen a ghost.'

'I have.'

'Who was he?'

I didn't answer at first. She waited for me to speak. 'Do do you remember years ago, when I'd come back from Wales and quarrelled with my mum and I'd walked across the park to see you. That summer in Wales had been horrible. Ifan and me...we'd tried to cross the river. I almost drowned. He disappeared. I never knew where or what had happened to him and he was my first love. I was devastated.'

'You never told me that. You were weird. You were going on about Gareth having sex in the woods.'

'I was weird because Ifan had vanished. I began to think he hadn't been real or he was dead.'

'And that was him?'

'Yes. You saw him, didn't you?'

'Yes.'

'I'm feeling weird again, Maddy.'

'Not surprised.' Maddy was looking at me closely. 'Annie, let's talk later about it because tonight you should be enjoying yourself. Don't get caught up in the past. Not right now anyway.' She looked in her bag, brought out a wrapped present. 'I loved your show. It was different, like you. I'm proud of you, you've done really well.' She leant towards me, kissed me, smiled and handed over a small package. She said, 'It's from all of us. We're so happy for you.'

I opened it and when I saw what she'd bought, I cried

again. It was an art deco necklace, with a black geometric design on a silver pendant. It was beautiful. 'You know what I like. Maddy, thank you.' I hugged her.

'Annie, promise me you won't think about him tonight. We'll talk tomorrow. I want you to enjoy this evening. Come round to my place tomorrow and we'll go out.'

I nodded.

The evening was fun, I drank too much but so did everyone else. We were all relieved to finish the course and hopeful the networking would pay off. But the whole time, at the back of my mind, I was thinking about Ifan.

My mother was out when I got back. The next morning she asked me how the meal had gone but she wasn't really interested, so I cut it short. She liked her new guy and she seemed happier than I'd ever known her. She could be funny and make me laugh but I marvelled at how little she knew about me. I felt like telling her about Ifan, but in the end I couldn't be bothered. I didn't have time or the energy because there was sure to be some kind of fall out. The world according to my mother, that's how it was with her, and there was never much space for anyone else's point of view or experiences.

Maddy rang later and we arranged to meet outside the tube in Camden. She insisted I chose where we ate. She said we still had to celebrate so I chose a Lebanese place because I loved the food, especially the mezze. As soon as we sat down, Maddy asked me about Ifan. I silently got out his note with his number on it and passed it to her.

She looked at it and said, 'Annie, what do you want me to do with this? I'm not a graphologist. Speak. Words.'

I laughed then. I said, 'Actually, that's a good idea, Maddy. I could take it to a graphologist.'

'Or you could just talk. Thought about doing that?'

'Living with my mother makes me verbally constipated. She's always on transmission and I'm always on reception.'

'Well, to continue with your metaphor, cut the crap. I'm on reception.'

So I told her. Everything. All of it, including how Ifan asked me to remove all my clothes, how I touched him, how he'd kissed me, how I'd nearly drowned, how he'd disappeared and then being told I'd imagined him, and that I'd thought he was dead.

Maddy asked, 'And where does Gareth fit into this?'

'It was after that I kind of got obsessed with Gareth. I was in the forest in the early hours looking for Ifan, but instead I saw Gareth with Chloe.'

'You were looking for Ifan in the early morning, in the estuary on your own, miles from anywhere?'

'I was distraught, Maddy, not thinking right.'

'I don't get it.'

'Well, whatever, that's how it was.'

'So what will you do?'

'Don't know. He did say he wanted to explain but I didn't want to listen. I don't want to know. He can get lost as far as I care.'

'But you still don't know what happened. He's got in touch. It's a waste of energy hating him.'

'I don't hate him.'

'Well, ring him.'

'Would you?'

'Too right, I would. You loved him.'

'Loved him? I was only fourteen. That's not possible.'

'You think so? I loved Theo.'

'And now?'

'Still do, but in a different way. Annie, I want you to contact him. For me.'

'Why should you care?'

'Because I do. I have a strong feeling he's okay and he had a good reason why he went off. Also because you need to find out for yourself. If you don't, you'll never settle. Will you? Besides, I want to know.'

I looked at her. 'I wish I was like you, Maddy. I've become cynical.'

'Maybe you have good reasons to be. So?'

'What?'

'Will you?'

'Okay. But I don't really want to.'

'Soon. Do it soon. The longer you leave it the more hostile you'll get and then you'll never contact him.'

'I will.' I smiled at her and said, 'And I'll let you know, you'll be the first.'

It was a couple of weeks before I finally rang. I'd chosen the time and place carefully but I was ambivalent so when he answered, I was cold.

'It's Anya. You wanted to speak to me?'

There was a long silence 'Yes, I'd like to explain.'

'For what?'

Another silence. Then, 'What do you think?'

'I haven't the faintest. It seemed not to bother you for years you hadn't been in touch.'

'That's because I didn't know where you were.' I didn't reply. He said, 'I do want to see you, Anya.'

'How did you know where I was?'

'I'll tell you when I see you.'

'No, now. Tell me now, before I see you. That is, if I do see you. You might be an impostor, for all I know.'

'You've seen me. You know very well I'm not.'

'So tell me.'

'It was a total fluke. I was at your Uni helping backstage with the lighting when I saw you walking along a corridor. I couldn't believe it. You've no idea how I felt... I want to see you...even if it's only once, for old time's sake.'

As soon as Ifan said, 'once', tears welled in my eyes. I said 'Alright. Just the once then.'

We arranged to meet a week later in the Wetherspoon's pub along the Holloway Road. It wasn't cool or trendy, but interesting. It had been a cinema and he'd said if we got there early we could talk in private. He was standing at the bar when I arrived and walked towards me to greet me. I thought he was going to kiss me but he shook my hand instead. He smiled, but I didn't. If someone close to you vanishes for years and you've grown up in that time, it's difficult to know how to be.

'What would you like to drink?'

'What are you having?'

'I'll see what's on offer.'

I restrained myself from making a quippy response. I could have, but I didn't want to wind him up. 'A large Chardonnay,' I said. I glanced round.

'Do you want to find a seat?'

I nodded, walked to the back and found a place furthest away from the bar and where we'd be on our own. While I waited, my mind ranged over the summers we'd shared. He'd been so important to me. I watched him banter with the barmaid as he bought drinks at the bar. He'd grown up. He was self-confident with an easy smile and I imagined women would fancy him. Perhaps he was a flirt. It was when he walked towards me I saw the old Ifan. His light eyes, the intensity of gaze – he was an outsider with the good looks of a Russian.

I'd chosen to sit at a table instead of a sofa. I didn't want him sitting next to me. He put my drink down and sat down opposite, looking closely at me. To avoid his gaze, I stared at the framed photos of old movie stars on the wall and the huge vintage movie camera placed in the middle of the pub.

'I should have dressed for the occasion, instead of my jeans.' He didn't reply or ask what I meant. Perhaps he knew. 'It's doing my head in,' I said.

'What is?'

'Seeing you, sitting there opposite. Are you really Ifan?' I picked up the wine, took a long sip and placed the glass carefully between us. I measured its positioning. It was exactly equidistant. I looked at him, 'How long have you been in London?'

'Three years or so. For my degree, electrical engineering.'

I restrained myself again, stopping myself from telling him a joke about engineers. It would have been funny, but a put down. Instead I asked, 'So how come you were at my finals?'

'I work for an agency. I do lighting and when I saw you, I couldn't believe it. I often used to think about you.' He smiled and went to take my hand but I pulled it away from him. He looked across towards the bar but said nothing.

I said, 'Why didn't you speak to me when you first saw me?'

'Because…I wanted to be sure it was you and to check you out.'

'Like the first time we met.'

'Yes, I'm still the same.'

'Was it you who sent me those flowers, there was no note on them?'

'I did send you some. Did you like them?'

'Thanks, I did. I expected to see a humming bird fly from them, they were so exotic.' I was feeling more and more awkward. 'Where do you live?'

'Clissold Park, borders of Stoke Newington.'

'Trendy… Well, have I changed much?'

He looked hard at me before answering. 'You're being flirty but of course you have. You're a woman now. When I last saw you, you were a girl.'

'I'm not flirting. It was a straight question. Is that all you can say?'

He smiled slightly before saying, 'For the moment. I miss Wales.'

'Like what in particular?'

'The sea. I miss the sea.'

His gaze made me feel uncomfortable. I wondered what he was thinking. 'There's no sea at Ffridd,' I said.

'No.'

'So where are you talking about?'

'We moved. After we nearly drowned.'

'We? You moved? You said you'd tell me.'

'I will. I'm trying to get my thoughts together. You're not the only one, Echo, who's stirred up.'

'Anya'.

'Sorry. Anya. Why did you change your name?'

'Because I was fed up being my mother's echo.'

'Echo and echo. Makes sense. You told me about her.'

'You remember?'

'Of course. Everything. How could I forget?' He was smiling, looking into my eyes. I felt myself blush as he said, 'Do you?'

'Of course, everything.' I hadn't eaten and the drink was getting to me. I looked down and studied my bag, twisting the handle round my fingers. 'So,' I said, 'what happened? Why the disappearing trick?'

There was a long pause. He seemed to be thinking.

'When that first wave caught us, I lost my handhold, and got washed off. I called out to you but the noise was too great. Your eyes were closed. You couldn't have heard me. I was swept away. I thought I would drown...the water carried me towards a bank... I was caught in a massive tree branch. Little by little I managed to pull myself out. I staggered to a nearby house, an ambulance was called... I was taken to a hospital in Cardiff.'

'Cardiff? Why not Chepstow? I went to Chepstow. That's why I couldn't find you.'

'You looked for me?' He sounded surprised.

'Don't be stupid, Ifan, of course I did. Sorry. I didn't mean to be rude but why wouldn't I? I'd almost drowned, and you'd gone, I wanted to find out where you were. But I didn't have your surname or your address. I knew nothing about you.'

'Is that all? To check I was alive.' He looked across the room and then back at me almost accusingly. 'You knew plenty.'

'Yes, but I didn't know how to find you.'

'I didn't know where you were either. You lived in London

but I didn't know where. I only had your first name and even that you've changed.'

'Why were you taken to Cardiff and not where I was, in Chepstow?'

'The emergency services. They were working flat out that day. Surfers riding the bore. We weren't the only ones in trouble. They took me to Cardiff but I was discharged straightaway. They said there were no ill effects...well, they were wrong because soon after I began having serious asthma attacks.'

He stopped, looked down at his beer mat, turning it round and round, then stood up. 'I'm having another pint. Would you like another drink?'

'Please.' I could see he was upset. When he returned he placed the glass by the old one and continued, 'So the asthma was investigated, they found no cause, but as you know, I've no medical history, you know, on my family, there's no history on file.' He stopped and looked hard at me, checking to see if I remembered. I did, but I wasn't going to interrupt.

'My adopters found out about us, the river, the pontoon, everything. I hadn't told them. They said I was too easily led. They were angry and blamed you. They were prejudiced. It was as if you were evil. I hated them and I wanted to go into care. I was sent to a child psychiatrist. She said it was psychosomatic and prescribed drugs. I refused to take them. They said it would be best to move so they put the house on the market and within the year we'd moved to the Gower. They said I had to forget, and that it was best that way. They forbade any contact with you. I thought I'd never see you again... What was going on for you?'

I was silent for a while. 'I tried and tried to find you. Then we went back to London. I didn't want to go back to the estuary ever again. Without you, it wasn't the same. They tried to make me believe I'd imagined everything. But I didn't believe them. Eventually I thought you must be dead. I gave up and I stopped thinking about you. Or that's what I thought.'

I paused, then said, 'Parents don't take children seriously, or respect our friendships. They lie, they cheat. How horrible taking you to the Gower to get away from me. As if I was evil. Didn't they know I didn't live in Ffridd?'

'Yes, they knew that and that we got together in the summer. Maybe they were jealous, frightened they'd lose me.' He paused, looked at me carefully before continuing, 'But to be fair, I was difficult.'

'Difficult?'

'Doing crazy things, stealing, petty vandalism, on the verge of delinquency, they said, and the asthma, all the time it was getting worse. They assumed it was your fault that we'd gone on the Severn, whereas in fact, it was my idea. I did tell them, but they didn't want to hear.'

'Head games, they make me crazy.'

Ifan smiled. 'Hah, but there's one thing. When it was really bad, I used to think about you.'

We looked at each other and smiled.

'Yes, but I still wonder whether I really was your first, the first girl you felt like that about.'

'What's it matter, Anya. It was more important than that. The psychiatrist guessed. She asked me some stuff I found embarrassing, but I never told.'

'Have you been with anyone since?'

Ifan looked away and said, 'What do you think, Echo? It's a long time ago and I'm normal.'

I felt irritated. 'Why do you keep calling me Echo? I'm Anya now.'

'You're still the girl in the estuary. Echo, Anya. Why do you care so much what you're called?'

That took me aback. For a moment I didn't know what to say, so I returned to my question, 'So you have slept with others.' It was a statement as much as a question.

It was his turn to get irritated, 'What's it to you? Of course I have. I'm a guy. Haven't you had sex?'

I looked away to avoid his eyes. 'Actually. No.'

'No? Well, I'm surprised... What's stopped you?'

He was staring at me as if I came off planet Zogg. I could have told him the truth but I didn't. He'd think Gareth was too old for me and anyway, I still felt raw about being rejected. I said, 'I could have, but for one reason or another, I haven't. I could have slept with some of the guys round my own age but I didn't fancy them.'

Ifan seemed astonished by this. He looked at me as if I was some kind of freak. Neither of us spoke and we continued drinking in silence. He suddenly asked, 'What are your future plans for work?'

'I've got several leads from NGOs. I'll follow those up.'

'Your show was stunning. I loved your dresses and the dancers. You're imaginative. I like how you dress, come to think of it.'

'Oh, this. Revamped. I got the dress from Camden Market, the cardigan from a friend, the shoes from a market stall.'

'So you practise what you preach. You look different. Feminine. Very feminine.'

I ignored that. 'What about you?'

'I'm signed up with an agency. I took an option in architectural lighting on my course, that's where I'm heading, that's what I want to do.'

'My best mate, Maddy, is doing architecture. Architectural lighting? Is that lighting up old buildings?'

'Old and new, exteriors and interiors.' He was looking at me as if he was thinking. He said, 'I don't live too far away. After you've finished, you could come round to my flat, have something to eat, a coffee and I'll walk you back. Where do you live?'

'Not far. Off Seven Sisters Road in Stroud Green with my mother, but I want to move, once I get a job.'

'No distance then.'

I nodded. 'Okay, that's cool.'

It was hard to believe that we'd found each other after all this time. Neither of us said much but after we finished our drinks, we walked round to his flat. It was large, on the first floor of a Victorian house and we had to squeeze past the bikes in the hall to get up the stairs, 'Is one of these bikes yours?'

'Yes, why?'

'Nothing. Just idle curiosity. Why aren't the others being used?'

'One guy is at his girlfriend's, the other's away for the weekend.'

It was a typical guys' flat, untidy, cramped, with yet another bike inside their sitting room. On the wall was a series of stunning colour photos showing trees lit up at night. A child's picture of fairyland. I was fascinated by them.

The bookshelves set in an alcove each side of the fireplace sagged under the weight of a random assortment of text books: electrical engineering, computing, zoology, but one shelf containing CDs was incredibly neat and arranged in alphabetic order. Someone with OCD, I thought.

Ifan went to make coffee, returned five minutes later and asked if I minded a takeaway, because there was no food in the fridge. I said, no problem. I was feeling awkward, like a spare part. I leant against the table trying to act nonchalant. 'I like the tree photography. Did you take them?'

He handed me the coffee and sat down on the floor. 'Thanks. I did. Second year lighting project. Anya, you're making me feel edgy... I wish you hadn't changed your name. I always liked Echo. Why don't you sit down?'

'Well, I didn't like my name, that's why.' I sat on the sofa. It was the only chair free of clothes. 'Look, I'm sitting down now, can you see?' I grinned. It was time to lighten up.

He picked up on that. 'Yes, I can see you. I'm looking at you and you're sitting down.'

He was smiling at me, talking the talk, and I was reminded of how we used to be, that we'd sometimes play with words as well as with dens, water, driftwood and pontoons. 'Do you mind if I sit by you?'

'No. As long as you keep your distance.'

'What if I don't want to keep my distance? What if I want to sit by you and you don't really want me to keep my distance, but you don't know that.'

'Men always say stuff like that or think it. Even if they don't say it.'

'I'm going to sit by you anyway. Then you can test your theory.'

'What theory?'

'That you want me at the other end of the sofa. Then you can see how you feel once I'm there. Anya. I'm going to have to practise saying your new name.'

'Ifan.'

'What do you want, Anya?'

'I don't know what I want.'

'I think you do. I certainly do. I want to continue where we left off ten years ago.'

That surprised me. I looked at him, searching his face for clues. 'Are you serious?'

'I'm very serious. But you don't trust me, that's what I think.'

I was feeling uncomfortable. I hadn't expected things to move so quickly but he was right, I didn't know what I wanted of him, and I didn't trust him.

I stood up and walked over to the CDs. 'Would you mind if I take a look at the music?' I needed some sort of distraction.

'No. Help yourself.'

I began sifting through the pile of vinyl and CDs. 'Somebody's a big blues fan. BB King "Rock Me Baby". Haven't heard that for a while. Will you play it?'

He didn't answer but walked over to the sofa and put on the CD. I remained by the hi-fi, leaning against the table by the window with my arms folded, watching him. The music was loud, rhythmic, the words raunchy. When the track finished, he stood up and moved over to where I was standing and said, 'Excuse me, Mademoiselle,' and pulled down the blind behind me. He put the same CD on and taking hold of me said, 'Let's dance.'

I wasn't going to refuse. He pulled me towards him but within a minute I felt so awkward, I stopped. 'It's not proper dance music. I've changed my mind. I don't want to dance.'

'Fine, is it the words that put you off?'

'What? Of "Rock Me Baby"? No. What about them?'

'Well, think about it, pretty babe, rock me all night long.'

I knew at that point where his mind was. 'Right. Yeah well. I didn't. Anyway, so what? It's written by a man. That's why it's crude.'

He sat down again. 'Well, you chose. Crude or not. Don't girls ever feel like that? Maybe you don't.'

'You're being sarcastic. But if you're interested, sometimes.'

'Seeing is believing. Here's a challenge. Do you know a song where a woman says what she wants?' He jumped up and walked across to the CD shelf, 'Actually, here's the same song, the same words, the same music, only it's Etta James' singing. I'll play it…if I can find it. Okay?'

I didn't answer beyond saying, 'Etta James, she sounds like a man.' He ignored that and continued looking along the lines of CDs on the shelves. 'Thanks to my flatmate, here it is, neatly filed under 'J', I'll put it on.'

I laughed, flew across and snatched it out of his hand, 'Oh no you won't, because it's the same as the other one, only sung by a woman. You're taking the piss, Ifan. Leave me to look for one I like.'

It was easy. I'd never seen anyone file their music alphabetically before but I could put my hand straight on what I wanted. It was filed under 'F' for Flack.

'This is "The First Time Ever I Saw Your Face" and – what a surprise, on the cover it says "To Chris with all my love from your Bubbles". A woman chose this. Is Chris your flatmate with OCD and Bubbles his girlfriend?'

'It's his boyfriend actually.'

For a split second, I was taken aback but I recovered fast. 'Well, same difference, the message is the same regardless of sexual orientation. It's women versus men, love versus sex, romance versus one-night stands.' I wanted to wind him up. Ifan laughed uproariously.

He said, 'Well go on, play it. I'm waiting, and don't give me that dirty look, Echo.'

'Anya.'

'Now I know how to annoy you. Echo.' He was grinning.

I glared, put the track on. I was going to pay him back. I knew what I was doing. One night, my mum was out and I was with my mates. We were having a laugh and spent the whole evening checking out Google and YouTube for the best songs by women. It was a competition. The unanimous winner was the Pointer Sisters with 'I Want a Man with a Slow Hand'.

I put the Pointer Sisters on, not thinking how provocative it was or recognising that both of us were circling one another to see how far we could go.

Ifan jumped up. 'You're preaching to the converted. I want Roberta Flack on.' He took off the Pointer Sisters and replaced it with Roberta Flack's 'The First Time Ever I Saw Your Face'. He'd caught me off guard. I just didn't see what was coming, probably because I was well out of practice. The mournful tones of Roberto Flack filled the room.

He pulled me towards him, drew me close and whispered in my ear, 'You can dance to this.'

Touché, I thought. I liked that he could outwit me. So I went with it and allowed myself to be physically close to him. Gradually I was becoming less wary, and beginning to forget my attitude problems. The song seemed to go on forever and the longer it lasted, the more I liked dancing with him. I wrapped my arms round his waist and leant against him. Being close to a man, especially Ifan, was new to me. But when that came to an end, and he put on Etta James singing 'At Last', I was done for. It was a major turn on.

I felt the warmth of his body and I wanted him desperately.

His body was against mine and we were dancing so close and so slow it was as if he'd already started making love to me. It could only go one way. I remembered the estuary and the two of us before we'd gone on the river and I was about to say something, but Ifan said, 'Don't,' put his fingers against my lips, bent down and kissed me. The music stopped but we didn't. It was a kiss so powerful that nothing I'd read, or heard, prepared me for the feelings sweeping through me.

He took me by the hand, led me to a bedroom and shut the door behind us. We stood facing each other. 'Echo?' I nodded. He came across and slowly undressed me. At that moment I'd have done anything he wanted. He pulled the duvet back. I lay back on his bed and I watched as he got undressed. I was falling in love with him. He sat on the edge of the bed, caressing me until I pulled him to me. He leant over, looked into my eyes, and brushing my hair back away from my face, whispered how long he'd waited for me. I closed my eyes. I wanted him.

I couldn't breathe. I was about to suffocate. Terrible feelings of dread, panic, fear took me over. Unbearable. Like the terror I'd felt all those years ago when the force of the river submerged us. I pushed him away. I didn't want him near. I didn't want to be touched. I didn't want him looking at me. I didn't want to see him. I didn't want to be there.

I hated him.

He was repellent.

I had to go. I almost fell out of the bed. I flung my clothes on. Breathless with fear I reached the door.

'What the hell's going on? I can't stop now. Are you crazy?' I turned round. He was still in bed, staring at me in amazement.

'I'm going home.'

He leapt out, hurtled towards to the door, stood naked, his arms raised, barring my exit. 'You're not.'

Furious. I looked round the room for something to hit him with, but there was nothing. He was breathing fast. I couldn't get past without pushing against him and I wasn't going to do that. He was eyeballing me.

He breathed in deeply. Then he dropped his arms and when he spoke he sounded calm. He said, 'Of course you can go, but before you do, let's talk. I have no idea what's going on with you.' He stood aside, opened the bedroom door. 'I'll get dressed now, make you coffee, then I'll take you back to your place.'

I walked into the lounge and sat down. The panic had passed but I felt bad. I didn't know why I'd behaved like that. The guys who'd called me a prick tease, maybe they were right but I hadn't intended to be like that, not with Ifan. He came into the lounge and silently went into the kitchen and made coffee. He brought it in and then sat right away from me on the floor and leant against the table. He was staring at the ceiling. When I spoke, the way he looked at me was as if he couldn't bear the sight of me.

'I'm sorry, Ifan. I didn't want to lead you on.' He didn't say a word. 'I did want to, you know, make love. I was going to. I wasn't play acting. But I can't, I mean I couldn't, go ahead. I got frightened. I don't know why. I've always felt I love you.'

He said, 'Oh really.' It was sarcastic the way he said it.

'I was angry with you, when you went. I'd hoped we'd meet again, I had memories, us together, before, the pontoon, they kept returning, the river, then you'd gone, I didn't know where or why, maybe you were dead, sometimes I'd think, what if you hadn't, what might have been, the next year I'd have been fifteen and so would you, and...'

He interrupted, 'Cut the crap, we're not fourteen and we're not fifteen, we're older and it's nobody's business if we have sex. It's allowed, nobody gives a damn if we screw each other, all day and all night long. You speak as if you're a child.'

His anger silenced me. He stood up. 'You know there's something wrong with you, did you know that? You tell me in the pub you've never slept with anyone. At your age, and with

173

your looks. I got a hint then something wasn't right despite all your bullshit about not fancying anyone. Are you frigid or something? No, I don't think so. You know damn well babies aren't found under gooseberry bushes. You know all about it, but act as if you don't. You know how to turn a guy on but then, bang. Finito. Do you think you're the fucking Virgin Mary? Who are you saving yourself for? How do you think I feel? Does it make you feel powerful? Is that your game?' He turned his face away.

I felt my eyes fill with tears. I said, 'I'm going, you've said enough. I get the message.'

'And what message is that?' He stood up, folded his arms, his eyes hard, ice cold.

'You'd rather we hadn't met. I said I'm sorry. What more can I say? I know your masculine self-esteem has taken a knock.'

'Oh, you know that. Thanks for telling me. What about applying your powers of analysis to yourself? Maybe you could find an answer to why you're so uptight.'

'I'm going.'

'Yes, so you've said. When?'

'And I don't want you walking home with me. I'll get a cab.'

'Actually I had no plans to do that. I got the message too. I can change my mind.'

I stood up and, leaving my half-drunk coffee on the floor, let myself out of the flat. Ifan didn't stop me. As I left he flicked on the television and sat staring at the screen. I was halfway down the stairs when I heard him shout, 'You need to see a therapist. There's plenty round here. Get your head sorted. Right? Shouldn't take longer than a decade or so.' He slammed the door.

I walked away down the street. I was shaking. It's almost impossible to say just how devastated I was. I truly had wanted to make love with Ifan, and I didn't know why I behaved the way I did. As soon as I saw a cab, I waved it down and within ten minutes I was back home. My mother was out because there were no lights on. I didn't know where she was and right then I couldn't have cared less.

I opened my bedroom door, shut it behind me, flung myself on my bed and sobbed until I fell asleep. When I woke it was morning and past nine. Another wave of sadness washed over me and I cried again. The whole day that happened: tidal waves of tears, tears, and more tears, until by the end of the day I didn't know what I was doing, and I was so exhausted I could hardly stand. I felt desolate. I'd hoped for so long to meet Ifan and knowing he hated me now felt like a knife in my guts.

I looked at myself in the mirror. My face was red, my eyes puffy and swollen and that made me feel worse. I was pathetic and ugly.

My mother came in mid-evening, took one look at my face and said, 'What's the matter with you?'

I said, 'I fucked something up with a guy, someone I thought I loved.'

She said, 'Love, don't be stupid. You'll get over it. If you miss one bus there's always another round the corner.'

That was the sum total of her concern. I didn't want to tell her any more. I could rely on her to put me in touch with cold reality. But the fact it had been Ifan, made it worse. I removed myself from her presence and went back to bed.

I wanted to play that Etta James number 'At Last' again. I downloaded it, but I couldn't play it, because as soon as I got to the line 'my lonely days are over' I burst into tears and had to switch it off.

Days passed and I still felt so bad I feared I was going to be ill. I wanted to tell Maddy but I was ashamed. She was wise, knew about men, I wasn't and I didn't. I went over and over what Ifan had said, but it continued to devastate me. That he could be so cutting was new and I didn't know he had that side to him. I didn't understand what had made me turn against him, but some of what he'd said was true. I did have sexual feelings, but when it came to actually making out,

I backed off. It seemed the more I fancied a guy, the greater the distance I'd put between him and myself.

He was right. I was screwed up. I was trapped in a cycle of repetitive thoughts that went round and round and I was going nowhere, except back to the start. I was driving myself mad.

Only my work kept me together. I could put all this aside while I worked. I was good at my job, I was appreciated and that made me feel less crappy. I'd been offered a job with an importer of fabrics. It was just what I wanted. It entailed working with the fashion industry, raising awareness of environmental issues and recycling.

Six months later, I had a review and my salary was raised which meant I could afford to move out from my mother's and into a flat with two friends. But I still wasn't feeling good and avoided going anywhere where I might see Ifan. That seemed like everywhere. I was becoming agoraphobic; I covered myself up, lost weight and like a nun, hid away from the world. I was frightened of myself, my desires and it was easier to keep away from men.

Ifan didn't get in touch. I didn't think he would, but I'd hoped he might. It was over for him but not for me because I couldn't get him out of my head. I thought of contacting him but couldn't. It wasn't pride that stopped me, but fear of his hatred and contempt. If he'd dipped me in a vat of boiling oil, the pain couldn't have been worse. His words were indelibly written in my head. I had to do something, get help from someone. It was then I decided to tell Maddy. She knew I was in a state and she'd begged me to tell her but I couldn't until I felt strong enough to cope with talking about it.

One Saturday afternoon I went to see her. Everyone was out. As soon as she opened the door, I burst into tears. She was as kind as ever, put her arms round me, told me to sit down and made me a cup of tea. She sat opposite and said, 'Okay, tell me all about it. Is it finding your long-lost love?'

I nodded and said, 'Finding him and losing him.'

I poured it all out. How I'd agreed to meet him in the

pub along the Holloway Road, how he'd told me what happened and why he'd disappeared all those years ago, going back to his flat, putting the music on, dancing, fancying each other, getting into bed to make love, but not being able to go through with it and how finally I'd jumped out of bed, flung my clothes on, and left.

'And how did he respond to that?'

'He was furious, so furious. He shouted at me as I left the flat that I should see a therapist. No matter how many times I said I was sorry, it didn't help. I haven't seen him since. It's unbearable. All those years thinking about him, hoping we'd meet up, then what do I do? I fuck it up.'

Maddy gazed at me and sat thinking for a while. She said, 'Do you know why you couldn't go through with it? Was it because you realised after all that time, that maybe you didn't fancy him?'

'Oh, no. I fancied him alright. He'd turned me on, well and truly.'

'So maybe you wanted to punish him? Was that it?'

'I don't know, Maddy. I felt frightened.'

'Of what?'

'Don't know. Having sex…it feels like being taken over, and kind of final. And as if, oh, I don't know, what's it matter now?'

'Well, it does matter, doesn't it? I guess from his point of view he'd be thinking you're taking the piss, you know, like asserting your power and just at the crucial moment rejecting him.'

'Well, it wasn't like that.'

'I know that, Annie. I'm just trying to work out what was going on for both of you. I can understand why he was so pissed off, even though it was pretty brutal how he was. Actually, almost bordering on the abusive. But what I don't understand was what was going on for you. But, if you don't mind my saying, we've been here before.'

'No, go ahead, that's why I'm here.'

'You never have had sex have you?'

'No. So what?' I was feeling defensive.

'It's a bit strange, isn't it? You come across as if you're up for it, you know guys find you attractive, you give them the come-on, don't you? And then? What happens then?'

'The come-on? I don't know what you mean. I don't know. If I knew, I wouldn't be talking to you. I'm a failure.'

'You're not. You just need to sort out some stuff. So leave it out.'

'Oh, what's it matter? About them. Or the others. It's Ifan. He's the one I wanted.'

I stood up, walked over to the mirror on the wall and stood looking at myself. I was about to turn away when Maddy came up behind me and put her arm round my shoulder. She smiled at me in the mirror, and said, 'What do you see?'

'I dunno. I don't like myself.'

'Why?'

'I'm ugly.'

'You're not. You know you're not. You're beautiful, Annie.'

I turned round to look at her, 'Inside, I'm ugly, and that's what you can't see.'

I sat down again. 'Maybe I should give up, put it down as just one of those things.'

'I'm not going to let you give up on yourself.'

Something about how she said that got my attention. 'What are you thinking?'

She didn't answer straight away, then she said, 'Look, Annie, I don't want you to take what I'm going to say the wrong way, but remember Saf?' She paused before continuing.

'Saf? The one in our IT class? The one who wanted to be a chef?'

'Yes, she fell in love with someone her parents didn't approve of and it was doing her head in, so she went to see a counsellor. She told me the counsellor really helped her.'

'I'm not going to a counsellor. I'm not mad. I'm insulted you've suggested that.'

'But it might help, talking to someone.'

'And it might not. Besides don't remind me. That's what Ifan said.'

'Which was?'

'He said I needed my head sorted. Great. Now even you think that. Would you go?'

'I would actually. You've got nothing to lose.'

'They charge a lot of money.'

'Not where Saf went, it was a charity for young people.'

'It's self-indulgent.'

'For chrissake, Annie, do you want help or not? Do you want Ifan or not?'

'I was hoping you'd help.'

'I am helping. That's my suggestion. You need to know why you're scared of sex.'

'And how will that help?'

'Look, it's not straightforward. Why you couldn't follow through. Until you know what makes you tick, it might happen again with someone else. In fact, I'm sure it will.'

'Do you think there's still a chance with him. Ifan?'

'No chance unless you get off your arse and do something. So listen up. You asked for my help and I'm giving it.'

Seeing a counsellor was against my better judgement but I agreed eventually to give it a go. I checked it out with Saf first and she told me how to go about it. She even gave me her counsellor's name. But when I rang there was a long waiting list and I was told they'd only see me if it was an emergency. I told them it wasn't an emergency, that I wanted to sort things out but I didn't want to wait six months or however long it was going to take. The woman at the end of the phone sounded nice and she asked if I'd like a list of their recommended counsellors.

A list was sent to me but when I saw it, I got an attack of nerves and decided not to go after all. I felt stupid. I didn't want to tell anyone about my problems, after all there were plenty of people worse off. When Maddy asked me how it was going and I said I'd changed my mind, she went bonkers and went on and on. She said she'd keep on at me until I went.

So I rang again but there was still a waiting list. I felt upset. I didn't believe her, it felt like I was being excluded so I said, 'I'm really pissed off now, how long will I have to wait? Until I'm on my death bed?'

The receptionist remembered me. She said, 'That's Anya, isn't it? I tell you what, I'll book you for an assessment and we'll see what we can do.'

I said, 'Don't book me in with a man.'

She said, 'It's only for a one-off, he wouldn't be your actual counsellor.'

'Maybe not,' I said, 'but I don't want a man, that's my problem. Men.'

There was a silence and she said she'd see what she could do.

Two weeks later I was at the Finsbury Park Counselling Centre, sitting in front of a woman for my assessment. I was about to enter shark-infested waters, although I wasn't to know that. Some counsellors and therapists are on a different planet. They see the world in a different way and you have to learn how to speak their language. They're serious, they don't joke about, and you need to know that before seeing one.

The woman I saw for an assessment sat opposite me. I could see her eyes raking over me. Like my mother, I thought, although she liked a laugh and this woman didn't. She looked cold and hard. I thought she was rude and she got under my skin right from the get-go. I didn't know what to make of her. She was eyeballing me so I did the same to her. I didn't know what to say or how to start. It seemed I was supposed to mind read because eventually I realised she wasn't going to speak to me and I'd have to speak first. I asked her what was to me an innocent question. 'Do you like your work?'

A look of annoyance passed across her face, so I said, 'Sorry, I didn't mean to be rude.' I smiled at her but she still didn't respond. I tried again. 'I don't know what to say.'

She spoke then. 'Well, perhaps you could tell me what's brought you to our service.'

There wasn't a trace of warmth in her voice. She was the ice queen reincarnated. I could almost see shards of ice dropping from her mouth. I thought that's a funny thing to say, 'our service' as if she was a waitress in an upmarket tearoom, like Betty's of Harrogate. But I didn't say that. I didn't want to annoy her again so I said, 'Lots of things,' and waited for her to encourage me, but she didn't. So I said, 'Would you like to hear about them?'

'That's why I'm here.'

I really couldn't make her out. She gave me the creeps and I began to think she found me threatening. It made me wonder why she was a counsellor. I saw myself through her eyes. She didn't like my irreverence or the way I dressed. It was what I call 'urban ethnic' and my mate had designed it. I particularly liked my tights, black and purple narrow horizontal stripes and I wore them with a black cardigan, flat black pumps and a silk dress. The skirt was lilac with a panel at the hem of pink lace. It was a version of rockabilly and I looked a little eye catching.

Neither of us spoke for what seemed an eternity. My mind was drifting away from her, when I heard her say, 'I think it's difficult for you to be here.'

She was right. I said, 'I think it's difficult for me to be here.'

She had that look again so I said hastily, 'I'm agreeing with you.'

I looked at my watch. I was thinking how much longer. It felt like torture. Any minute I expected an arc lamp to be switched on and directed at my face.

I said, 'You're difficult to talk to, if I'm allowed to say that.'

'There's no rules here.'

I looked at her in disbelief. 'You can't be serious. No rules.'

But as I said that, I saw there was no point because she wouldn't answer. I was wrong. She did answer. What she said was, 'You want to engage me in an argument.'

I felt a flash of anger. 'If you call having and expressing a different view from you, wanting an argument, you're right.'

Her lips tightened, she stared icily at me. She was so uptight, it was frightening. I stood up. It was getting as if I'd like to smack her one, although of course, I wouldn't in reality. I looked at my mobile.

'Oops, omigod, I have an urgent appointment. I have to go. So sorry.' I stood up.

She didn't get up out of her chair. I walked towards the door and as I turned the handle, I heard her say, 'I don't think you're ready for this.'

I looked over my shoulder and said, 'Enjoy the rest of your day.' I winked at her and stayed just long enough to see her glare at me.

I couldn't wait to get out and as I passed through reception the woman at the desk said, 'You're early, didn't it work out?'

'No, I didn't know you employed people off the street with emotional handicaps. Is this "social services" or something?' She looked blank. 'People with an empathy deficit. The woman I just saw, she has an empathy deficit. She needs a counsellor.'

She smirked and said, 'Don't let it put you off, sometimes it happens, two people don't get on. I'm sorry. Shall I book you in again?'

'Thank you, but no. I need to check out one or two things first.' I smiled. 'Pity I couldn't see you.'

She smiled back, 'Well, I just do the bookings but I hope to see you again.'

It had been a bad experience. I left the building and went to the community coffee shop just down the road and sat drinking coffee, pondering what I should do next. Saf had told me North London was full of therapists and counsellors.

'What's the difference?' I'd asked. She said 'Not much, they both work with people. Therapists have a longer training, but what's important is you feel safe with them, and they're on your wavelength.'

Well, that hadn't happened for sure. It felt as if I was at a dead end. I sat stirring my coffee, idly looking at the notice board. There were lots of ads including, I noticed, some for therapists and counsellors.

My eye was caught by one in particular. It was a professionally designed A5 leaflet, with a photo of a good looking, middle-aged man. Underneath his picture was a list of questions like, 'Do you suffer with shyness? Are you anxious or depressed? Do you have problems with your partner, with work or at home? Have you suffered loss?' It went on, 'I'm a trained therapist and work with all types of emotional problems, including domestic violence, abuse survivors, sexual problems, eating disorders.' All sessions were completely confidential and he offered 'A fast, friendly service, with a sliding fee scale.' It said, 'Call me on my mobile and I'll return your call within twenty-four hours.'

There was a short biography. His name was Jason Fellowes and it said where he'd trained, but that meant nothing to me. He seemed to have done lots of things: teaching, importing and exporting, working on a pig farm and keeping a small holding in Spain where he'd kept bees and sold wild herb honey.

He came across as friendly and normal, and after my experience with the counsellor I'd just seen, I was too scared to try another woman. What with her eyeballing, her looking for a fight and then blaming me for how she felt, maybe, I thought, it was time to try a male counsellor. Jason also reminded me of Mr Harris at school, which made me feel better. I took one of the leaflets, stuck it in my pocket and caught the bus back, intending when I got home to get on the net and find out more about him.

There was more. He had his own website with photos.

He seemed to work all over London and one photo showed him with a herd of pigs all gathered round. I laughed when I saw it; they were looking up at him as if he'd descended from heaven. I thought, pigs are supposed to be intelligent so he must be alright. There was another of him holding a jar of his honey, presumably made by Spanish bees.

It said he believed in self-determination, non-judgementalism, total acceptance and valuing the authenticity of the client's story. How good is that, I thought. He certainly knew how to appeal and after my ghastly interaction with Mrs Frosty, I needed a positive experience. I rang him straightaway and left a message. A woman rang back the next day.

We arranged to meet at his place of work which was in a building in one of those huge London squares at the back of John Lewis. It seemed he shared it with other therapists and counsellors because the waiting room was almost full. No one spoke. It was like a doctor's waiting room minus the coughs. There was a rather snooty, smart-looking receptionist sitting behind a huge modern desk, but it turned out she was actually friendly. She offered me coffee while I waited for Jason and spoke as if we knew each other already. She reassured me he was expecting me, then she sat down and her attention was glued to her computer screen, except when she answered the phone. The phone rang constantly. Jason was in demand. She'd ask their name, how they'd heard of him and according to their answer would fix an appointment or tell them he was fully booked. I thought I was lucky I could see him so quickly.

I waited fifteen minutes. I was becoming more nervous. Eventually he called the receptionist and she showed me to his room. He was waiting outside and as soon as he saw me he smiled and shook my hand. His hand was clammy. I walked in. His room was large, painted that drab green you see in National Trust properties, with oak window shutters and wall-to-wall carpeting in a golden colour. Underneath the window was a huge mahogany desk, but he didn't sit behind that but gestured to a leather chair and invited me to sit down. He sat diagonally opposite. So far, so good. A different experience to Mrs Frosty; he was friendly and he initiated conversation.

He smiled, and leaning forward, he said, 'I can see how nervous you are, Anya. Well, you needn't be. Tell me what's brought you here today. That is, if you're ready. It's disconcerting to open up to someone you've only just met, isn't it?'

I didn't answer straightaway. I looked round. There were signed portraits of famous actors on the wall, thanking him for how he'd helped them. I looked from them to him. He could have been one of them. He was slightly tanned, just enough for it to be flattering. His hair was close cropped, grey. He could have been a dead-ringer for George Clooney. He oozed self-confidence, charm and style. He leant back in his chair, crossing one leg over the other, his ankle resting on his knee, and smiled. He seemed never to stop smiling. I noticed his shoes, expensive, tan brogues and his tweedy shawl-collared sweater – the rural look, aka known as smart casual. It might have looked poncy but he carried it off.

'You know I haven't got much money. I can't pay you much. I'm not famous and I'm not rich.'

He threw his head back and laughed, theatrically some might say. 'Please don't worry about that. It's the person I'm interested in, not their wealth. The rich subsidise the poor here. I'm more of a Robin Hood character.'

I looked at him suspiciously, bit glib, I thought. I said, 'Where's your tights then, your green tights, shouldn't you be wearing them?' Not funny, but the best I could do given my nervousness.

He laughed again. 'I can see you and I are going to get on, Anya. But we have work to do and what I'm really interested in is you.'

You bet, he was. Looking back, I was completely taken with him. He knew how to put me at my ease and his manner

185

was easy and open. He had a ready smile and made lots of eye contact and in his presence I felt valued and attractive. Perhaps he put me in mind of Gareth when I'd first met him all those years ago in Ffridd, before things had got complicated between us. My mind began drifting again.

I heard him say. 'Okay, Anya, give it to me. What's going on for you?' I was surprised by his informality. It was the type of thing Maddy might have said. I paused to get my thinking straight, looked across the room but he knew what I was trying to do. He said, 'Don't bother to organise what you want to tell me, because I want to see for myself what's the most important and the most disturbing for you. Speak as you feel.'

My words tumbled out, one after another, chaotically tripping over each other, the flow of thoughts and feelings stopping only when I paused for breath and before the inevitable tears that followed. I was hardly aware of Jason when I re-lived the humiliation of the night with Ifan. I told him everything, how we'd first met, our friendship and how, just before we'd been separated by the river near-drowning experience, he'd seen me naked, and how he'd kissed me, but after that he'd disappeared and I thought he was dead.

Now and again Jason interrupted with a question so I knew he was listening. He made only one comment, 'So Ifan sexually aroused you, but after meeting him again, something stopped you. Can you say more?'

I glanced at him and as he said this, I noticed his tan, his white teeth, his sensuous mouth, but for some reason I felt wary and I closed up. 'No,' I said, 'I can't.'

'You've had no other sexual experiences?'

I shifted my gaze away from him while I wondered whether to tell him about Gareth. There was a long pause. He noticed.

'Tell me everything.'

'There was somebody before him, but that didn't work either. He's a poet, called Gareth, he's older and after Ifan vanished, I became obsessed with him. One night I got drunk and tried to seduce him. He didn't want to know. It was devastating. Humiliating.'

'How old were you?'

'Nearly sixteen.'

'And what about him?'

'Maybe thirty-five. It doesn't matter. Not to me.'

He didn't pursue that line of questioning but said, 'I'd like to return to your early history, you've said nothing about your parents, neither of them, in fact.'

'What is there to say? What little I know about my father is that I'm the product of an affair, my father was married already, and my mother? She's angry, spiteful, unfulfilled. But she does her best, so I'm told.'

After this, he sat for a while thinking. I didn't mind the silence, then he said, 'Well, Anya, life's been difficult for you, brought up by a mother who sees you as a "product" – is that your word or your mother's? – of a man who cheated on her. A father of whom you know little.'

At that point I interrupted him to say I'd forgotten about my uncle Harry and that I'd gone to Liverpool to find out more about my father. But Harry had other things on his mind. I told him I'd been frightened and how repulsive I'd found him when he came on to me.

Jason asked 'Why?'

For a split second, I thought he must be stupid but I replied politely. 'It's obvious, isn't it? He's my mother's brother, my uncle.'

'Yes, of course.'

He was silent again, then he continued, 'Your absent father, the unexplained loss of Ifan, whom you see as your first love, then grieving, you transfer that love and affection to Gareth, but Gareth, from your point of view, rejects you, and your uncle attempts to exploit your vulnerability. It's hardly surprising you find it difficult to trust men. They either leave you or they reject you. That seems to have been your experience.'

I was impressed. 'I see what you mean. But can you help me?'

'How would you like me to help you?'

'I don't know, you tell me, that's why I'm here.'

Jason said, 'I think you need to come here, regularly. You need space, to talk, reflect, think. You need to feel accepted but do you want that commitment?'

I answered immediately. 'Yes, but what about your fees?'

'Don't worry about them, Anya, tell me what you can afford.' He stood up and, smiling, held his hand out. 'Make an appointment with my secretary before you leave. You can cancel later, if you have second thoughts.'

I thanked him and as I left his room, he said, 'You're a very attractive young woman. You must know that.'

That observation took me aback big time. I could have done without it; I didn't want to know how he saw me. But I was ready to forgive him. He'd put me at my ease and with the exception of that last comment, he'd said the right thing at the right time. I made an appointment with the receptionist and began seeing him on a weekly basis.

I looked forward to those sessions and gradually I began feeling better. I don't know how it worked, but Jason called it 'the talking cure', and I did talk. I talked about anything and everything, until the fragments of my life began connecting up and I saw the big picture. All was going well, until the inevitable happened. I saw Ifan.

London's a big place and unless you work or live in the same locality or hang out in the same coffee bars or music venues, it's unlikely that your path will randomly cross with someone you know, but it does happen.

It was a Wednesday, late afternoon. I'd had my session and was walking down the steps of the building when my eye was caught by a familiar figure. Ifan. I was a little way down the street and he was hoisting his bike up and attaching it with a D lock to some railings.

I couldn't move from where I stood and I stopped breathing. It had been almost a year since that last disastrous meeting but he was never far from my mind. I stood wondering what to do, when a girl ran down the steps. Like me, she must have just seen a therapist. She ran towards him, calling his name. He looked up, smiled, then he saw me.

That wiped the smile off his face. Our eyes met. His gaze was direct, intense. When the girl reached him, she'd put her arm round his waist, and kissed him, but he must have said something because she looked back at me. They walked away leaving his bike still attached to the railings. It all happened so quickly, I was left standing unsure of my next move.

I continued watching them until they reached the traffic lights and turned into the next street. I saw Ifan glance over his shoulder towards me. Spontaneously I raised my hand to my shoulder and gave him a shy little wave. I was filled with a longing to speak with him and I felt my eyes fill with tears. I walked to his bike and stood for a moment wondering whether to leave him a note or wait until he returned. What would his girlfriend make of it? Yet admitting to myself he had a girlfriend was painful because rightly or wrongly, I still felt he and I were destined to be together.

I took out my 'Re-Vamp Designs' business card, and tucked it under the saddle of his bike. I didn't care if his girlfriend saw it or not. I didn't leave a message, he'd know it was from me. I walked home and cried but I had to wait another week before I could tell Jason. I tried to avoid thinking about Ifan and his girlfriend by keeping busy at work. I knew my feelings of jealousy and betrayal were irrational, but knowing that didn't make them go away. All the old memories resurfaced. Then I began to dream and they were bad.

It was the same one for five nights. I was back in the forest and hiding behind the tree, only this time it wasn't Gareth and Chloe I was watching, it was Ifan with his girlfriend and as they were about to have sex, I'd wake in a panic. After that, I couldn't get back to sleep and I'd be awake for hours.

I became exhausted. I couldn't wait to see Jason. I needed his help to make sense of my feelings.

The day came, I arrived early for my appointment and was sitting in the waiting room impatiently flicking through the magazines, when Ifan's girlfriend walked in. It hadn't crossed my mind I might see her.

She sat down and stared at me coldly. She must have known who I was, but neither of us said hello. I put my head down. She was pretty in an ordinary way, but dressed as if she'd just come from work and her work must have been boring because her clothes were boring. She had no style. I thought she looked like an office worker in her black skirt and white blouse and, knowing Ifan, I was surprised he was with her. Maybe she was more interesting than she looked, or after his experience with me, he wanted someone conventional.

She couldn't have positioned herself further from where I was sitting but I was aware of her eyes drilling through me. I felt myself blush and began wondering how much Ifan had told her. Would she know I had a hang up about sex? No matter how boring she looked, perhaps she liked sex and she had no problems. She'd be safely predictable and wouldn't suddenly jump out of bed at the crucial point and cry she couldn't go through with it. But if she was so together, why was she seeing a therapist? Just as I thought I'd have to go to the loo to avoid her eyeballing, the receptionist said Jason was ready to see me.

I was relieved, walked quickly to his room and flung myself on to the chair. Jason looked at me curiously. I didn't speak straightaway but seeing him made me tearful.

'What's going on? You look stirred up.'

'I am stirred up. Last week, by chance, I saw Ifan. It was after my session. I was walking along the street, and I saw him locking up his bike so I was standing there wondering whether to speak to him, when a girl ran down the steps. He must have been waiting for her because they walked away together. That was bad enough, but now she's in your waiting

190

room. We didn't speak, it was all so fast, but you can imagine how I felt. She must see a therapist here. She's fair haired, dresses like an office worker and wears high heels. Do you know who she might be?'

He didn't answer. I hesitated before adding. 'It's a shock. After all this time, seeing him with someone else. I thought I was over him. But I'm not. My feelings are the same. I miss him and I feel terrible.'

'Terrible?'

'Yes, I keep having this dream. It's like it's about Gareth and Chloe in the forest but this time it's Ifan and her, the one in your waiting room. I don't know her name. The dreams wake me up, just as they're about to have sex. I've hardly slept since last week.'

'Why do you think that is?'

'How should I know?' I was irritated. 'I want you to tell me, that's why I come here, isn't it? If I knew, I wouldn't need to come.'

For a change he didn't seem to know what to say, and was silent. He was thinking. Eventually he said, 'Perhaps you wake from the dream to protect yourself from watching them. Watching them make love would make you jealous. Having sex is something you haven't achieved yourself.' I glared at him, but there was more to come. 'You feel excluded and inadequate; as if you're not pretty and it hurts that he's chosen her rather than you. If you stayed asleep the dream would become a nightmare, so you wake and that way you maintain your control and avoid the pain.'

That pissed me off. Big time. It was unexpected. I felt as if he'd thrown a bomb in my face. My response was immediate. 'Why do I have to listen to such crap? What you've just said is cruel and it's as if you want to hurt me.' I glared at him, stood up and gathered my things. 'You know what? I'm going. I can do without your shit. I came here to feel better, not made worse and you've made me feel worse.'

He didn't move. His face was expressionless. I was on

a roll by then and nothing would stop me. 'I think,' I said, 'actually, it's you who's jealous. You're jealous because I still have feelings for Ifan. I think,' I paused as I found the right words, 'I think that's why you want to hurt me. It's as if I've betrayed you because I still miss Ifan and you want me to be totally involved with you.'

That got to him. He was as angry as me now. He looked furious and waved his hand imperiously in the air. 'Transference. Your problem, not mine.'

'Whatever that means. But I can guess. Do you think I haven't noticed?' He didn't answer. 'Your clients, they're all young women, attractive young women but they never last long. I've been seeing you now for a year and I must be your longest-standing client. Why don't they stay? What's your game? Are you married? Don't you get enough? I think not. That's why you're so interested in my sex life.'

'You haven't got a sex life.'

That was way out of order. I retorted, 'And neither have you. That's obvious.'

He must have lost it by then because he said, 'None of your business.'

He got out of his chair and we stood glowering at each other. I was halfway across the room when he stepped across my path, blocking my exit to the door. 'You're a creep,' I said and then I delivered the killer line, 'You remind me of Harry.'

When I said that, he seemed to pull himself together. He spoke slowly and quietly. 'You're here because you need my help. Therapy is a difficult process and it requires that you trust me and recognise I have your interests at heart. This is our first difficulty but you immediately want to run, which is something you've always done. I suggest you stay and see it through.'

'What is there to see through?'

He paused, then said, 'It's not Ifan you want to have sex with, the dream is about me with someone else, but I'm unavailable and it's this which causes you anguish.'

That shocked me. I laughed sarcastically. 'You,' I said. 'Don't make me laugh. You're wrong.' I repeated what he'd said to me, '"Transference", it's your problem. Anyway, I don't go for your type, a George Clooney look alike... And I'm still going.' I side-stepped round him, reached the door and turned to look at him. 'I'll think about it, whether I'm coming back. It's my decision, mine alone.'

I walked out. I wanted to get out of that building fast. I ran down the stairs. There was still ten minutes left to my session and the last person I wanted to see was Ifan waiting for his girlfriend. I headed towards Cavendish Square for the back entrance of John Lewis. I was desperate for anonymity and figured I'd get that in John Lewis.

It was, as I thought it would be, busy. I drifted round looking at the various displays. I was upset and wanted some sort of distraction. Eventually I found myself in the handbag department.

I looked around. The more expensive the bag, the more seductive the display. Before long, my eye was caught by a solitary, beautifully coloured leather bag. You couldn't miss it. It was lit up with a back light, and balanced high on a clear plastic plinth. It was azure blue and put me in mind of the one I'd bought off eBay. The one I'd called my Anya bag, but after the Gareth debacle I'd put it away.

I stood in the middle of the crowds surging round the glass display cabinets, but my mind was in that hotel room, remembering when I'd got drunk and how I'd tried to seduce Gareth – and I would have, if he'd let me. Now seven years later, I was still looking for that wonderful experience but it hadn't happened. It was then, I realised, big time, I was a mess. Despite seeing a therapist, I was destined, it seemed, never to have a good relationship with a guy and included in this list were male therapists. But then a wave of defiance came over me. Right now, I didn't give a shit.

A woman assistant interrupted my reverie. 'Can I help you?' I was pulled back into the present. I was standing in front of the blue bag. 'I was wondering how much that bag is? It's so beautiful.'

She took it down and placed it in my hands. 'It is, isn't it? It's one of my favourites. It's Italian leather, of the best quality and hand made in Florence by Forzieri.'

The bag clicked open with a clasp. 1 peered inside. Lined in deep blue silk, it had pockets for a phone, a purse, a notebook. 'It's stunning. How much is it?'

'Seven hundred, just under to be precise.'

'Oh. Well out of my price range, but to be expected. Thanks. But actually, I have a beautiful bag at home. I bought it off eBay, but maybe, when I'm rich and famous I'll buy this one. Then I'll have two.' I smiled at her, handed back the bag, left the store and caught the bus home.

It was crowded but upstairs there were some empty seats and I found myself sitting next to a very expensively dressed woman. She was carrying a Selfridge's bag and wearing a perfume I recognised. It was familiar. It was Coco Mademoiselle. I stared at her but as I did, I heard the voice of Anya, my namesake telling me she could help me. The woman must have become aware I was looking at her because she looked sideways at me. I said to her, 'Anya is the perfume, the perfume is Anya and I want to be Anya.' She stood up and moved away to sit somewhere else. She must have thought I was mad but I didn't care.

Three days later I received a letter from Jason. It said he recognised how upset I was and apologised for being 'wrong-footed' and that he'd see me at the usual time. I couldn't have cared less. My feelings for him had changed. I looked cynically at what he'd written. It was what I call, 'therapese'. It said the right things but there was no emotion. I was sure he wouldn't care if he never saw me again, and the thought of going back to where he worked and sitting in that waiting room and seeing Ifan's girlfriend was excruciatingly embarrassing.

I didn't know whether to return or not, but the comment

he'd made about running when there was a problem had got to me. Maybe he was right. Then I had an idea. He worked in other parts of London so I emailed him and asked if it was possible to meet elsewhere. That way, I could avoid Ifan's girlfriend and still check out more about what he'd said. Otherwise I wrote, I'd look for another therapist. It wasn't an idle threat. I meant it.

He emailed me back. He said that was fine. He worked near Hackney Downs Station and gave me two possible dates and times.

I chose Tuesdays at seven. Although Hackney isn't so far from Stroud Green, I wasn't familiar with the area so I was there early and I ended up loitering outside. It was a basement flat and totally different from the elegant and professional place in Wigmore Street where I'd seen him before. I wondered if he lived there so I walked up the steps to the front door to look at the flat name plates. There were three flats but none with his name.

I went back down to the basement, rang the bell and stood waiting. A safety light snapped on. When he opened the door he didn't greet me or smile, just stood aside and gestured towards an open door inside the flat. The heat hit me. I looked around the room. It was painted white and either he or his partner must have been to Ikea because I recognised the style of the two tub chairs. They were covered in that bold flowered pattern the Scandinavians love. The blinds at the window were a subtle violet colour. On the walls were some Chagall prints and the carpet was rough sisal. It was all new and very tasteful in a modern kind of way. I liked its simplicity.

I sat down. I had no idea what I was going to talk about but I felt indifferent and a little contemptuous. I'd thought more about the last session and disapproved of what he'd said. It had been unprofessional and it was this which was on my mind. But I covered these thoughts up.

'I like your room. Very Ikea. I didn't know Ikea sold Chagall prints.'

'They don't. I got them elsewhere.'

He was leaning back in his chair with his fingers pressed together, studying me closely. My eye was caught by a bed along the wall.

'Why have you got a bed in here? Is it a spare guest room?'

'It's not a bed. It's a couch. Some people prefer to lie on the couch as they talk.'

'How peculiar. That's weird. And where do you sit?'

'Behind them.'

'Behind them? But they couldn't see you. You never had a couch in the other place.'

He didn't answer. We were staring at each other.

I said, 'Did you see that staring cat on YouTube? It out stared its owner.'

He said, 'A battle of wills.' He remained unsmiling.

I ignored that. I was now reminded of that woman therapist I'd seen, the one who didn't like me. The atmosphere was similar. Hostile. I began drumming my fingers on the arm of the chair. I looked in my bag for my oyster card for something to do and wondered how much longer I could stand the silence. I smiled uncertainly at him. I was regretting coming.

'I could do with some tea, but I know you won't get me one.' Silence. 'I just thought I'd say something. You know, to break the silence.'

'You seem jumpy.'

'Not surprising, is it? *The Silence of the Lambs*, did you ever see it?'

'You fear being slaughtered?'

I gave him one of my looks. The type of look that wound my mother up. A quick glance, purse my lips, look away, then up to the ceiling. Contempt. I was good at it. He didn't react.

'I've got nothing to say. I didn't know whether to come or not, and now I wish I hadn't.'

'But you have come.'

'What's the point?'

'Of what?'

I sighed, 'What's the point of coming here?'

'Maybe there was something drawing you here.'

'Like what?'

'I think we both know that.'

I didn't answer immediately. Then I said sarcastically, 'Are you a mind reader? You seem to know something I don't. Perhaps you can enlighten me.'

He said, 'The couch. It attracts you, doesn't it? But it's difficult for you to speak of your desire; you dream but even in a dream, you wake. You're frightened. You must be in control.'

'What are you talking about?'

'I'm talking about desire between men and women and your difficulties in acknowledging your own.'

He stopped. He was watching me carefully. He was monitoring my reaction but I was out of my depth. I didn't know what was going on or what he was talking about, but something wasn't right.

'Anya. At some point you need to let go. You need to give in and stop fighting. Until you can do this you'll remain in a childlike state, conflicted, unhappy, isolated... Your nightmares reveal your true feelings. You're desperate for love and affection.'

I glanced at him and looked away. What he'd said had got to me. I saw myself as he saw me. He felt sorry for me. He saw me as pathetic and screwed up.

Images of me as a child, searching for my mother, her shouting, Harry sexually excited, lurching drunk across Gareth's room, and Ifan– even he no longer wanted me.

I was alone in the world, a nobody, a failure, a total failure. I fought back tears. The estuary at dusk came to me. I wanted to go back to those times when I played with Ifan, to how it used to be, when life seemed safe and easy, but that was the past and I was frightened. I didn't understand what was going on. I didn't know who I was or what life was about. I wished I hadn't come. I began crying. I turned away to hide my face from Jason. Through my tears I heard him speaking softly.

'Anya, let me help you. I know what you want. You must trust me. I won't hurt you. Let me help you. Please.'

I didn't answer. He was getting up out of his chair, slowly walking towards me. He's standing over me, gesturing towards the couch. I did what he wanted. I lay on the couch, looking up at him. My mind is empty. I'm mesmerised by his voice.

I trust him. I want him to make me feel better. Neither of us speak. I wait for him to sit in the chair behind me. But he doesn't. He crouches on the floor. He's close to me. He's smiling. He slowly pulls up my jumper, fondles my breasts, he puts his hand up my skirt, then into my pants. His fingers explore my body. He's breathing heavily. But I can't move. My body is inert, my mind blank. I allow him to do what he wants. Everything that follows is in slow motion. I can hear him talking but not what he says. I'm staring at the ceiling until the room spins round and round. My body isn't mine. I feel a searing pain. I pass out.

When I come to, he's gone. I'm sleepwalking. I get off the couch. My pants lie blooded on the floor. I pick them up. I put them in my bag. I'm shaking. I want to leave his flat. I walk to the door. Open it. Look back over my shoulder. He's standing in the hall. He has a mug of tea.

I hear him say, 'You're not leaving yet, are you? I've made some tea for you.' Everything normal. Except it's not. I look at him. Who is he? I feel nothing. I leave. I make my way across the Downs. It's dark. I stop under a tree and retch. Then I vomit. I stay there until there's nothing left inside my body to spew out. I catch a cab back to my mother's flat. She's not in. I remove my clothes and stand in the shower. I let the water cascade over me but I can't get clean. I don't know how long I'm there. I sleepwalk my way to my bed and lie for hours, half-awake, half-asleep. I don't cry.

Hours later, I start searching. I have to find her. My Anya bag. I get up, become more and more focused. More frantic. I empty drawers, boxes, wardrobes. I go to my mother's room. I find it. I hold it close. I open it. Her fragrance, Coco Mademoiselle, enters the room. I've unleashed her. She was right. I need her. She's been waiting for me. It was time.

Part Six

I couldn't tell my mother. She didn't know I was seeing a therapist and I didn't trust how she'd respond, but I told Maddy. She was furious and said I should go to the police, but I didn't want that. There were no guarantees of a sympathetic hearing and I couldn't bear the humiliation of a medical. There was no danger of a pregnancy because I remembered later he'd worn a condom, but Maddy still insisted I visit a clinic and get myself checked out. She came with me. Physically, I was alright. It was my mind that wasn't.

I took two weeks off work. I told them I wanted a holiday and retreated to my bed. For days I was in a state of shock. Over and over, the scene would be replayed in my head. I felt humiliated and dirty. Bits of it came back. I blamed myself. I must have been provocative. I tried to understand what led to it. My behaviour? But I hadn't been seductive. Nothing I'd said could be interpreted as a 'sexual come-on'. My dress? I'd dressed the way I usually dressed, vintage style. Perhaps I shouldn't have gone to his flat, but he was my therapist, I'd trusted him. Perhaps I shouldn't have got on his couch. My mind was full of self-doubt and self-recrimination.

At first, I'd thought it was a 'seduction' because I should have refused him and I hadn't. I'd never said 'no', but when Maddy realised I was thinking like that, she corrected me. She said it wasn't seduction. It was rape. She said I'd been in a childlike, vulnerable, dependent state and in that state of mind I couldn't give consent. He'd exploited that. She was angrier than I was, but I was in a state of shock.

Everything and everybody had become strange. I could see people talking but there was a delay before I could hear their voice. Their mouths moved, but there was no sound. I could see the words floating into the air as they spoke, drifting away, slow and distorted, like tortured musical notes. I retreated from the world and for days I lay in bed, refusing to eat. I'd entered a twilight world, halfway between dreaming and sleeping.

Maddy came to see me every day. She looked after me, stayed with me, talked to me. She said what he'd done was unforgivable. She played me the music I liked. She wanted me to go to specialist rape counselling, but I refused. I'd had enough of counsellors and therapists. She brought me books written by rape survivors and slowly, gradually I was able to face the truth. The truth was I'd been raped by my therapist and once I'd accepted that, my thinking changed, from a victim to thoughts of revenge.

Acknowledging what he'd done filled me with hate. I couldn't bring myself to use his name and when I spoke of him to Maddy and my mates, I called him JF. They wanted me to put in a complaint to his professional organisation. They said I should, not only for myself but for other women. They said he might do it again. They were adamant it would help, so I began the research, but it wasn't long before I realised that complaining would be a waste of time.

Therapist organisations are powerful. They advocate for therapists and they have a number of wonderful let-out clauses, mostly based on familiar stereotypes about women. I came across blogs written by ex-clients of therapists. Someone who wrote 'Fifty Shades of Getting his Way' and called herself 'Angry Bird' wrote sex between a therapist and his client was common. Whether that was true or not I didn't know, but I was out for vengeance. I objected to women being seen as fantasists or crazy. I didn't buy the 'therapeutic relationship' had finished or when he said, 'I loved her' or 'she misunderstood the nature of our relationship'. I bitterly opposed the envy, jealous, malicious motivation matrix where ordinary human emotions were elevated to murderous, violent intent and ipso facto, by sleight of hand the victim has become the offender.

I began to see psychotherapy and its practitioners as the conveyors of myths and ideologies. Patterns of beliefs, theories, and words, fireworks of meaning, images and affects; they'd spun round my head with their promise. Seductive, enthralling, a dozen nuanced languages to enslave and entrap the inarticulate, the confused, the victimised, the vulnerable, the curious, with the promise of a better world. I'd been hooked.

But I was no longer. I'd come to my senses and it was payback time. I wanted him to suffer the way I had; to feel the betrayal, the humiliation, the shame and powerlessness, the fear, the shock, the apprehension, the incomprehension, the rage. These feelings stalked me. They'd taken up residence in my mind and I had to erase them and since they originated with him, he had to be erased. It was necessary. It was essential. It required the sense of timing and purpose he'd shown me. It required an intervention that was as powerful and as destructive as he had been.

I came to a decision. I was going to attack him the way he had me, but my attack wouldn't be physical but psychological. He'd invaded my body and I wanted to invade his mind. It was the slow-burn approach to revenge.

For a while I had no idea how to go about this but the idea came unexpectedly. It was a month later and I was back at work. I'd woken early and I'd placed my Anya bag on a chair where I could see it as I woke. Its presence was reassuring. Maybe I was half-asleep and still dreaming, but that morning I felt as if a magnet was drawing me towards it. I stumbled across the room and picked the bag up, and as I opened it, Anya entered the room. I knew she was there because of her fragrance, Coco Mademoiselle. I could hear her saying what I should do and that she'd protect me.

I was to stalk him and take her with me and she'd look after me.

From then on, just before I slept, I placed the bag on the chair so I could hear her when I woke. She always spoke to me first thing. She told me I needed to get my confidence back and the way to do that, was to start in little ways and work up to the more spectacular. The little ways she called 'interventions', the more spectacular, 'invasions'. That's how my stalking began.

It started with checking out JF's movements; when and where he was, and for how long. I had two addresses, the one in Wigmore Street and the one near Hackney Downs. That was enough. It gave me a choice. I'd go before work, lunchtime, after work; whenever the spirit of Anya moved me. I'd stand outside, wait, watch his comings and goings. I got to know his routine. Each time I made sure to carry my Anya bag. I made no attempt to hide myself.

The first time he noticed me he approached me, holding his hand out. 'Anya, how lovely to see you. How are you?' How shameless he was. I didn't answer. I looked coldly at him, turned and walked away.

It took a while and several sightings before he realised what was going on. At first he seemed oblivious or indifferent as to why I might be there and how that might connect to the consequences of his actions. Either that or he was deeply stupid.

But I was determined he would get it and if he needed time, I had the time, the motivation and the patience. I became a forensic observer. I began keeping a record of his psychological deterioration, monitoring the corrosive effects of my attack. I had no overall plan of action but scientifically recorded my observations, incident by incident and with each sighting I carefully watched his face, his gestures, his movements.

Once when I saw him get out of his cab, he must have

thought I wasn't there, because he looked nonchalant. I ran towards him. I ran fast and the fearful look on his face when he saw me amused me no end. I got there first. He pushed past me and ran down the steps. He fumbled for his keys but he was so nervous, he dropped them. He wasn't quick enough. I stood at the top of the steps looking down on him. The safety light had snapped on so he could see my face. I was unsmiling. That time I did speak. I took two steps towards him and spoke softly and reassuringly, using the same words he'd used before he raped me.

'You look frightened. You needn't be. I know what you want. You must trust me. I won't hurt you.' The look of utter terror on his face made me laugh. 'See you soon,' I said and as I walked away I turned to look over my shoulder, 'And take care. You never know who's watching you.'

I was pleased with that incident because each time I saw his fear I felt empowered and I regained some self-respect, but I was becoming bored. I wanted a new intervention, something less obvious than hanging round where he worked. It was too predictable. I wanted to increase the intensity of my attacks. At any time he could put in a complaint to the police, tell them that a mad client was stalking him and I didn't want a police visit. It was time for something new. I went back and waited for inspiration and sure enough it came. Was it Anya? I don't know, but I like to think it was.

I'd come home late. I switched on my computer, and as I did the disembodied voice of Etta James floated out of the computer and into the room. She was singing 'At Last'. I was transfixed. It was the song played by Ifan after I'd met him in the pub and we'd gone back to his place. The song we'd danced to before everything had fallen apart and Etta James' harsh, expressive voice brought it all back.

Hearing the lines of the song was gut wrenching. All the old pain returned and tears welled into my eyes. I walked round my bedroom. I couldn't sit still. I walked out of my bedroom, I sat at my table. I got up from my table, I paced back and forth. I was buzzing. I wanted to get in touch with him. I didn't want to get in touch with him.

I was so taken with this song and the memories it brought back, it took a while to register that someone had hacked into my computer. Then I freaked. I had no idea who it could be, but whoever it was, knew my taste in music. I wondered if it was JF but discarded that thought. The song was too beautiful for him and I couldn't imagine it was his type of thing. Besides, he didn't go for retro, he was too conventional and he was on the run from me. I couldn't see him counter-attacking.

It could only be one person and that was Ifan. I'd left my card with my email address on his bike the day I'd seen him in Wigmore Street. He was an electrical engineer, he'd have the right techie background, and he knew the significance of Etta's songs for both of us. It was still creepy. He would know how to do it, but why didn't he just ring me? Ask me out? What was his game?

Two weeks later, I switched on my computer and another of her songs drifted out. This time it was 'I've Been Loving You Too Long to Stop Now'. I sat and listened. The lyrics were beautiful. I wanted it to be from Ifan so much but the irony hadn't escaped me; Ifan was stalking me. But in an alternative way. After all if you're a 'hacker' with an offbeat sense of humour, it could be seen as a special way of sending an anonymous love letter. But, it occurred to me, this was a game two can play and the idea came to me that I could play Ifan at his own game by hacking into his computer.

It was a small jump from that, to a decision to hack into JF's computer. That way I could still stalk him but online. It was a way of getting into his head. I'd invade his mind so that every time he opened his computer a song would play. But it had be disturbing.

I began my search. I soon found one on YouTube. The song? 'Every Breath You Take.' I planned to get it installed on his computer. He wouldn't be able to switch it off. It would spread through the computer's hardware and like an actual biological virus it would infiltrate, penetrate, insinuate, destroy all expectations of rationality and predictability. The infection would cross the boundary from the machine to his mind, and from there it would invade, colonise and control his thoughts – just like he had mine.

I imagined him switching on his computer at home, in Hackney, at Wigmore Street, on the train, at home. Wherever he was, he couldn't escape. The lyrics of 'Every Breath You Take' would follow him. Only a specialist would be able to clear the virus. It would be expensive, time consuming, disturbing and the disruption it would cause gave me pleasure every time I thought of it. I turned to my Anya bag and gave her a wink. 'Keep the ideas coming,' I said.

But I didn't know how to go about this so I had to ask around. I found out that hacking, like stalking, is a crime, and infecting someone's computer with a Trojan virus doesn't stop there; it can spread. That slowed me down for a while. I thought about it long and hard before I made the decision to go ahead and when I did, I justified it on the grounds he'd raped me.

I continued my research and through friends of friends of friends, I discovered within the cyber world some hackers will hack 'for free' if they think someone or some organisation has done wrong. They're a kind of cyber social service, an updated Robin Hood or SAS patrolling cyberspace and although I never found out who it was who helped me, I'm eternally grateful to him or her. Let's hope it was a 'her', anyway.

As for Ifan, I still planned to contact him but I wasn't sure how he felt about me even if he had sent the two Etta James tracks. There was only one way to find out; I had to take a risk. I turned again to my Anya bag for inspiration, but this time there was nothing and I had to make up my own mind.

In the end, I sent him via email an attachment of a track from the Etta James CD. It was simple, straightforward and legal but I chose the track carefully. My song had to have the right lyrics and since he'd communicated his thoughts and desires with her lyrics, I did the same. I chose 'Teach Me Tonight'. Having made that decision, I danced round my flat. I loved that song and I loved him. But now I knew that I was filled with an insecurity so strong, I wanted to run away. What if, I thought, he was still with his girlfriend and they'd had a tiff and he'd contacted me to just make her jealous?

Yet, I'd trusted him when we'd been together in Wales all those years ago. Since then life had changed me, but had it him? I wondered how Philomena and Gareth were in Ffridd, and whether they were still together. My mother used to talk about them but no longer. Since she'd met her new fella, all her time was spent with him.

I was filled with a wild yearning to return to Wales. I wanted to visit the estuary. I hadn't visited since my failed seduction of Gareth all those years ago and I wasn't sure how he'd react when he saw me. Despite that, I still wanted to go back, to the time when life had seemed straightforward and predictable. The next morning I was ready to visit Ffridd.

A week later, I was standing in the queue at Newport Railway Station waiting for a cab. I'd taken advantage of the absence of appointments in my diary and organised a long weekend away. I hadn't contacted Philomena and Gareth to say I was coming because I wanted my visit to be spontaneous. Besides, they weren't the type to need notice and if, when I arrived, they weren't there, I'd stay somewhere else.

A cab drew up. I asked for the farmhouse at Ffridd. The cabbie seemed to know of it and gave me a look, but didn't say anything. We headed towards Ffridd. Eventually he turned off the main road and we bounced along the tracks through the fields towards the farmhouse. It was winter. The landscape was bleak, the sky grey, the trees bare but there was no wind. It had been raining and muddy water splashed up from the potholes, spotting the sides of his immaculately maintained BMW. He loved his car. He said, 'If I'd known I'd be bringing someone here, I wouldn't have bothered to wash it.' I didn't respond but stared out of the window. He spoke again. 'It's a long time since I've come here. Used to visit a lot, bringing all kinds from the station. Weird. Artists. What they get up to. All their comings and goings. They all slept with each other, but then it takes all sorts. Been before?'

'Yes, I used to come every summer with my mother.'

'So you know about it then.'

'Not really. Not when I was young. Do you know if the same people live there?'

'No idea, can't help you there. Sorry.'

I could see the farmhouse now. It lay in a hollow but it looked different from how I remembered it in the bright summer days of my childhood.

'You can stop now. I'd like to walk the rest.'

He turned round briefly. 'Sure?'

'Yes, your car will get splashed more. Drop me off here.'

He pulled the car to a halt, silently took the fare, turned his car round and with a wave drove off. I watched the car bump away, picked up my bag and began the short walk to the farmhouse. I heard the geese before I saw them. They were the same as when I used to come, they rushed at me, but I knew how to ignore them. In terms of the noise they made, they were better guards than dogs. I stood waiting, half-expecting to see Philomena standing in the doorway, but she didn't appear. I closed the farmhouse gate behind me, put my bag down by the porch and began wandering round the grounds.

I was filled with nostalgia. Memories of past summers flooded back. I walked to the orchard at the back of the farmhouse and in my mind's eye I could see Gareth sitting under the apple trees writing his poetry. He was sitting in his favourite chair, the high-backed, rush-seated chair, and drinking cider. It was warm then. The wind had got up. I turned to make my way back. There was a new sculpture under the trees and I stood looking at it. A figure with a long neck, small breasts, folded wings, it was a cross between a woman and a swan. It had a plaque entitled Leda, and I remembered from Greek mythology, Leda was raped by a god in the form of a swan. I turned away. I didn't like it. It disturbed me.

I'd reached the porch, put my hand up to ring the bell, when the door opened. Philomena stood smiling broadly. She held her arms open, stepped towards me, and clasped me to her. 'Anya. Amazing. Do you know I was dreaming of you a few days ago and I thought that was an omen and you might visit. I was upstairs and saw you in the orchard. It's been a long time, far too long since you last came. Come in.' She picked up my bag and said, 'I'll leave this in the hall. Let's go to the kitchen and I'll make some coffee.'

She looked the same as she had eight years ago but I felt shy, as if I was still the child I had been when we used to visit. All I could do was smile. I looked around. 'You've changed the colours of the kitchen. It's less vibrant. More contemplative.' The colours were sludgy and reminded me of the mud of the estuary when the tide had gone out.

'Well, it was Gareth's turn to choose.'

'Some turquoise, still in the same palette, would have lifted it, don't you think? Needs a bit of contrast, if you don't mind my saying.'

'Tell it to Gareth. There speaks a designer. Your mother told me you worked in the fashion industry. You always did have an eye for clothes and colour.' She paused while she made the coffee and then sat down opposite me. 'You know I've missed you, Anya. I used to look forward to your coming. What's kept you away?'

'This and that.'

'Gareth told me you'd fallen out with him but he wouldn't say any more, and your mother hasn't been here for five years.' She sighed. 'Sadly those summers have passed. I used to enjoy them.'

'She has a boyfriend now and he keeps her busy. Another

teacher, she met him at school. I see her now and again.'

'I always thought it a shame you two didn't get on.'

'It happens. We get on better now. Now she has someone, she keeps off my case.'

'But how are you? I've often wondered. But I gathered that you and Gareth weren't speaking.' Her voice trailed away, she was watching me, waiting for a response but I was silent. 'You know, he was upset when you two fell out.'

'Was he? I'm surprised. I thought he didn't care. Anyway...stuff happens, so I thought it best not to.'

'My curiosity is roused. What on earth happened? You know, he always saw you as the daughter we never had, but after that, whatever it was, he felt as if he'd lost you. Did you know that?'

She'd caught me totally caught off guard. I stared at her, before shifting my gaze away. I stood up, took my coffee and walked towards the window and looked out on to the orchard. I could feel my eyes filling with tears. I'd been so caught up with myself, I'd misjudged him. What he'd said in that hotel room about protecting me must have been true. He was a good man but I hadn't recognised it. I turned round and for a moment Philomena and I looked at each other. She was waiting for me to tell her, but I couldn't. It still felt raw.

'Where is Gareth?'

'You haven't heard?'

'What about?'

'He doesn't live here anymore.'

'No, I didn't know.' I stared at her, wondering how she felt about that.

'Gareth moved out seven years ago, not long after you had stopped coming. After his book came out, he told me he was in love with someone else, someone called Chloe. It had been going on for years and she was married. I always wondered if you knew. You were an astute child. You may remember her, she was at the meeting, the day we went to Chepstow. I'd suspected something was up, after all I'm no fool, but I waited and I hoped it would blow over like the others. But this one lasted. When I married him, I knew what I was taking on. He's a poet, he has to get his material from somewhere.'

So she had known about Chloe. Even so, I wasn't about to tell her anything. It would be like rubbing salt into a wound. There was a long silence before she continued.

'But it doesn't stop there. Chloe was pregnant, not by her husband, but by Gareth, and he wanted to be with her and the baby. Her husband was very unpleasant, well he would be, wouldn't he, and Gareth wanted to protect her. He moved out some time ago.'

I felt a rush of sympathy for Philomena. 'I'm so sorry. It's been tough for you. I had no idea. If my mother knew, she never told me.'

'It has some advantages, Anya, living on one's own. For one thing I can get on with my work and Gareth visits regularly, with or without the child, so I have the best of both worlds.'

'So you're still friends with him?'

'Of course and Gareth was always a good lover.'

Had she misheard me? I stared at her with astonishment. 'I'm sorry, I didn't mean that.'

Philomena laughed and for a moment she sounded just like before. It was a smoker's laugh, husky, dark, with a hint of bitterness and of illicit love affairs. 'It's of no consequence. Life goes on as usual.'

'Where's the child?'

'Ceri? She's with her mother and Gareth. They live in the Black Mountains on a small holding. Chloe teaches Welsh but she's also a weaver, of the non-traditional sort, modern designs using the colours and dyes of nature; berries, lichen, roots, that kind of thing. I like her work actually. It's beautiful and quite subtle.'

'You're very generous, Philomena. But what of Ceri?'

'Ceri is the apple of Gareth's eye or as he prefers to put it, she is "the gift of love".'

My mind went back to the time I hid in the forest and saw them about to make love. 'How old is Ceri?' I asked.

'Eight. She's a lovely child. Always singing and when she's not singing, she's humming.'

I smiled. 'A love child.'

'Yes, Gareth always wanted children and I didn't, maybe that was it. Anya, you will stay, won't you? I know Gareth would like to see you, if he knew you were here. Shall I ring and let him know?'

'Go ahead. Actually, I'd like to see him too.'

'And Ceri? Would you like to see her?'

I felt that familiar feeling of jealousy. The truth was I wanted Gareth to myself but I couldn't and wouldn't exclude his daughter. I was non-committal. I said, 'It's his choice, whatever's convenient.'

'I'll ring him. But you must be tired. It's a long journey. Would you like to go up to your room, the one you used to have? The bed's all ready. Make yourself at home, like you used to.'

'Is the bike still here, the one I used to ride to the estuary? I'd like to go there.'

She nodded and smiled, 'Yes, it's still here.'

I spontaneously crossed the room and hugged her. 'If it's alright with you, I'll go for a walk first?'

'Of course. Do whatever you want, I'll see you later. I want to hear what you're up to.'

'You will. I'm glad I came, we can catch up later.'

I went back to the hall, picked up my bag and carried it up the stairs. The house was just the same; painted in bright colours, untidy, interesting, stuffed with quirky objects, the walls covered with strange images and photographs. The ostrich with the human face had been moved from the kitchen and now stood on a half-landing at the top of the stairs. It had the same notice, 'This is not an ostrich'. I stood looking at it, wondered who'd made the Leda sculpture in the orchard. It wasn't the type of thing Philomena would make.

212

The bedroom was the same as I remembered it; walls painted white, bare floorboards covered with a brown Kelim rug, and standing against one wall the same old pine chest of drawers. A patchwork bedspread made of old pieces of fabric covered the double-sized iron bed; it creaked as I sat down on it, but it was comfortable, I knew that.

I sat for a minute thinking about what Philomena had told me. It was sad she and Gareth had separated but she seemed philosophical about it. It wasn't the same without him. I was curious about Ceri, what she looked like and whether he'd bring her. The house felt empty. The atmosphere had changed. I lay down and fell asleep straightaway and when I woke it was dark and too late to go for a walk.

I jumped up, put on the light, drew the curtains and unpacked my bag. Philomena must have come in while I was asleep because a purple glass vase filled with evergreens had been placed on top of the pine chest of drawers. It hadn't been there before. She'd also put water out for me. Just as I was about to go downstairs I heard a car draw up on the gravel outside. I stood hesitantly at the top of the stairs waiting to see who it was. Whoever it was came straight in.

It was Gareth. I recognised his deep voice immediately and for a moment I felt panicky. It was eight years since I'd met him and whenever he'd contacted me, I hadn't responded. But I felt mean after what Philomena had told me. I owed him an apology. I decided to brazen it out and act as if I'd forgotten all about it.

Even so, I wanted to look attractive for him, even though I felt critical of myself thinking in this way. I'd brought a change of clothes so I took off my jeans and put on a simple black dress I'd packed. It wasn't tight but straight and elegant with a scooped neckline. It was one of my few 'bought as new' dresses and I wore it with the artdeco necklace Maddy had given me, a silver bracelet, black tights and high heels. I studied myself in the mirror, blocking the endless self-criticism – the voice of my mother – and then descended the stairs to the kitchen.

Gareth and Philomena were sitting round the large kitchen table drinking wine and talking, when I walked into the room. I couldn't have wished for a better entrance. They stopped talking. Gareth eyes widened. He got up, walked towards me, 'Anya, you've... I don't quite know what to say.' He continued staring.

Philomena said, 'Well I do. Anya, would you like a glass of wine?'

'Please.'

'Red or white? You look stunning by the way. Very elegant.'

'Red, please, Philomena.' I smiled. 'I try.'

Gareth didn't say anything. I wondered if I looked over the top and it flashed through my mind how I used to feel intimidated when I saw Chloe. I'd admired her style and it was strange she now lived in the mountains, but I had a role to play now, that of the urban sophisticate.

'It's good to see you, Gareth. I must apologise for my lack of communication. I've been really busy, with one thing and another.' I didn't stop for a response but ploughed straight on. 'I hear you're well established now as a poet. I'm pleased for you, really pleased. Philomena also tells me you have a daughter and live up in the mountains with Chloe. Of course, I'm sorry you two split up, but happy for you and Chloe.' I paused before saying, 'Tell me about Ceri. I do hope I'll meet her sometime. If not this visit, another time.' I looked directly into his eyes.

Philomena handed me a drink. I sat down opposite them both. He hadn't said a word. I smiled encouragingly at him. He was sitting with his head resting on one hand studying me and the gesture reminded me of how he'd looked in that hotel room. It was the same. I felt a little apprehensive. I dropped my gaze.

'You've changed, Anya. What's happened to the child I knew? There's a hard edge to you.'

It wasn't what I wanted to hear.

Philomena said, 'Shut up, Gareth. That's no way to talk to a guest.'

'Anya and I used always to speak the truth to each other. It was something I liked about her. Her honesty.' He paused. 'Where's that gone? Have you changed so much?'

He was looking at me so intensely, I felt uncomfortable. I put my drink down, crossed my arms and sighed. I decided to play it straight without giving too much away. 'You're right, Gareth. I've grown up. I have changed and maybe I am a little harder, but I'm still the same underneath. I still feel. I still care and I'm sorry I lost touch with you.'

I was beginning to feel upset and he must have picked up on that.

'That's alright, Anya, don't think twice, it's alright.' He smiled.

'I love that song. Bob Dylan, isn't it?'

'You know it?'

'Of course. My mother used to play it. Do you have a photo of Ceri?'

He gave me a look. I said, 'I mean it. I want to see a photo.'

He took out his wallet, pulled out a photo and handed it across to me. She was pretty with long dark hair, sitting on a field gate and smiling. She had the innocence of a child with none of Gareth's intensity. She looked more like Chloe, but I made no reference to that. I was thinking of Philomena and how hard it was for her. 'She looks a happy child, and she's pretty. I'd like to meet her.'

'Yes, I'm very proud of her.'

I gave the photo back and said, 'And how is Chloe?'

'Well. She's happy. She loves her work and looking after Ceri. What about you?'

'I love my work too. I'm in the fashion industry, recycling clothes.' They waited for me to say I was happy, but I couldn't.

There was an awkward silence. Philomena stood up and pushed her chair back noisily. 'I'll make some food. Why don't you two go in the lounge and catch up?'

Gareth said, 'Much as I'd like that, I have to go back. I was passing by and hadn't expected to see you, Anya. Chloe and Ceri will be waiting for me.'

'You didn't know I was here?'

'No. Not until Philomena told me. I must go. We've got visitors. How long are you here?'

'Till Monday.'

'Not long then. I'll tell you what. I'll come tomorrow and maybe we can go to the estuary. You always loved the estuary. I'll take you.' He stood up.

'Thanks, Gareth. I had planned to cycle there, assuming the weather's okay. That would be my preference.'

'Then when?'

He was looking down at me with those intense blue eyes. I felt uncomfortable again but I wanted to see him; talking to him in Philomena's presence was difficult. 'I could meet you there. How about that?'

'That's good. In the new car park at the edge of the woods. Philomena will tell you where it is. Twelve?'

I smiled, stood up and put my hand out to him. 'Twelve it is.' For a split second he looked puzzled and then he shook my hand. He held it for a second longer than was necessary, but maybe that was my imagination.

Philomena stood watching. She said, 'Gareth's right. You have changed, but whether you're hard edged, I'm not sure. But I'll say this, you're certainly wary, if you don't mind my saying.'

There was a long silence. Gareth didn't respond to her comment and neither did I. Then he smiled and said, 'I'm going. See you tomorrow.'

I said, 'I look forward to that.'

It was late when I woke the next morning. I pulled back the curtains. It had rained through the night, the sky was heavy with dark clouds, the garden holding its breath for the next downpour. I decided to go down for breakfast before I got dressed. I could hear Philomena in the kitchen. She was listening to classical music but switched it off when I opened the door. She'd always welcomed me as a child and she hadn't changed. She asked if I'd slept well and what I'd like for break-fast. She said Gareth had rung and as it was raining, he'd pick me up and drive me to the estuary. I thanked her, said that both of them were kind and sat down to drink my coffee.

I'd never been an early morning talker so I was happy to listen to her. It gave me a chance to wake up. She told me about the Leda sculpture and the artist who'd made it. A man, of course. I said I didn't like it. She agreed it was disturbing and laughed as she said this. I don't know why she thought it funny but I couldn't be bothered to ask.

I was still eating my toast when Gareth arrived. He walked in as if he still lived there, made a coffee for himself, sat down at the table and asked if I was on for the estuary. I said I wanted more time to get ready so they continued chatting but what they said floated past; I was half-awake, in my own world.

I finished my breakfast, returned to my room and stared vacantly at my clothes. I didn't know what to wear. I hadn't really packed for the country, so I threw on a retro black wiggle skirt, boots, and a dull pink-and-beige Fair Isle knitted sweater bought from a North London boutique. It was new but vintage looking. At the last minute I grabbed my Anya bag-for reassurance.

An hour later I was sitting in Gareth's car and we were driving towards the estuary and I was wondering if it would ever stop raining. On and on it went. 'Do you know?' I said, 'When I used to come here, it never rained.'

'Yes, like my childhood, the sun was always out.' He flashed a smile at me.

We reached the new car park. The rain had stopped, and I was thinking I wasn't sure whether I wanted him with me walking through the woods, when he asked, 'Would you prefer to be on your own?'

'I don't mind, Gareth, if you want to stay, that's okay or if you want to go, that's okay too.' He came.

I picked out the path I took when I used to meet Ifan. Gareth followed behind until we reached what had been Ifan's den. It was so overgrown it was impossible to see the entrance and I only recognised it because of the tree standing outside the entrance. It was still there, standing like a sentinel. I'd always liked that tree and I stood looking at it. It seemed magical but maybe that's because it reminded me of childhood.

I said, 'Do you remember me telling you about Ifan? The boy I'd been with when I nearly drowned on the river? The one you and the others thought I was making up?' I didn't wait for an answer. 'Well, this was his den. It's overgrown now but it wasn't then. This is where we used to meet.'

I glanced at him but I couldn't tell what he was thinking. He smiled and said, 'Well to be fair, I never knew if he was real or not. Tell me about him.'

I said, 'When we get back to the car, I will, but I'd like to go to the river first. I want to see it.'

Neither of us spoke. We reached the river. It was strange, like a disconnect between then and now. I felt Ifan was there, not the Ifan I'd met in London but the Ifan of my childhood. The one who had made me laugh and had ideas and had listened to me. The one who'd loved me but that was before I'd lost him. I wondered if he'd got the Etta James song and whether he knew it came from me. It all seemed crazy now.

Then I thought of JF. I was still out to get him and I still had to organise hacking into his computer. I'd do it as soon as I got back. That cheered me up and I began humming 'Every Breath You Take'. We stood looking at the river. The tide was coming in. It was in full flood and its force and power was the same as I remembered it the day Ifan and I tried to cross it on the pontoon.

I turned to Gareth and said, 'We must have been mad.'

He looked at me, but intuitively he knew what I meant because he said, 'Just children – innocently playing.'

'Not really,' I said. In that moment I was undressing for Ifan. I remembered the desire in his eyes and how he'd kissed me. I remembered my own desire. 'Not so innocent,' I added and as I said that, I caught Gareth's glance. 'Let's go back,' I said, 'before it rains.'

It was raining heavily by the time we got back to the car. I threw the waterproof jacket Philomena had lent me on the back seat and for a while we listened to the downpour and watched rain drops race down the windows. Gareth didn't drive off straightaway and seemed to want to talk.

He said, 'I'm glad you came to visit. I've missed you, you know. Why did you leave it so long?'

I didn't answer that, but instead said, 'I wanted to come because of the summers we spent with you and Philomena, but as well as that, because...' I stopped. I didn't want to say any more.

'Because?'

'Ifan. That's really why I came. To remember him, as we were. I wish I could go back to how it was.'

'Why don't you tell me about him?'

'I'll only tell you if you believe me, and before, you never did.'

'Try me,' he said, 'but don't you remember, you mentioned him before. It was the night in the hotel, when I upset you. You told me Ifan was the only one who understood you and loved you. I knew then he was real.' He was looking straight ahead.

I said, 'Don't remind me of that. I'm sorry.'

'For what?'

'My behaviour.'

'Think nothing of it. It doesn't matter. Not any more.' He turned to smile at me. 'So Ifan. Where is he now?'

'No idea. Probably in bed with his girlfriend.'

'You're no longer friends? But it seems like you miss him.'

'What do you think? Do you still read John Donne?'

'Yes. I do. He's an important poet. Why do you ask?'

'You introduced me to him, indirectly, because reading your poetry books put me on to him. I like him, how he writes.' I paused and then said, 'That's the only way I know about sex, because I still haven't been to bed with anyone, not properly.'

Weirdly, in that moment I'd pushed the horrific rape out of my mind. I just wasn't conscious of it. But I was of him. He was so close to me that I could smell him and see the rough pebbly texture of his tweed jacket. I glanced at him sideways on. He turned and looked at me. 'Why are you telling me this, Anya?'

'Don't use my name. It's better not to. I'm dangerous, you see.'

He laughed. 'I don't think so.' I didn't like that. His laughing at me. I stared ahead through the windscreen. A mood was coming over me. I looked at him coldly.

'You'll see. The spirit of Anya. I've just called her up. She tells me what to do. I'm not joking. She's over there.' I gestured towards my bag lying on the back seat.

'And what is she telling you to do?' He was teasing me.

I glanced at his mouth. A nice mouth. I liked it.

'This is what she's telling me to do.'

He wasn't quick enough. I leant over, put one hand behind his head, pulled his face towards mine and kissed him. It was a lingering, open-mouth kiss. It was the way Ifan had kissed me and I made sure it lasted a long time and I didn't stop until I was ready. Eventually I pulled back. I looked at him with a slight smile because he could have stopped me, but he hadn't. He stared at me. Perhaps he was shocked, but I was about to play games with him. The first time I'd failed. This time I wouldn't. I'd entered another zone of being. One where I wasn't myself. Kissing him had turned me on.

'You shouldn't have asked. She'd told me not to wear underwear. So...no pants...no bra. I left them off. Does that excite you? It does me. I'm old enough now and I still want you. Right now. Here in the car while it rains, in the middle of the forest, just the two of us. What do you think? Shall we make love or shall we have sex? It doesn't matter to me. Not really. Either is okay. You know much more than me. Show me what to do, pretend you're John Donne. What do you think, Gareth?'

I half-expected him to jump out the car and escape like when he'd locked himself in the bathroom in the hotel, but he didn't. He said nothing and did nothing, but when I pulled up my sweater and pulled it away to expose my breasts, for several seconds he couldn't take his eyes off them.

I leant across to him. I felt as if I was possessed. I'd become like a witch. I wanted to seduce him and I wasn't even drunk. I said, 'You seem shocked. Why don't you touch me? You want to, don't you?'

I took one of his hands and brought it to my breast. He seemed in a trance but he didn't remove his hand. He began caressing me. I'd won. I closed my eyes and gave myself up to the sensation but just as I thought he was losing himself, he stopped. I opened my eyes, stared at him. He'd turned away and was peering through the window. The windows had steamed up and he'd cleared a space so he could see out. I was angry. Monumentally angry, when I saw that.

'You're a disappointment. I don't want you to stop. Why stop? It was getting good.' I sounded petulant.

He turned to face me. His eyes were narrow. His body tense. 'Maybe you don't want it to stop, but I do. It's madness, and I'll say why and this time you won't cry, you'll listen. You're beautiful, you're young, you're desirable, and any man in his right mind would want to make love to you and if I knew you in some other circumstance I might do exactly what you want, make love to you. But you know I don't see Anya. I see Echo. I don't know who Anya is but I do know Echo and she's still growing up and she needs protecting from herself. Understand this, because I'm not going to repeat it. I don't have sex with children and you're a child.'

I felt a flame of anger rage through me. He'd rejected me.

And for the second time. Without thinking, I pulled off my jumper, flung it at him, hitting him in the face, yanked open the car door and ran into the woods. It was raining and cold.

When I was out of sight of the car, I stopped and stood half-naked under a tree. I hadn't gone far but I knew he'd come looking for me. I shivered. I didn't have to wait long. He knew where I was but as he strode towards me, I ran off. He could outrun me and when he caught up, he flung his jacket round my shoulders. He didn't say a word, but pulled me roughly by one arm, dragging me towards the car. Then he pushed me into the front seat and got in. He locked the car from the inside. I tried getting out but I couldn't. I was trapped. He was breathing heavily.

'You've locked me in,' I said.

'Yes, I've put the childproof locks on.' He looked straight at me. I pushed against him violently but he sat stolidly, glaring at me. 'Just pack it in Anya. I've had enough.'

We sat there, neither saying anything for what seemed hours.

Then I said, 'Bastard. You hurt me. Didn't you like my breasts? Is that why you covered me?'

'Put your top on.'

'No.' I pulled my skirt up.

He shouted, 'Put your top on and pull your skirt down.'

He switched the engine on, but I knew he wouldn't drive off with a half-naked woman next to him. Besides if he did, I had other ideas and my thinking by now was well out of order. I didn't move. I was possessed.

'Make me... Why don't you put it on. You've had plenty of practice dressing and undressing other women.'

'I stay here until you make yourself decent.'

I twisted round in my seat and was about to hit him, but he caught hold of my wrists and said, 'No, you don't. Now put your top on.'

'Why? You want me. I know you do.'

That got through. His eyes burnt through me. 'Listen,

Echo, stop playing games with me. Right now I hate you and if I never saw you again, nothing would give me greater pleasure. You're behaving like a whore. Do I make myself clear? Do you hear me? Shall I repeat myself?'

I'd seen Gareth angry before but I never thought he would say something like that, let alone to me. I became silent. I looked away and whispered, 'Okay.' In that moment I saw myself through his eyes. I was shocked. I returned to my senses. I turned and looked at my bag. Nothing. It was a bag lying on the back seat. I glanced again at Gareth. He was watching my every move but he didn't say a word. I pulled my jumper back on, pulled my skirt down and stared through the windscreen.

'I don't know what got into me.'

He just looked at me, turned the key in the ignition, pulled off the handbrake and the car slowly moved off. 'I'm going back.'

'I don't want to go back yet. Please, Gareth. I'm not ready. Give me a few minutes.'

He switched the engine off but continued looking straight ahead.

'I'm sorry. I feel ashamed. Please don't tell Philomena.'

'What gets into you?'

'Anya, the spirit of Anya, she takes me over.'

'Crap. Don't talk crap. And grow up. It's no one's spirit other than your own. Anya is you.' He turned and looked at me. 'Why are you so angry? Why do you hate me so much?'

'What are you talking about? I don't hate you. I want you.'

He looked at me, shook his head, 'Never, not if you were the last woman left on this planet.'

'You said I was a child just now.'

'Yes. You are.' He paused. 'I used to think I knew you when you were younger, then there was the hotel incident, and now this. I don't know you anymore and what I see, I don't like. There's a hardness in you. I don't find it attractive.'

I didn't answer for a long time. I sat and thought about

what he'd just said before I spoke. 'Maybe there is, but so what? Maybe I need to be hard to protect myself.'

'You weren't protecting yourself. You were attacking me. Why?'

'To pay you back.'

'For what? I haven't hurt you. You know that.'

'For being a man. For being like the others. For abandoning me when I did nothing. For victimising me. You're right... I do hate you.'

Gareth was silent. He seemed deep in thought, then he turned towards me. 'Now I understand. It's not me you hate, but who I represent.'

'Represent? What the fuck are you talking about? Go back to Chloe and Ceri. They need you.'

'And what about you, Echo? Who do you need?'

'Nobody. I need nobody. I'll get along.'

'I don't believe you. You're full of bravado, but it's bullshit, the bravado of a defiant child.'

'You won't tell Philomena, will you?'

He didn't answer, so I repeated it, 'You won't tell her, will you?'

He switched the engine back on and reversed. I caught the look in his eyes as he turned his head to manoeuvre the car. We bumped slowly along the track back on to the road and then he turned the car towards Ffridd. We'd gone about a mile before he stopped the car and turned off the road into a farm gate.

'Where are you taking me? Why are you stopping? What are you going to do?'

'Nothing. What do you think I'm going to do? We're going back to the farmhouse. Just tell me, Echo, what's happened to you?'

'Why should you care?'

He sighed. 'I've known you since you were nine years old. I liked you, I took to you. I used to think if ever I had a daughter, I want her to be like you. I admired your quirkiness, your spirit, your feistiness. You still have those qualities, but they've become distorted. You use them to attack and I want to know why.'

For ten minutes I said nothing. I was weighing up whether to tell him about JF. Gareth was silent, leaning back in his seat with closed eyes.

'Don't fall asleep,' I said.

He opened his eyes and for a moment and I saw a hint of amusement. 'I'm not,' he said.

'What's Ceri like? Is she like me?'

'No, she's not like you.'

'Do you love her?'

'Yes, of course.'

'There's no "of course" about it. Not everyone is loved by their parents.'

He didn't answer, but gave me a look before closing his eyes again.

'How is she not like me?'

'She's uncomplicated.'

That shut me up but not for long. 'Maybe I was once but that was when I was young. I'll get my own back.' He opened his eyes then and was looking straight at me. I continued, 'I'm not telling you how. Wouldn't be fair but there is someone and I'm going to terrorise him. What he did to me, he could do to others. If he hasn't already. Revenge. That's what I want.'

'Are you talking about Ifan?'

'Ifan? No, not Ifan. I still love Ifan. I messed that up.' I looked out of the window to avoid his gaze. 'And it looks like I'm about to mess up my friendship with you and I don't want that. Not you. I'm sorry.' I opened the car door and began to get out.

'Where are you off to?'

'I'm going to walk back. I need to be on my own.'

He leaned across and pulled the door shut. His face was so close to mine I felt that familiar feeling of panic but he didn't touch me. 'No, you're not. You're staying. I want you with me. You don't need to run. You want to get even. I don't know why, unless you want to tell me, but I care about you, Echo, and I'm not going to let you walk out on me.' I stared at him in surprise. 'Does that surprise you?'

'After all I've done?'

'Yes, after all you've done, which is nothing actually.'

'I want you to kiss me.'

He turned his face away, then said, 'No. Stop it, for Christ's sake. It doesn't work.'

I glared at him.

'You must resolve what's gone wrong between you and Ifan. It wouldn't work. I don't see you like that. I don't feel that way about you. Your heart is lost to Ifan. I can see that. I'm not Ifan and I'm not who you think I am, and who you think you want. I'm driving you back.'

'You won't tell Philomena, will you?'

'Why do you keep asking me that? Why's it so important?'

'Because she'll hate me if she knows the real me.'

'Listen, Echo, we love you the way you are. Why should I tell her?'

'Love, how can you love me? And how can she love me?'

Gareth turned to look at me and then he said, 'I'll tell you something. Philomena and I have never had a child but when you started coming with your mother we looked forward to the summers because when you were there, it didn't matter so much.'

I was silent at first. 'You have Ceri now. But I don't know what to say.'

He smiled and said, 'Yes, Ceri, and if you don't know what to say, say nothing, and keep it like that. Try it for five minutes.'

Neither of us spoke again until we arrived back at the farm.

Part Seven

What happened in the estuary with Gareth affected me deeply. I felt ashamed. Yet I had a sense of someone caring about me, of being accepted, and that was new. Just as I was leaving for the station and about to step into the cab, Philomena stopped me. 'Don't leave it so long next time,' she said.

'Maybe next time I could come in the spring and meet Ceri and Chloe,' I said, although I knew as I said that I'd still have to deal with my, by now, familiar feelings of jealousy.

I did think about what Gareth had said, that I should resolve my feelings about Ifan. I wanted to, but I didn't know how. It required an input from Ifan and so far, it wasn't forthcoming.

I arrived back in London, switched on my computer, there was a new song – Etta James singing 'Body and Soul'. I played it over and over. I loved that song, especially the lines 'my heart is sad and lonely'. I'd never been particularly romantic but as time passed, I was becoming more so. I realised I was in love with Ifan, but I was apprehensive. We couldn't go on like this, communicating through the computer, exciting though it was. At some point we had to meet up and as Gareth said, sort out what was going on between us. But I wasn't ready to contact him. I feared being rejected.

Gareth's observation that I'd become harder made sense and from his point of view, he was right, although I saw it as becoming tougher. I'd lost my innocence, but what hadn't changed were my feelings of revenge towards JF. I was as determined as ever to punish him; he had to know how I felt when he raped me.

It was a week later and I opened up YouTube and listened to 'Every Breath You Take'. It could have been written for me, the words were almost perfect, not all of them but enough to frighten him. The song had a possessive menace. JF had had my body without my consent or participation and without love; now I was about to have him, albeit in a different way. I was going to screw him, not just for my own revenge but for all women who'd been hurt, tricked, used and abused by men. My way was the slow burn approach but such was his arrogance, it would take a while before he understood he couldn't do what he liked, and not everyone admired him.

I wanted to make sure his computer was infected. I knew he'd be working in Hackney that night and that probably he'd open his computer after his day's work. His last client would leave at eight.

I looked out of the window. It was dark, nearly six. I had just over an hour to get there. I remembered his white Apple Mac lay on a table just under the window. Sometimes he pulled down the blinds, sometimes he left them. I had to see his reaction. I wanted to see the fear in his eyes. I'd be watching him, every breath he took, and every vow he broke.

This was to be special so I prepared meticulously. I had to wear something dark so I could dissolve into the shadows. I pulled on black jeans, a black parka and pushed my hair under a black beret. I came across a mask in a box, one I'd forgotten about. I'd used it once at Halloween when I was a student. It was red, made of rubber, and was a realistic copy of the terrorised and tortured face in Munch's *The Scream*. I pulled it over my face and looked in the mirror. It was grotesque. Nice one. I put my Anya bag and my perfume Coco Mademoiselle in my backpack.

I paused. There was something else I had to have with me. It was a poem, written by Anne Sexton and called 'Her

Kind'. It was about a crazy woman, but she's powerful in her craziness because she's indifferent to convention. I liked that poem and I'd kept it tucked inside the cover of a book of modern women poetry. I retrieved it, sat down and read it over and over until I felt at one with the character. Anya and Anne Sexton's poem; they were my sources of female inspiration.

Then I left. I caught the bus and got off at Hackney Downs. No one looked at me. Wearing black is almost a uniform in certain parts of London so I easily merged into the shadows of the night. I was about to become an unknown force, unsettling, unpredictable, malign, otherworldly.

As I walked towards JF's flat I recited some lines of the poem to myself. 'I have gone out, a possessed witch, haunting the black air, braver at night, dreaming evil, I have done my hitch, a woman like that is not a woman, quite.' I felt crazy, but as I got nearer his flat another thought came to me which was so funny, so bizarre, I laughed out loud. The poem, I realised, was my version of a 'Hakka,' the war cry of the Maoris, a ritual chant designed to instil fear and trembling in the enemy. I was 'going equipped' as the police say, not with the tools of 'breaking and entering' but with a poem. It was like a 'Hakka'; and symbolic of the power of women who defy convention in seeking revenge.

I crossed over Hackney Downs. There were few people about. It's not so smart to walk over the Downs at night, but I felt invincible. I arrived at JF's street and walked slowly along, casually looking into the flats. Most of them had the curtains drawn or the blinds pulled down. Hackney isn't the type of area where you advertise your possessions to passersby, but JF seemed not to know that. His blinds were up. An invitation.

I positioned myself on the other side of the road. It was almost eight and the end of the day for him. I watched as a young woman came up the steps from her session. She was crying and in a rush to get away, half-running and half-walking, but this wasn't the time to offer help. I had an intervention to complete.

I waited for ten minutes and then I closed in on him. I could see JF sitting at his desk under the window. His hand was on the touchpad of his computer and he was looking intently at the screen. I had to be fast. I stood on the pavement in the shadows, pulled on my mask, then keeping to the wall, slithered down the steps. I reached basement level. I stood watching him. He was oblivious to my presence and to the security light which snapped on.

I tapped lightly on the window. He glanced up. I pressed my contorted rubber face against the glass, dragging my hands down it, as if I were clawing my way in. I stayed like that, a visible nightmare, long enough to have maximum impact. I was silhouetted from behind by the security light. I must have looked demented, but that was my intention.

I'll never forget the terror in his eyes. I didn't know if he'd heard 'Every Breath You Take', but it didn't matter. He stood up, saw me through the window and backed away. He almost fell over his chair. I would have laughed but the rigidity of the mask prevented that. He stood staring. I saw his hand move towards his mobile. Time to go. As I left, I sprayed his door with Coco Mademoiselle, my symbol of universal femininity, then I ran back up the steps, crossed the street over to the Downs, tore off my mask, pulled off my beret and slowed down to a steady walk.

A success, a massive success. I was so high on adrenaline I felt capable of anything. I looked round, over my shoulder, to make sure I wasn't being followed. A cyclist was coming slowly towards me, heading in my direction. I stepped sideways off the path to let him pass and avoiding eye contact, continued walking.

'Anya.'

I knew that voice. I stopped. Looked round. Ifan was standing astride his bike. He looked serious. I don't know why I wasn't surprised.

He said, 'What are you playing at?'

'Getting my own back, what else would I be doing? What are you doing cycling round in the dark?'

We stood looking at each other. It was over a year since we'd seen each other. Gareth had said to sort it out. I was in the mood and high with my success. Anything was possible. Now was the time.

'I've been watching you.'

When he said that, I laughed.

'What's funny?'

'Watching me, watching him. "Every breath you take, every move you make, I'll be watching you".' He didn't answer. 'I was at the farmhouse last weekend. I saw Gareth and Philomena, and I went to the estuary.' He hadn't said a word. 'You know your den? It's grown over now. I went to the river as well.'

I took a step nearer to him and looked at him straight. 'But is it true? Or is it somebody else?'

'What are you talking about? Somebody else? You're weird. Echo.'

I ignored that. 'Your heart. Is it "sad and lonely"? I know it's you. So don't deny it.'

'If that's what the song said.'

'Yes, but is that what you say?' He still didn't answer, so I said, 'You seem to be struck dumb.'

'I'm trying to get my head round what I just saw.'

'How much did you see?'

'Enough. You were wearing a mask. What's got into you?'

'Anger, revenge. I want to frighten him.'

'You're frightening me.'

'I don't think so. You know me too well.'

'Not as well as I thought I did, but well enough.' He was still standing astride his bike. He put his bike on the ground and moved towards me. He took hold of my hand but I pulled it away. We stood silently looking at each other. He said, 'Anya, I've missed you. I'm sorry for what I said.'

I looked at the ground, my head full of the images of the

night we quarrelled. 'You said some cruel things to me, Ifan. You hurt me.'

He was silent, then he said, 'I know. I'm truly sorry. Can we forget it? I've thought about it often. I still have strong feelings for you. Will you let me make it up to you?'

'How?'

'Well, for a start, a coffee – or a drink.'

'Right now? You still want to, after what you've just seen?'

He paused, then he said, 'I like you.'

I glanced at him shyly, thinking only like? But I said, 'Well, I've got nothing to lose, I suppose.'

He grinned. 'Good. A lift?' He gestured with his head towards his bike.

I wasn't sure what he meant so I said, 'Do you mean on your bike?'

'Yeah, on my bike.'

He picked up his bike, sat back on the saddle and patted the crossbar. 'Come on, Ms Anya, aka Echo, get on, like you used to.'

I laughed, 'Okay. On your cross bar? You won't let me fall off?'

'No way. Be my guest. Sideways, you have to sit sideways and hold on to the handlebars, like you used to and I won't let you go.'

I got on, sat sideways, but I held on to him, not the handlebars, and we wobbled across the Downs until I fell off laughing.

We picked up as if we'd never quarrelled. I told him why I was stalking and about the rape. Not everything but enough. He was so shocked he didn't speak. I asked him what he was thinking, but he just shook his head. He wouldn't or couldn't say. He asked why I didn't go to the police and I explained to him if I had, I'd have been called a fantasist and JF would have wheedled himself out of it. That's why I was stalking him, to get my own back.

'Is there anything I can do?' he asked.

What he'd just said, about making up, was an opportunity not to be missed. 'Were you thinking about something in particular?' I asked.

He wasn't, but his offer made me think. I'd already decided to increase the pressure on JF and Ifan's willingness to help had given me another idea. It was risky and it required someone with technical skills. Like him.

'Ifan... I can think of something. I want to break into his Wigmore Street office. It'll be hard. It'll have to be at night and I need someone who can disable the security light and pick locks.'

'Why do you want to do that? It's illegal.'

'I know it's illegal, but I have to up the ante. Shake him up. Make him think he isn't safe anywhere. Break into his mind, like he did with my body.'

He looked at me thoughtfully, 'But when's it going to stop?'

'No idea. I shall have to assess that later. Right now, I need your techie know-how.'

He wasn't too willing. 'Picking locks wasn't part of the curriculum.'

My answer was fast. 'And neither was hacking into my computer, but you did that.'

He laughed. 'It's a way of getting your attention, and I knew you'd know it was me. You liked "At Last", didn't you? Remember?' He looked me straight in the eye.

'As if, of course I remember.' I was giving nothing away. 'So, will you help?'

He paused, shook his head as if he didn't agree, then he said, 'Okay, but there's a condition. It has to stop and soon, because the police are gonna catch up with you.'

I knew he was right. 'Thanks,' I said, 'for agreeing to help.'

'Promise?'

'Yes. I've said.'

'I've got to go now. Here's my landline and mobile number.'

I didn't ask why or where he had to go, but as he cycled off, he said over his shoulder, '*Ti yw fy nghariad ers erioed ac mi fyddi'n gariad i mi am byth.*'

I shouted after him, 'You still speak Welsh then. What's it mean?'

He stopped, blew me a kiss and said, 'I'll tell you one day.'

I couldn't sleep that night. Terrorising JF was a major buzz, but meeting Ifan was even better. I was well and truly smitten. It was spooky the way he'd hacked into my computer, but it amused me. I thought more about what Gareth had said, that I needed to sort out what was going on, because it was like we couldn't get it together but neither could we separate.

The following week I rang him. A female voice answered. 'Hellooo.' She sounded ultra friendly. That put me off and for a moment I floundered. 'Oh, I must have the wrong number,' I said.

'Who is it you want?'

'Ifan Baranov.'

'He's here. Just a moment. I'll call him.' I could hear her calling him and then she came back to the phone. 'He's in the shower. Who is it? He'll call you back.'

'Anya Morgan.'

It was clear she knew who I was. 'Hi, Anya, yeah, he'll be another fifteen minutes. He'll ring you.'

Oh, will he? I thought, no he won't. My response was immediate. The thought he was now living with the woman I saw in the waiting room really screwed me up. I got angry, and it put me in a bad mood all day. I tortured myself imagining him talking to her, dancing with her, making love to her, so I blocked him. I switched off my personal mobile and made sure I wasn't accessible by using my work phone. I didn't want to talk to him, ever. End of story. But predictably none of it worked. I just couldn't get him out of my head.

Eventually I told Maddy. We arranged to meet and within five minutes of speaking I was in floods of tears.

'Anya,' she said, 'how do you know she's his girlfriend? She might be a flatmate.'

I stared at her in disbelief. 'I never thought of that.'

Maddy smiled. 'Well, I'm telling you. You need to check out stuff before going into distraught mode, and giving up on him.'

'God, you're so Mrs Sensible, I don't know how you do it.'

I looked at her, wondering whether to tell her about my stalking because she still didn't know, but I decided not to; she wouldn't approve and it would put her in an awkward position.

I got home, and as usual looked at my computer first thing. There was a new piece of music and it wasn't an Etta number but Chopin's 'Nocturne'. I sat listening to it over and over. It was unbearably sad and it made me think about when we'd first met and how we'd played together and how after the incident on the river he'd disappeared. Our friendship seemed never to have recovered from that. Life was too complicated and I wasn't up to it. By the morning I was totally exhausted but I'd reached a kind of resolution. If Ifan was living with someone else, then so be it, but he had offered to help and I needed him, if only for that.

I dragged myself to work. Fortunately it was a day when I didn't have to be at my best so I spent it looking at fabric designs from Sweden and became so absorbed for several hours I forgot about Ifan. Eventually, I opened my phone. There was a long list of texts and missed calls from him asking me to contact him. I rang him.

'I like the Chopin.'

'Where have you been?'

'Busy. Work.'

'Too busy to contact me?'

'Sorry. Thought you might be otherwise engaged.'

'When shall we meet?'

I wanted to see him there and then but I couldn't say that. 'Tomorrow evening?'

'Fine, the pub down Holloway. At eight?'

'Look forward to it.' Then I said, 'Have you moved?'

'Yeah, nearer to Clissold Park now. Why you asking?'

'Just wondered.' I didn't want to ask who the woman was, the one who'd picked up the phone. He didn't answer, which raised my suspicions but I thought I'd wait until I saw him and see the lie of the land.

We sat in the same place, everything was the same, like before. He watched me walk towards me and handed me a glass of wine. This time I sat next to him. I looked at him. I was thinking, I really, really fancy you, Ifan Baranov. Especially when you smile.

'Same again?' He smiled and looked directly in my eyes. How did he know?

'Thanks.' There was a silence until I broke it. 'Here we are again.'

'Yep, here we are again. You want help?'

'How are you?'

'Fine, that's not why you're here though, to ask about my health. You don't want me, you want something of me.'

'That's fighting talk.' I glowered at him. Within a minute, we were in fight mode.

'What's with you, Anya? I'm picking up bad vibes. What's going on?'

'Nothing. At the moment. Who's the woman who answered the phone, when I called you?'

'Aaah. Now I know. So. You do care.' He leant back, putting his arms behind his head, smiling like a Cheshire cat.

'Don't look so smug.'

'Why not, I'm pleased.'

'Don't be. You're neither here nor there to me.'

He grinned. 'Okay, we'll play it your way. So why tell you? Since you don't care, what's it to you?'

'I don't play games.'

'Nor me. How can I help?'

'Another of your conquests?'

'How can I help? Disabling security lights? Breaking and entering? For you, Anya, anything. I'm your man.' He was smirking. 'I have some uses, it seems, not the one I want, but there you go, *c'est la vie*.'

I stood up, 'Want another?' I gestured towards his empty glass with my head. 'Same again?'

He nodded. He had a look on his face, one I couldn't make out. When I came back, he was on his mobile. He put it down immediately. 'Okay, let's get down to business. I haven't been wasting my time. I can do it. Fix the lights and get in. And then what?'

'I haven't decided.'

'Well, you need to. You need to know exactly what you want to do once you're in. After all, I'm putting myself on the line for you, I might get caught and bang. The end of my career.'

'We can go together. I know the building.' He had a look that said, no. 'Don't you want me with you?'

'I think not. No.'

I stared at him. I hadn't really expected him to agree. I distracted myself by gazing round the room. The pub was filling up with local characters. The old men from the nearby estate there for the cheap booze were staring morosely into their pint; lines of casually dressed young men with loud voices blocked access to the bar; clusters of young women dressed in tight jeans and high heels screamed with laughter; and at the side, a couple of women. They were talking intently, their heads nodding in agreement with each other.

'Is this your local?'

'Yes, but you need to tell me soonish what you want, because I have to go.'

I couldn't help it. I blurted out, 'To see her, I suppose.'

'Who?'

'The one who answered your phone, when I rang your flat.' I stood up. 'I'm going.'

'Sit down. You're jealous, aren't you?' He gave me a look. 'You're pissed off with me. The girl you spoke to is a flatmate. End of story, but I still have to go.'

'A female?'

'Get off my back, Anya. You've been telling me you don't care. Do you or don't you? It might make a difference.'

'What about breaking into his office? Having a look round, seeing what we can find?'

He did a double take. 'Ah, we've changed the subject. His office? Which one?'

'The Wigmore Street one.'

'I'll think about it, and I'll let you know.' He stood up. 'Have to go, in a rush.'

'You haven't finished your drink.'

'True, I haven't, but I will.' He picked up his drink and downed it in one. 'See you soon,' he said and walked out.

He had to be going to see her. I was seething. I waited for a minute and then I left by the side door. There was a bike rack at the back of the building, I crossed over, walked a little way down the street and stood in the shadow of a tall hedge in someone's garden. I could see Ifan unlocking his bike, putting on his lights, then he made a call, got on his bike and cycled down the street towards me. I moved further into the garden waiting for him to pass.

He stopped right by me. Got off his bike and smiling, stood by the garden gate. 'You know, Anya, you'll never make MI5.'

'Maybe I wanted you to see me,' I said. I didn't believe that but I said it.

'Maybe you did. But for what?'

He leant his bike against the wall and came towards me and we stood in the shadows looking at each other. He moved even closer but just as I thought he was going to kiss me, he turned round and said he'd be late. He got back on his bike. I said, 'Aren't you going to kiss me?' That stopped him, he turned round, looked at me for a long while, or that's what it seemed. 'Maybe someday I will,' he said. 'When the time's right.'

'It is right.'

He laughed. 'Not yet it isn't.'

'So when?'

'I'll know when and so will you.'

He cycled off. I shouted after him, 'Enjoy yourself wherever you're going.' He waved and disappeared down the road. Another wasted opportunity. I should be awarded a prize for messing things up.

The next two weeks I made sure I was busy at work, meeting new clients, making appointments to see designers, but my mind was never far from thinking about Ifan. It felt like he was playing games but I didn't know the rules. The last meeting with him had annoyed me but at least we hadn't fallen out.

When I wasn't thinking about Ifan, I was thinking about JF but I was getting nervous. The more I upped the ante, the closer he'd get to cracking up, and the greater the risk he'd contact the police for help. But knowing that didn't stop me.

The following Saturday I'd been up early shopping along Oxford Street and I was on my way to meet Maddy when life presented a delicious opportunity. It was a coincidence that, if planned, would have required the skill and split-second timing of a trapeze artist. As I passed Euston Station I saw JF walking on the opposite side of the road. I was heading in the same direction and walking parallel with him. He was accompanied by a young woman and laughing at something she said. Even from where I was, I could see she was well and truly enamoured with him. She was looking up at him as if he was the most interesting man in the world.

They swung into the Quaker Meeting Rooms. Was she his latest conquest? Had he seduced her under the same guise he'd used with me, claiming to know what she wanted? A wave of repulsion passed through me. I wasn't going to miss this opportunity of harassing him, although how I didn't quite know.

I threaded my way across the Euston Road traffic and stood outside the meeting rooms. A poster announced a conference, called 'Key Concepts for Therapists and Trainees'. I ran my eye down the speakers. None of them meant anything to me with the exception of Mr Jason Fellowes. He was talking on 'The Erotic Transference'. I couldn't believe my luck. It was a moment of serendipity that only my alter-ego, Anya, could have organised. I walked into the foyer and hung around.

When the crush died down, I spoke to the woman on reception. 'I wonder if it's possible to register for the conference. I tried yesterday but the lines were always busy so I thought I'd just turn up and see if it was possible.' I smiled sweetly, 'That's of course, if there are vacancies.'

The woman had grey hair in a bun and was wearing a long, multi-coloured skirt and flat lace-up shoes. She looked over the top of her glasses at me. I seemed to be specimen number one. I looked at her hoping she wasn't into mind reading, mine in particular. Her dress sense was 'Charity Shop' minus the charity. An odd ensemble of ill-matching clothes, and looking so severe she reminded me of the therapist in Finsbury Park, the one I'd walked out on.

'Which organisation are you training with?' she asked.

I blagged it. I said the first thing that came into my head. It happened to be where JF had trained and it had jumped off the poster, the one I'd just read. 'I'm applying for the London School of Transferential Phenomena. I'm waiting to hear from them actually, you know, if I get in.'

'Yes,' she said, 'it's very popular. One of the speakers represents that organisation.' She looked down her list of names. 'If you can wait until just after the start, I'll be able to see who hasn't turned up and I'm sure I can find a place for you.' She smiled.

'That's so kind of you. I'm most grateful.' She wasn't as bad as expected. I walked away to the other side of the room and rang Maddy. I told her I was going to be very late and whispered, 'Wait till you hear this.' She wanted to know straightaway but I told her I couldn't speak right now.

'Anya Morgan.' I turned round. The woman on reception was waving a programme at me and smiling. 'Several people haven't arrived, so do go in. You can pay me later.'

I thanked her and walked into the hall. It was packed. On a raised dais behind a table was the chairperson. He was dressed in a grey suit, to give himself gravitas presumably, and in the middle of a welcoming speech. He was impressively tedious and self-congratulatory, so much so I felt like laughing. It felt as if I were back in the classroom in front of a particularly uninspired teacher, who covered their lack of talent and personality with verbal layers of pomposity.

I looked round the room for a seat and found one towards the back at the end of the line. I had no idea how I was going to use this opportunity but being able to make a quick getaway seemed a good idea. I looked down the programme for JF. He was on just after lunch and his event was billed as a 'masterclass'.

Out of curiosity I listened to the first two talks which were about the different trainings and the personal qualities necessary for becoming a therapist. I didn't find either interesting, maybe because I had no desire to become one, and for another, everyone looked intense and lacking in humour. They also dressed badly, so for an hour I amused myself by imagining them in some outfit I'd designed. At the coffee break I made a break for freedom, and checked out the book shops off Tottenham Court Road, planning to return just after lunch.

I was late and JF had started by the time I took my seat. He was on stage and in the middle of an introduction to 'transference', running through its origins, which apparently started with Freud. Even I'd heard of him. Sitting opposite and acting as his stooge was the young woman I'd seen earlier. She was very obligingly asking him leading questions which he answered unfalteringly. Well rehearsed, I thought, let's hope you get your reward in heaven and not on your back.

He moved on to present-day usage, giving several case studies, his point being that love and sexual feelings were imagined by the client and little to do with the therapist's own behaviour. It was all so perfect and all so wrong and the more I listened, the angrier I got. When he commented how seductive female clients could be, I'd had enough. I sprang out of my seat, brushing away the microphone someone passed me. I hadn't planned it, it just happened.

'Does transference justify rape?' I shouted. 'Does it justify seduction? Why do you portray the therapist as the innocent victim of a powerful client? The reverse is true.'

There was a silence. People turned their heads to look at me and then at each other, shuffling their papers with embarrassment, some looking disapproving, a few smirking.

For a moment JF looked nervous but not for long. 'I'm sorry I have no idea what you're talking about, but I'd be happy to speak to you later.'

'You know very well what I'm talking about, but this audience doesn't. Tell them the truth, Mr Fellowes. Tell them what happens in your sessions.'

The chairperson leant forward, whispering to him. Two porters appeared, took hold of my arms and bundled me outside. As I left the room, I shouted again, 'Check the web, look at "Fifty ways of getting his way", then you'll know what I'm talking about.'

JF got out of his seat, jumped off the dais, and was making his way to the exit, when I broke loose from the two porters and stood blocking his exit. I was quick. I said, 'You can run but you can't hide. I know where you are and every breath you take, every move you make, I'll be watching you.' He pushed past me. He was wild-eyed.

He was followed by a woman from the conference, who also seemed in a hurry to leave, but she came towards me and

242

stopped. 'Go for it, I couldn't agree more.' That's all she said, then she left the building.

I was so touched by her support, I was close to tears. The two porters were still standing by me, waiting for my next move. 'Don't worry, I'm going,' I said, and the lines of the poem 'Her Kind' came to me. 'A woman like that is not a woman quite, I have been her kind.' Still shaking, I left and caught the bus to Maddy.

When I told her what had happened, she thought it funny. But, she asked, had it achieved what I wanted, his public humiliation? I wasn't sure. Maybe he felt safe among his colleagues and I'd be judged as an embittered ex-client and as someone not quite right in the head. I thought more about it. I wanted something spectacular, something which would simultaneously humiliate him and catch the imagination of onlookers and I was prepared to wait until an idea came to me. I didn't have to wait long.

I returned to observing him at Wigmore Street. He'd changed his routine, probably to avoid me, and because I kept out of sight he must have assumed I was off his trail. How wrong he was. It was easy to conceal myself amongst the crowds of the West End, but also I'd borrowed a bike from a friend and now wore a cyclist's helmet and cycling gear. Armed with a street map, I'd stop opposite where he worked and pretend to study my mobile. I passed off as a ditsy tourist and since my head and face were obscured I was unrecognisable. I got to know his hours.

Wednesdays he always worked late, very late. I knew he was in the building because I could see his light, and when he left round about ten, he'd lock up, and walk towards the West End. What for? I had to know. The third week, I followed him. I left my bike locked to railings and followed on foot. He began walking towards Oxford Circus and from there made his way down the back streets until he arrived at Dean Street in Soho. It was easy keeping him in sight. He never looked over his shoulder.

Soho at night is unbelievably tacky. It's the underbelly of London, full of tourists and sad, desperate-looking men on the hunt for sex, either by themselves or in groups. It's London at its most ugly and rapacious. I guessed what was coming and I was right. His interests were in the numerous strip clubs, pole dancing clubs, and 'gentlemen's clubs'. Here he paused to look at the young women whose bright, brittle smiles did nothing to conceal their inner emptiness. Spray-tanned orange with augmented, unnatural-looking breasts and wearing badly fitting bras, they stood in doorways on display, supposedly enticing, their arms folded, vacant looking, bored, high on drugs to ease the pain of collusion with a system designed to profit from their bodies. Sad, depressed women with few choices, imported like cattle from Eastern Europe and with nowhere to go. I stayed just long enough to see him enter one of the clubs and then left. I'd seen enough and couldn't bear watching the exploitation of my own sex.

I returned home and sat thinking. JF's whole persona and attitudes towards women disgusted me and seeing what he got up to when alone, made me even more vengeful. I wanted to hit him with something dramatic, something dark, something he wouldn't forget. A plan began formulating in my mind. It took a while but by dawn I knew what I was going to do and how to do it. If he had a voyeuristic interest in women's bodies, I'd give it to him, but it would be a version he wouldn't like.

I remembered my first foray into buying underwear, when the woman in Marks told me about burlesque dancers. Since then, the idea of the burlesque fascinated me to the point I'd used some of the ideas in my designs, mainly for shock value. It was a paradox. Women selling sex in a highly stylised way, emphasising their bodies and their sexuality but without any resolution, seemed to me an ironic comment on men's lust. Meanwhile they were being sent up.

I began investigating the 'burlesque stripogram'. The agencies selling these services stress how much 'fun' they are, but like I say, the 'fun' lies with the stripper. She controls when and how to humiliate. The joke is on men.

My plan involved one of these burlesque dancers. I was about to expose JF's hypocrisy with a dash of humour. It was a little like defrocking a priest in public and the thought of it amused me no end. I employed a stripper from an agency, a stripper whose specialism was burlesque. She called herself Cherie Dear and she had the right mix of attributes; a sophisticated veneer concealing the underlying vulgarity, humour and brashness of burlesque. An out-of-work actress with a liking for comedy, she based her act on the night clubs of the thirties and forties.

It had to be carefully planned and there had to be an element of surprise. I rang Ifan, reminded him he'd offered to help and said I was ready. I asked if he'd disconnect the security light and alarm system and set up a simple sound system in the reception area.

'Okay, but what's that for?' he asked.

'Rather not say.'

'And I'd rather not do.'

'Why not?'

'On a need to know basis. Those are my terms,' he said.

I sighed. 'Okay, I plan to humiliate JF at his place of work with a burlesque stripper.'

He laughed, then said, 'Sounds good to me. Just deserts and all that. You're on, leave it to me and I'll call you when I'm ready.'

It was as easy as that. He saw it as a challenge. Two weeks later, I was watching a film on television when the phone rang.

'Anya, are you ready?'

'Ready? For what?'

'To break in. You can be my apprentice.'

He'd changed his mind about me going. I was ready. I'd been waiting for this moment. I pulled on my stalking outfit. Black jeans, black motorbike jacket, black beret. I stuffed into my backpack disposable gloves, a Swiss Army Knife, my mask, my poem, my Coco Mademoiselle and my beautiful Anya bag.

We were going separately. Ifan would cycle. I'd catch the bus. We arranged to meet near Wigmore Street. Ifan was dressed in black too, wearing a hoody which he pulled up and over his head. Like me, he carried a backpack for his gear.

It was almost midnight. There were a few people around but no one looked twice at us. We must have looked normal. Ifan had done his preparation. He'd called in earlier that week and told them he was doing a safety check on the electrics. He'd disabled the security light and the alarm system. It's amazing how trusting people can be. We looked around. The street was clear. We walked quickly up the front steps.

I'd expected Ifan to pick the locks but he didn't have to, he had a set of firemen's keys which could open any locked door. He'd acquired them, he told me, through his contacts but he had to return them within twenty-four hours. I didn't know such things existed, but they were about to be put to an illegal use. After trying several keys, one worked and we could enter the building. It was creepy. We didn't put on the lights but used large flashlights to get around. I showed him the reception room and left him setting up the sound system. That had to be concealed.

I went to JF's room. I was curious. I wanted to see what it was like without him. I tried the door. He'd locked it. I went back to Ifan, got the bunch of keys and tried each of them until I found the one that fitted. Once inside, I walked over to a large cupboard. It was unlocked and contained a new looking computer. I took it out. Opened it. There was no password. It was dead easy to look at the files and I could see he'd written about each of his clients but out of respect to their privacy, I skipped reading them.

Necessity is the mother of invention. Here was an opportunity to cause more trouble. I took it. An idea had come and it was one that made me smile. I walked back to reception and asked Ifan whether he'd seen a printer. He was fixing a cheap music player at the top of a cupboard and placing a box to the front of it.

'I think that's one.' He gestured with his head across the room. 'Why do you want one?'

'You'll see.'

I examined the printer. It was impressive with an industrial capacity to churn out a thousand copies of a document. It must have served all the computers in the building. I set it to print the maximum number of copies, removed the paper tray, and returned to JF's room. I typed out on his computer the lyrics of 'Every Breath You Take'. I clicked print, but not start. I'd wait until Ifan had finished and we were ready to leave.

I pulled out my Coco Mademoiselle from my backpack and sprayed the fragrance around the room. I knew it was a desecration of a beautiful perfume but I didn't care too much at that point. I wanted him to know it was me, that there was no let up, that I was still around, still active, still persecuting, still out to get him. For my finale, I left the crumpled mask of Munch's *The Scream* on his desk. Then I left. I locked the door behind me.

Ifan had just finished setting up the sound system when I walked into the reception. 'Try this, point it towards that cupboard, then press.' He handed me the remote control, 'Now press.' The music flooded out. I'd loaded on to a USB some tracks for the stripper. It worked but it was too quiet. He showed me how to make it louder.

We'd finished and stood looking at each other. I threw my arms around him and kissed him. It was the kiss of a friend not of a lover but enough to startle him. 'Thanks,' I said. He looked astonished. 'Let's go now.'

'One more thing.' I walked across to the printer, pressed start. Paper shot across the room. Ifan picked one up, read it, grinned.

I said, 'That's the first. Nine hundred and ninety-nine to go and every page printed with 'Every Breath You Take, Every Move You Make, I'll Be Watching You'. Just in case he hasn't got the message.'

Ifan didn't say anything, just gave me a look. We left as silently as we'd come.

A week later and I was ready to go. Speaking through the intercom, I told the receptionist I wanted to make an appointment to see Jason Fellowes. She was new and didn't know me. She buzzed me in. Once inside I hung about in the hall until just before six, then I shot up the stairs to find a seat in reception. It was busy, every chair taken with clients waiting for their therapy session. Good, I thought, the bigger the audience, the greater his humiliation.

The phone rang on the receptionist's desk. She said, 'Special delivery? Fine. Bring it up, I'll tell him and he can sign for it.'

So far, so good, it was going to plan. A couple of minutes later, three men staggered in carrying a large square box. I heard one say to the other, 'Fucking 'ell, what's in this? It'll break me bleeding back.'

No one said a word, just watched impassively as they dumped the box by the receptionist's desk. 'Need a signature from Mr Fellowes, mate.' The receptionist picked up her phone the same time as, coincidently, JF walked in. He caught sight of me, came to a halt, turned to leave. He was quick but not quick enough. He'd reached the door when the receptionist called out, 'Before you go, Jason, I need a signature for this box. It's special delivery, addressed to you.'

I watched. He hesitated, walked rapidly across to the receptionist and, with his back to me, avoiding my gaze, signed. I said in a loud clear voice, 'Mr Fellowes, can I speak to you for a moment?' It was the signal for Cherie.

He ignored me. He'd reached the door when the box burst open. She sprang into the room, rushed over to JF and in a simpering voice, asked, 'Is that you, Jason?' That stopped him, he stood open mouthed, his hand on the door knob. He didn't answer. I repressed a laugh. He looked exaggeratedly surprised, like a character from a pantomime.

I'd seen and met Cherie before and together we'd worked out her routine and her dress – if you could call it that. That evening she surpassed herself in the vulgarity stakes. She was heavily made up, her mouth a red cupid bow, her blonde hair curling round her heart-shaped face. She was wearing an electric-blue, sequined satin bra, a tight long skirt in the same colour split at the back and an assortment of feathers and balloons, some of which she contrived to burst as she sprang out. She looked like an old-fashioned movie star in a Hollywood musical.

She stood for a moment wobbling on very high heels, her arms outstretched, her gaze taking in the occupants sitting round the room. She spoke in the little voice of a child-woman, seductive yet innocent.

'I'm been looking for you, Jason. My name is Cherie Dear. I'm here to entertain you with my dance and my music.' She smiled. 'In my very own special way.' She winked at the audience. 'Enjoy.'

She had a slight lisp which I think was put on but it added to the farcical atmosphere and to make doubly sure she knew who her target was, I was to indicate with a slight hand gesture who he was. But it was obvious. It was a set-up and he knew it. He stood by the doorway twisting his hands like a frightened schoolboy about to be caned. There was no sign of his bravado, his arrogance, his confidence; all that had gone and what remained was a middle-aged, pathetic-looking man with a weak mouth.

I walked towards him and pushed him roughly in Cherie Dear's general direction. He licked his lips nervously, his eyes shooting round like a lizard, and when he caught my gaze, he tried to run back towards the door, but it was too late. Wiggling exaggeratedly, Cherie ran over to him and pulled him by the hand into the middle of the room. I, meanwhile stationed myself by the door so he couldn't get away without passing me.

'Come here, Jason. I know who you are. Don't be naughty, you mustn't run away when Cherie Dear wants to play with you. I promise I won't hurt you.' She giggled and looking at the audience. 'We won't hurt him, will we? We like games with boys, don't we? We like having fun.'

I pressed the remote for the music. It was in the burlesque style; vulgar and loud. Cherie began twirling round, gyrating her hips, clicking her fingers to the music. She grabbed his hands, trying to get him to dance, but he refused and the more he resisted, the more outrageous she became and the funnier it got. She treated him as if he was shy, and that he needed more encouragement, but that made him squirm even more. I took a quick look round the room. The audience were transfixed, most were smiling, some were embarrassed and two left the room, looking disapproving.

She was moving in on him now, enjoying herself, enjoying the attention, enjoying tormenting him. She danced around him, sinuously bending her voluptuous body, waving her long feathers in his face and around his neck. She ran her hands down her body, miming undressing herself, before she removed her skirt. With a flourish she waved it in his face and smiling and without self-consciousness, she stood dressed in nothing more than a black satin thong and a miniscule blue top which barely covered her breasts. Very little was left to the imagination. He was transfixed. Not with pleasure but terror.

She began pulling off his tie and his jacket. He stood, his eyes starting out of his head but he didn't move. He acted as if hit by a thunder bolt. She glanced towards me. I gave her an encouraging wink.

'Jason, you need some help, you must be hot darling. Look at you. The sweat's pouring off you.' She turned towards her audience. 'He needs help, doesn't he? He doesn't know what to do. Shall we help him?'

The receptionist pushed past me and didn't return. She must have thought she was employed by a madhouse. I moved away from the door so anyone could come in. The word was getting round. I'd only met Cherie Dear once before but by now I knew we were on the same mission – his humiliation.

She could do whatever she liked with him because he was paralysed with fear.

She pushed him round, stood behind him, put an ornate mask over his eyes, then, dropping her top off, she covered her breasts with feathers, and moved back in front of him. She pulled off his mask, removed the feathers from her breasts and after tickling him with the feathers round his neck and face, moved her body close to his.

I glanced around. The room was full. Where they'd all come from, I had no idea, but they didn't look as if they'd been waiting for therapy. These were office workers, professionals, men and women, they'd come off the street to watch the fun. The word was out. Some of them took photos with their mobiles, the men guffawed, one shouted, 'Go for it, Cherie.'

That gave Cherie the green light. She really began hamming it up and the more sexually suggestive she became, the more pathetic he seemed. She was a natural exhibitionist; she leant back on the receptionist's desk on her elbows, crossing and uncrossing her legs suggestively, but when he didn't respond she jumped off, ran towards him, and pressed her virtually naked body against his. He seemed incapable of protecting himself from her assertive female sexuality, faked though it was, but the best was to come.

'Won't you dance with me, Jason? Don't be shy. You and me together and don't bother about them. Forget them.' She giggled, ran around the room and whispered loud enough for us to hear, 'I have a song for Jason. It's called "Move Closer", it's one of my favourites.' That was my cue to start the music. She began singing, 'Move Closer'. I turned up the volume.

The tune and the words are highly sexual and she interpreted them in such a way as to make him look an impotent fool and a figure of fun. The audience loved it but the more he tried to resist, the more outrageous she became and the more we laughed. He refused to dance but this played right into her hands. It gave her the opportunity to move on to her finale. She stood in front of him, her hands on her hips, shaking her head, wagging her finger.

'Jason, sweetheart, I'm disappointed with you. You won't dance but I can help you. It's a song I've chosen for you. It's about a psychologist, like you. Listen carefully, then I'll let you go home, you naughty boy.'

Sweating profusely, JF was becoming smaller, meaner, more rat-like with every second and I swear to God, if he could, he would have crawled his way under the reception desk. He was well and truly trapped. She began clicking her fingers to the music, a swing jazz number with a jaunty clarinet and as she walked round the room, she smiled and giggled at each one of us.

'Now,' she said, 'I want you all to join in,' and on the down beat, she began singing 'He Ain't Got Rhythm'. It was an old Billie Holiday number from the thirties which she sang in a mock American accent. 'He's the loneliest man in town 'cos he ain't got rhythm' and as she pranced and danced all around him, she periodically turned to us and asked, 'Why is he the loneliest man in town?' and we shouted back, 'Because he ain't got rhythm.'

I had no idea how Cherie Dear had planned to finish her act, but when she began pulling his tie and shirt off, and said he looked so hot that she wanted to take off his clothes, he bolted out of the room. I ran after him. As he disappeared down the stairs towards the front door, I shouted, 'Frightened, are you? Humiliated, are you? Now you know how I feel.' He didn't look back, just slammed the front door behind him.

The party was over. I gave Cherie Dear a hug and told her I'd be in touch. She said she'd enjoyed every minute and she'd add it to her repertoire, then she flung her clothes on and raced down the stairs. We were on a high. It's true what they say, revenge is sweet. I glanced at my watch. Time to go. I was to meet Ifan. I let myself out. As I walked down the street the police arrived, closely followed by the press. Someone must have called them. I stopped to watch the fun, until Ifan appeared.

He grabbed my arm, 'For Christ sake, Anya, let's go.'

'Why should I, I haven't broken any laws.'

'Maybe not now, but what about "breaking and entering"; they'll easily put two and two together, and come up with a motive.' He put his arm round me and said, 'I insist, let's go.'

We walked quickly in the opposite direction down the street. 'Where are we heading?' I asked. 'Pizza Express,' he said, 'it's on me.'

'Why?'

'Well, why not, shouldn't we celebrate? I presume the plan worked.'

'It did, it worked really well.' I began laughing, 'You should have seen his face. I'll never forget it. That stripper, Cherie Dear, she's wonderful, the sound system was ace, everything went according to plan and, I have you to thank for that.'

'Appreciation at last, but...' He never finished his sentence.

A police car drew up beside us and two police officers jumped out. They stood in front blocking our path.

'Are you Anya Morgan?'

I looked at Ifan for support, 'Yes, why?'

'You're wanted for questioning at the station.'

'What for?'

'Get in and you'll find out.'

'What if I don't want to?'

It was then Ifan spoke, 'It's easier to do what they say, Anya.' I looked at the ground.

'You heard what your boyfriend said.'

I smiled. 'I always do what he says, don't I, Ifan?'

He was serious. 'No more games,' he said. I stared at him and got in the car.

We were there all night. I discovered how the police had found out. After the Wigmore Street break-in when I'd flooded the reception with the lyrics of 'Every Breath You Take' the police were called. Everyone was interviewed, including JF. He told them that I was an ex-client and stalking him, but he'd no idea why.

Ifan and I were separately interviewed by two of the police, one female, one male, but by then I was so overwrought and tired I hardly looked at them. They said it was just a preliminary enquiry, and questioned me for hours, eyeballing me the whole time. So I told them. Everything. I had no choice actually. How I'd first met JF, the sessions at Wigmore Street, the argument, his suggestion we meet in Hackney, then the worst thing that happened, the rape.

The only thing I noticed was how poker faced they were, with the exception of when I told them about my bag and how the spirit of Anya helped. I could tell by the expression on their faces they thought I was mad.

'So why didn't you report this alleged rape?'

'Because I knew no one would listen and I knew he'd say I was making it up and that I was mad. That's what men do, don't they, and he's a therapist.'

'And...? What's that got to with it?'

'Everyone who has a different view to them is called mad.'

'How do we know you aren't making it up?'

'My friends can tell you the effect it had on me. I was falling apart.'

'Did you go to a rape counselling service?'

'No, I'd had enough of counsellors. I did go to a STD clinic to get checked out.'

'Which one, and don't lie because we'll find out.'

'The Whittington, near Archway. I'm not lying.'

Eventually they stood up, leaving me in the room on my own. When they came back, I asked where Ifan was. They said he was outside, waiting for me. I'd had enough by then. I began to cry. I wanted to see him, but they said they had more questions and if I told the truth, then I could go.

'So at what point did you decide to stalk?'

'It was sometime after. After what he did. Can't remember too well.'

'Days, weeks, months?'

'Weeks but it went on over months.'

'Was it your boyfriend who suggested it?'

'Ifan, is that who you mean?'

'You tell us.'

'He's not my boyfriend. No, it wasn't him; the idea came from my bag, Anya, my namesake. She understood and told me what to do.' There was a long silence. They were staring at me. I continued, 'Yes, I know it sounds strange but that's what happened. It's the only way I can make sense of it. You took my backpack away and if you look inside there's another bag, made of indigo-coloured leather. The spirit of Anya is inside the bag. She helps me, that's why I carry the bag with me when I go on an intervention. The perfume is Coco Mademoiselle and when the fragrance enters a room, I know it's Anya and she'll help me.'

They looked at each other. 'You think I'm mad, don't you?'

They didn't answer. The man said, 'Intervention? You mean when you stalk.'

'Yes, to frighten him, so he knows there's no hiding place and wherever he is, I'll get him.'

'It's an offence, do you know that?'

'I do, but what he did was an offence and I reckon rape is far worse than stalking. I trusted him but he abused my trust and raped my body. That memory will never go away so it's in my mind too. Don't you understand, I had to punish him. No one else will.'

'So you decided to take the law into your own hands?'

I didn't answer.

'Answer me.'

'Yes, I wanted him to suffer like I had, terrify him, destroy him, take my revenge.'

'And this latest, hiring the stripper, that was also part of your revenge?'

'Yes, whatever he'd done to me, he had to suffer too. So he knew how I felt, humiliated, powerless, shocked. You're a man so you don't know, but what if someone forced something into your body. How do you think you'd feel?'

He didn't react but looked at his colleague, stood up, and said they'd be back soon. They were gone ten minutes and when they returned, they told me they were going to write a report and I might or might not be prosecuted.

It was dawn by the time I was released. Ifan had waited for me. He said it was time to go home but first he had to pick up his bike. Neither of us said much. I was so exhausted, I could hardly put one foot in front of the other.

He glanced at me, put his arm round me and said, 'Would you like to come back to my flat?'

'Yes, I would. I don't want to be on my own. I'm so tired, I feel like a zombie.'

Ifan gave me his keys, put me in a taxi, gave the driver the address, and said he'd follow on his bike. I arrived before him. I let myself in. His flatmate wasn't there. I lay on his sofa and within minutes was asleep. I couldn't have been asleep longer than ten minutes before the front door bell went. I dragged myself up and let him in. He left his bike in the hall and we sat down. He sat right by me and I didn't move. I wanted him there.

He said, 'I'll make you a cuppa, if you want.'

'Please. I'm exhausted.'

'It's been a long night, what do you want to do?'

'Sleep.'

He got up, went into the kitchen, made a cup of tea, handed it to me, and said, 'Okay, use my bed. I'll sleep here.'

'Are you sure?'

'Yeah, I'll sleep on the sofa.'

'Do you have something I could borrow to sleep in? I've been wearing these clothes all night – and the day before.'

I thought he was going to say something, but he didn't. He stood up, retrieved a shirt off a hanger and silently handed it to me. I went to the bathroom, washed, and changed into it. It was white cotton, and I rather liked it.

He was on the sofa, lying on his side and almost asleep by the time I finished. I stood in front of him. I said, 'Ifan... what if?' He looked up into my eyes, didn't reply, but turned on to his back, lightly running one of his fingers along the line of my leg under the shirt.

'Suits you,' he said, then sat up, paused but must have had second thoughts. He said, 'Anya, the bed, it's in there.' I didn't move. He said then, 'Anya, please, it's better that way.' He lay back down, and half-turned away.

I said, 'I don't know what to say.'

'When you know, tell me.' He turned again, looking intently at me before saying, 'It's better to be sure, don't you think?' His eyes closed.

A month or two ago this comment might have crushed me but by then I didn't take it that way. I stood uncertainly looking at him. 'Thanks, Ifan for all your help.' He didn't answer. He was asleep. I walked into his bedroom. It was untidy, but I didn't care. I got into his bed and fell into a deep sleep.

The newspapers, especially the 'red tops', were full of the incident. Someone must have tipped them off. I always wondered whether it was Cherie Dear but I never asked her. She told me it was the best opportunity she'd ever had and that she'd received loads of offers for musical theatre. Eventually she stopped being a burlesque stripper and made a name for herself as an actress in light comedy.

Once the press discovered JF was a therapist, they were out for his blood. They don't trust the touchy-feely therapeutic world. They saw through his hypocrisy, and having linked it with the rape and seduction of some of his clients, subjected him to a second version of stalking.

The police didn't prosecute either me or Ifan; we were let off with a caution, but JF didn't get away so lightly. I wasn't the first to be raped by him and they were collecting evidence for a prosecution. He was bailed on a surety. He couldn't go abroad and live with the pigs, which I thought was his rightful place. I told Ifan I was going to send him a jar of lavender honey, with a note saying 'You'll need more than this to sweet talk you're way out of court,' but Ifan stopped me. He said enough is enough and that I'd achieved my aim.

It's strange though, revenge brought Ifan and me back together. We stopped being uptight with each other and became the best of friends. I knew I loved him, yet I couldn't tell him because of my insecurity. And I still had a problem with sex. It was still a big deal and what JF had done had made me even more nervous. I knew Ifan had had girlfriends but I never asked him about them and he didn't mention them. We both knew I had a strong jealous streak, so we had this weird relationship, where I suspected, but wasn't sure, that sometimes he slept with other women. At the same time I wanted him like crazy but I couldn't talk about it or act on it.

We were seeing more and more of each other, but neither of us made a move. It was safer the way it was, safe but stupid, I thought. I talked it over with Maddy. She was incredulous.

'For Christ's sake, Annie, that's unbelievable. You're not a child.'

'I know, but it's easy the way it is, and sex has never worked for me. Look at what happened when I came on to Gareth and then later, when Ifan and I tried to make out. Disastrous.'

'Gareth's different. Do you fancy Ifan or not?'

'Yes, I guess, but...'

She interrupted me. 'So do something, and then tell me. If it's good, I'll be over the moon for you, if it isn't, so what, it's not the end of the world. Go for it, Annie, and stop pissing about.'

'He's more like a brother.'

'Well, the two of you need to stop behaving as if you were still children, come out of your den, get off your pontoon, do what you want to do. It'll come naturally.'

I laughed. She was right of course, but she set me thinking. I still valued my childhood memories – the times we'd spent in the estuary and I wanted to relive them. Maybe I was stuck in the past, but I didn't care. That's when I decided to line up another long weekend. It was over a year since my last visit to Wales and Philomena had contacted me again and asked when I was coming. I told Ifan. I wanted him to come too, but he said he'd got stuff to do. I even asked my mother. She was interested but she'd got a prior engagement that she couldn't cancel. So I left it at that and made my own arrangements.

It was a Saturday and I was back in Wales, sitting in the farmhouse kitchen with Philomena. She was plying me with tea and homemade cakes when she told me she had a garden party to go to and asked whether I'd like to accompany her. It was a beautiful hot day and I was tempted, but I decided against it. 'No, thanks,' I said. 'If it's all the same to you, I'll just hang out. I don't want to do much. Maybe I'll go to the estuary this afternoon, or I could even visit Gareth.'

'That's fine. But he doesn't know you're here, so give him a ring before you go. He might be out but he'd want to see you and you could meet Ceri. I'll show you on the map where he lives. You'll need to get a cab.'

She found a road atlas, pointed out the way and disappeared upstairs to get dressed for the party. It wasn't long before she came back down. She was wearing a simple 'A' line dress in burnt orange linen with a brass bangle on her wrist. It suited her colouring.

'Wow,' I said, 'what a transformation. I love your outfit.'

She walked to the mirror and as she put on her earrings she saw my reflection in the mirror. She turned round and said, 'You look good yourself. I was wondering earlier – if that dress you're wearing, is it vintage? It shows off your figure.'

I stood up, smoothed down the dress, smiling. 'You think so? It's a bit short and it may look old, but it's not. It's a copy of the "land girl" style, modelled on the dresses of the forties. I picked it up from some fashion show. I guess they used to go out jitterbugging wearing this style.'

'Well, it very much suits you and I like the padded shoulders.'

She walked past, leaving a trail of perfume behind her and sat down in one of the chairs.

'What's that perfume?'

'Something Gareth bought me. I always forget the name. It's French, that's all I remember.'

'Gareth. I'm surprised that you two, in a way, are still together, despite everything. You must have something going.'

'You can't live with someone like Gareth for that long and not grow to love him. He's a good man.'

'I know that, he is a good man.' She laughed. 'What's funny?' I asked.

'Nothing. Just…resistance in the face of enemy action. I've got eyes and ears you know.'

I wondered then how much he'd told her, but I didn't really want to know. I felt embarrassed as I remembered that last scene a year ago in the forest. I looked away.

She stood up. 'I'll have to be off.'

'Are you driving?'

'Yes, I'll stay the night with Tim. Will you be alright on your own?'

'I will. I love it here, it holds happy memories, besides you're usually here on your own and you don't get scared. Who's Tim?'

'My latest. I met him in the library. Cardiff.'

'You don't care, do you, you know, what people might think?'

'No. I don't care about convention, if that's what you mean, but what about you, Anya? Your love life, it seems non-existent. You tell me nothing. Do you really live like a nun? You shouldn't be on your own. What happened to the boy you used to play with years ago? The one round here? The one you were with when you almost drowned; you were like brother and sister together.'

It was my turn to laugh. 'You mean Ifan? If only you

knew. He disappeared but then, years later, turned up. We're good friends, but nothing more. I see a lot of him, but maybe not enough.'

'That sounds mysterious, so what's going on? Anything or nothing?'

'There isn't any more to tell you. Actually, maybe there is, but it's long and complicated.'

I didn't know whether to tell her or not about my problems. We stood facing each other. Philomena sensed my discomfort, took my hand and said, 'I do want to hear about it, but when I have more time. I have to go. Sure you won't come?'

'Yes, I'm sure.'

'Well, if you change your mind, ring me. I'd like you to meet Tim.' She blew me a kiss, left the room, the front door banged, and she drove off. I heard the car crunching the gravel as she left.

I sat for a while in the kitchen enjoying the peace and quiet, thinking about the summers I'd spent there, my elbows on the table, my chin in my hands. I missed those times. I remembered the past meals we'd shared outside on the lawn, trips to the estuary, watching the rise and fall of the river, meeting Ifan, climbing trees with him. It was so peaceful... until my dreams were interrupted by the geese. The racket they were making pulled me back into the present. Something or somebody had disturbed them. They were honking, hissing, loudly, aggressively. I pulled the door open and glared at them. But they ignored me. I ran at them. They scattered, but soon came back together and huddled in a tight circle of resentment. I thought there must be somebody there and I looked around, but I couldn't see anybody.

I walked across the damp grass until I reached the orchard. The orchard had always been a favourite place. The sculpture of Leda, the one I hadn't liked, had been removed. I imagined Gareth sitting under the apple trees in the orchard drinking cider and writing his poetry. Writing poetry and drinking cider – they went together for Gareth.

I sat in his old chair still under his favourite tree, listening to the evening bird song, watching the sun dipping low in the sky until it was almost too late to visit the estuary, but I was determined to go.

I went to the outbuilding and looked for my old bike. It was still there. I wiped the dust off the saddle, blew up the tyres, went back to the kitchen, made myself a flask of coffee and within half an hour I was cycling down the back lanes. I didn't bother to change, there was no time. I felt the exhilaration of the air rushing past my legs as I sped along. There was no traffic and it was still warm. It was twilight by the time I reached the estuary. I looked for the place and the trees where Ifan and I used to hide our bikes, but it was impossible to locate. The new car park concealed where it could have been. One solitary car remained but it didn't unduly concern me. It probably belonged to someone fishing or a couple taking a late-evening walk.

I propped my bike out of sight against a tree and slowly followed the path down to the river. The old willow was still there, its feathery branches trailing the surface of the water. It was where we'd played, and where I'd first seen Ifan launch his frog on the raft. I took off my sandals and dangled my feet in the water. It was cool, the river running fast, the tide on the turn. Across the river I could see the fields and distant lights of England. I wanted to stay until darkness enclosed the estuary and I fell asleep and became part of its silence. I lay back, enjoying the warmth and the solitude and closed my eyes.

I became aware of every sound. A twig cracked. Someone was walking through the woods. I sat up and waited. But there was nobody. Nothing, except the shrill startled alarm of a blackbird. I got to my feet. I heard then a song sung so quietly and so softly, it was difficult to hear except as the singer came nearer, the song became louder. I recognised the song, I recognised the voice. I'd first heard it years ago, the day I met Ifan. 'Calon Lân'.

I waited for him to emerge through the forest. He smiled

when he saw me. I felt shy standing barefoot in my pink dress looking hot and dirty after my bike ride. But I was aware that evening of his strong physical presence, his height, his tan, his light grey eyes. He came to a halt. We stood facing each other.

'I thought you weren't coming to Wales.' He didn't answer. 'How did you know I'd be here?'

'I changed my mind and I wanted to surprise you. I guessed you'd come here...besides I wanted to see the river myself.' He picked up a small stone and passed it from one hand to the other and back again, watching me as he did so.

'You've been following me. It was you. Wasn't it? You disturbed the geese.' He smiled, but didn't answer. 'It's a bad habit, stalking,' I said.

He threw the stone into the air, caught it, then said, 'You think so?'

'I know so...where are you staying?'

'Chepstow.'

'It's getting dark.'

'Yes. But I'm in a car.'

'Well, now you're here, before you go, you could see the farmhouse. You never did get to see it before. There's only me there, so you don't have to be sociable.'

He dropped the stone, folded his arms and looking straight at me said, 'Why not, it's on my way.' He seemed indifferent but I ignored that. I was pleased he was coming.

'I'll race you. I'm on my bike and I know a quick way.'

'No, you won't. I want you with me. And the bike can go in the boot.'

His directness took me by surprise. I didn't answer straight away. 'Okay, I'll show you where it is.'

'I know where it is. I saw where you left it.'

'Oh,' I said, 'I might have known.' I pushed him playfully.

I wanted us to joke about like we used to, and I thought he would, because he smiled, pulled me against him but then he let me go, as if he'd had second thoughts. I was puzzled. There was something different about him. He seemed preoccupied and I didn't understand what was going on. We reached the car.

He put my bike in the boot. 'What are you thinking?' he asked, as he opened the car door.

'Nothing, I'm not thinking anything. Do you know how to get there?'

'Of course. I've had a good teacher.'

I didn't answer but sat in the front staring straight ahead. I was wondering whether his reference to 'having a good teacher' was to the Etta James song 'Teach Me Tonight' or to my stalking. He drove without speaking but I was keenly aware of his presence. Every now and again he'd turn to steal a look and that made me self-conscious. I pulled my dress over my knees.

It was dark when we arrived, the house still warm from the heat of the day. We walked into the kitchen. I clicked on the lights.

'There's nobody in. Philomena's out and Gareth's left. He spends his time between here and with Chloe and Ceri, his daughter. This is his second home.'

'Where's his first?'

'In the mountains. He writes his poetry here, in the orchard if the weather's good, that's his favourite place. I'll show you around.'

We wandered through each of the downstairs rooms. It still smelt of wood smoke, it was still full of quirky objects, strange pictures. I still loved it.

He said, 'It's full of eccentricities.'

I said, 'No, it's a house filled with the surreal. That's different.'

'Eccentric, surreal, either or both, it's weird,' he said, 'but whatever rocks their boat.'

We returned to the kitchen. 'Like a coffee?'

He nodded and sat down in one of the sagging armchairs. 'You used to talk so much about your mother, and Gaby, was that her name? What's happened to them?'

'My mother has a partner so she's off my case, and Gaby,

I don't know about. It's a shame we've lost contact with her.'
Ifan sat watching as I rinsed out the Bodum, ground fresh
coffee, and poured boiling water over it. I waited for it to
percolate and stood in front of him, leaning against the table.
'I've never been here before on my own, not at night.'

'Scared?'

'Of course not.'

'So why mention it?'

A good question, I thought. Maybe I wanted him to stay
a while but I didn't say that. I just shrugged my shoulders.
'Dunno,' I said.

'Where's Philomena?'

'Somewhere in Chepstow. She said I could ring if I wanted
to join her.'

'I can give you a lift.'

'I was going to stay here.'

'Fine, if that's what you want. What about the rest of the
house? You haven't shown me upstairs.'

I looked at him, warily. 'I'll show you later but I need to
eat and I want to shower, get rid of the bike-ride dust. I'm hot
and sticky.'

'Which way round, eat or shower?'

'Shower.'

'Good, while you shower, I'll make the food.' He stood up.

'But you don't know what to make or where everything is.'

'I'll find out. How long will you be?'

'Ten, fifteen minutes, thirty minutes. It depends. You'll
stay then?'

'Is that an invite?'

'Yes.'

'Great. I'm in no rush. Have your shower and take your
coffee with you.'

'It can wait, I won't be long.'

'I'll put it in your room.'

'You don't know where it is.'

'I'll work that out too. I'm good at that type of thing.'

265

'Finding a girl's bedroom? I'd noticed.'

He smiled.

I ran upstairs to my bedroom and pulled off my dress. I was hot. I hadn't packed many clothes and I was in one of those moods when I didn't know what to wear. In desperation I opened the wardrobe and found a dress I'd left years ago. It was perfect for this weather, a sun dress, blue, floaty, strappy, pretty, not the type I wore now, but it would do. I lay it flat on the bed, took out my Coco Mademoiselle, wrapped myself with a towel and made my way up the stairs to the bathroom. It was even hotter at the top of the house, and just like a sauna.

I loved that bathroom. It was huge. It was built into the roof space and designed by Philomena. It had a roof lantern with hanging plants, but Philomena called it a wet room because of the walk-in shower in the corner. She'd said that creating a steamy atmosphere was good for the plants and they deserved a treat now and again, because like people they shouldn't be neglected. The floor was in terracotta with tiny insets of small colourful Mexican tiles, the walls rough plastered in deep blue, and there was an old-fashioned white bath with claw feet underneath the roof lantern. It was very arty and as a child I'd lie in the bath and imagine I was in a tropical rain forest.

But right then, it wasn't the bath I wanted, but the shower. I hung my towel on the hook and stepped underneath the enormous metal disc suspended from the ceiling. I turned it on. A powerful force of water gushed out. It was cold, so cold, I lost my breath for a moment, but it warmed up quickly, the water surging from the round shower head like gigantic rain drops, saturating my hair, running down my face, cascading down my body.

I held my hands and face up to the water and laughed with delight. I experimented with the flow, the force, the temperature. I danced, I twirled, I sang, I ran in and out the water. I made the water hot, cold, strong and weak. I was as happy as a carefree child, and in my imagination I was running naked in and out of a mountain waterfall.

'Anya. Anya.' I turned round, water streaming down my face. Ifan was standing just inside the door. 'You've been here almost an hour. Your coffee's cold and your food's ready.'

Immediately I was self-conscious. I spoke primly, attempted to hide myself and switched the water off. 'I'm taking a shower, you shouldn't have come in, pass me my towel, please.'

'You didn't lock the door and there's no towel. I can't see a towel.' He was smiling and walked further into the room.

I glanced around. The towel had disappeared. I glared at him. 'What's so funny? There's no towel because you've taken it, haven't you?'

'Maybe I have. Maybe I haven't. Actually I can see it. It's there, on the chair, where you left it. You know what, you're going to have to come and get it.' He sat on the side of the bath, smiled, folded his arms. 'No good looking at me like that, Anya, because I'm here and it's impossible to intimidate me. I'm staying. Besides, I like looking at you. You're beautiful... especially without clothes on.'

'I'm soaking wet and I don't want you staring at me.' I scowled, turned to put the shower back on, wrestled with it unsuccessfully and said, 'It's broken and it's your fault it isn't working and you're making me nervous standing there. You'll have to fix it.'

He walked across to the shower, which gave me time to retrieve my towel and wrapping it around me, I returned to stand next to him.

'I can't see anything wrong with it,' he said.

'Really?' I said. 'You'll have to try harder. Let me try.'

I turned the shower on. A jet of warm water streamed over his hair and clothes. He was momentarily shocked, then he laughed, but he stayed where he was, looking intently at me as the water cascaded over him. I turned the knob to increase the force of the water. He didn't move, but looked straight into my eyes, oblivious to the water cascading over him.

I laughed. 'Look what's happened. You're saturated. Now you'll have to take your clothes off. Go on. All of them.'

He gave me one of his looks, pulled off his t-shirt, unbuttoned his jeans, removed his boxers, and threw them one by one across the room towards the bath. He changed the water flow to its gentlest and warmest. He stood close and slowly unwound the towel from round my body.

We faced each other. The water poured over us. I took a step back. I wanted to see him. Seeing him naked took me back to when I'd had the disastrous panic attack. It was different now. I'd changed. Now he looked good and I wanted him like crazy.

He was tall with an athletic build, powerful muscles in his legs – must have been his cycling. His skin was fair. He had a scar which ran from his knee up his thigh. I traced its line with my finger. I looked up at him. He was watching me. 'A bike accident,' he said, 'don't stop.' I didn't. His grey eyes shifted away from my face, followed the flow of water across the curves of my breasts, down my body, through my dark pubic hair and down my legs. We were silent, the warm water cascading over us. He was aroused. He touched me all over. I took a step nearer.

He spoke then, 'Anya...what do you want?'

I knew exactly what I wanted. 'You. I want you.'

He was so close, I was aware of his breath. He switched the water off, pushed the wet strands of my hair away, kissed my mouth, my neck, my belly, and slowly drew and held my wet body against his. In a soft voice said, 'Here? Now?'

I looked directly at him. 'Yes.'

That was all either of us said. We went to bed but we never made it back down to the kitchen.

Someone was knocking on the bedroom door. 'Anya, Anya, are you asleep?'

I had been. I struggled to sit up, and smiled. Ifan was lying on his stomach next to me, one arm stretched across the bed, the other round me. Sunlight streamed round the edges of the closed curtains.

'Who is it?' I was sleepy.

'It's me, Philomena. I've got coffee for you.'

I covered Ifan with the duvet and pulled one corner up to my shoulders. 'Come in.'

She walked in, her usual chatty self. 'I saw the car outside. I guessed you were with someone. Ah, the clothes on the bathroom floor, they're his. Who is this?'

Ifan was pretending to be asleep but I knew he wasn't. I wriggled away. He was making it difficult to concentrate.

'Ifan, you know, my childhood friend and the one you asked me about. What time is it?'

'Late. But you didn't say you were going to see him.' She seemed at a loss for words. 'Well, good. That's good. I'm pleased. I'll get another coffee. I wasn't sure what was going on and who was here. I didn't recognise the car.' She got to the door and then said, 'Your perfume. What is it?'

'Coco Mademoiselle. I wear it for special occasions.'

'It's a lovely fragrance.'

'Yes, it has a definite presence.' I smiled to myself and looked down at Ifan. He sat up, offered his hand to Philomena, 'Hello,' he said, 'I'm Ivan Baranov. I've heard so much about you.'

'Have you now, good things, I hope.' She hesitated, 'Well, if you two want to stay longer, and I think you do, you can come down later. There's plenty of coffee and croissants. Tim's here, and Gareth rang to say he'd be over later for lunch with Ceri and Chloe. But take your time.'

She pulled the door behind her, then opened it immediately. 'I put the clothes I found in the bathroom into the dryer, they should be dry soon.' She walked out and I heard her run down the stairs.

We looked at each other. He lay back on his stomach and began lightly caressing me. 'So, Ms Morgan, why's it taken so long?'

'To do what?'

'You know what I'm talking about.'

I pulled away from him, sat up, got out of bed and stood up. 'I dunno. Maybe self-protection. I really don't know. Maybe fear. That you'd leave me and if we'd, well, had sex or whatever, and I'd got fond of you, that would be even worse.'

'Fond. That's a stupid word.'

'Well, what word would you use?'

'How about love?' I didn't reply. I pulled my night shirt back on and walked towards the door. 'Where are you going, Echo? Stay here.'

'Ifan, don't sound so indignant. I've an idea; you know the bath, it's really big, what about trying that out?' I leaned seductively against the chest of drawers like Cherie Dear did.

'I see you've got over your shyness, but I want you here, not there. So remove that shirt you've just put on.' He jumped out of bed, took hold of my hand and pulled me back. But I wasn't to be put off, 'Just a minute,' I said, 'I want to ask you something.'

'Go ahead.'

'Do you remember the time, we were by the river, it was when we were very young and you asked me to take off my clothes?'

'As if I'd forget.'

'What was it you nearly said, but never said? Do you remember?'

'I'm not telling you because I want to know something.'

'Say what it is and I'll tell you.'

'It's about me and you… I want to know if…?'

He was looking into my eyes. I knew what he wanted me to say. I took a deep breath and I told him the truth. It was a big, big moment for me. I said, 'Ifan, I'm crazy about you and I've been crazy about you since we first met. I love you – more than I can say.'

'You mean it?'

'I do. But you won't leave me?'

'No. There's no one like you. You're wonderful. You're funny. You make me laugh and above all... I love making love to you.'

'Ifan... You may say that but I still don't know...you know, if I can trust you?'

'Give me a chance. He smiled 'Come here. You've forgotten what I told you. Listen. *'Ti yw fy nghariad ers erioed ac mi fyddi'ngariad i mi am byth.'*

'No, I hadn't. But I can't pronounce it, and you never told me what it meant.'

'You want to know?'

'I do. I really want to know.'

He patted the bed. 'Then come here. Come lie with me and be my love. Like the poet said.'

I leant over and kissed him. I whispered 'You're irresistible, Ifan Baranov.'

He pulled me to him. 'Anya Morgan, aka Echo Morgan, I want you to lie with me. Closer than that.'

He pushed my hair away from my face then whispered into my ear, *'Ti yw fy nghariad ers erioed ac mi fyddi'n gariad i mi am byth.* It means, you are my love and always have been and always will be. Can you say that? *Ti yw fy nghariad ers erioed ac mi fyddli'n gariad i mi am byth.* Say it after me.'

Acknowledgements

My thanks to Andy Aiers, Kate Dee and Jenny Collingridge for reading an early version of the manuscript, to Tony Collingridge for advising on the Severn Bore, to Richard Grove for his computer know-how, and to Kris Moen for his last minute, masterful proofreading.

To Susan Steinberg, film maker extraordinaire, for her inspirational creativity and whose (real) Welsh farmhouse was the basis of the (imagined) farmhouse in Ffridd.

Special thanks also to Sally Berry and Tom Ryan of the Arbours Association whose outstanding commitment to working with and understanding the emotionally troubled stood me in good stead as a psychotherapist and now as a writer.

Also by Marguerite Valentine

Between the Shadow and the Soul

Flori is a successful, attractive young woman living and working in London when in the early hours of the morning, in a moment of madness, she steals a tiny baby. With the reluctant assistance of her best friend, Rose, and Matt, an erstwhile lover, she flees with the baby to Jura, a remote Scottish island.

Living in extreme isolation and without the support of Rose or Matt, traumatic memories from her childhood return to haunt her and her life begins to unravel. Calling again on her friend for help, Rose insists she tells her the truth about her past. Confronted by Rose's determination, Flori is forced to reveal a secret, a secret she has kept since childhood but which leaves Rose with a terrible dilemma.

Between the Shadow and the Soul is about the conflicts of love, trust and betrayal and how friendship can be tested to its limits.